C. L. Roth

BONE WEARY

BONE WEARY

First C.L. Roth Publication May 2013
All Rights Reserved

Cover Design
DreamSpring Design Marion Sipe
http://marionsipe.blogspot.com/
Author Photograph: Red Jasper Artistry
Rebecca Rowe
www.redjasperartistry.com/
Copyright © 2013 by C.L. Roth

C.L. Roth Publishing
Box 77
Seneca, IL 61360

www.clroth.com
carolenglehaupt@gmail.com

ISBN: 13: 978-0-9846619-2-3
ISBN eBook: 978-0-9846619-3

Published by C.L. Roth Publishing

No journey is ever travelled alone. The concept of Bone Weary came to me from several different sources. It started with a series of 'what if' questions. It expanded from hearing various in-laws hint that my family isn't 'normal'. It grew when I started to list the questions people asked me about how I communicate with my non-verbal son, Joshua.

So I thank my siblings: Marilyn, Sharon, Phyllis, Bill, Nyla, Rhonda, and Kathy. They were the models for Charly's siblings and many of the characteristics and family stories are true. They may not have happened exactly as written but they add honesty and depth to the story.

I need to thank my extended family; the in-laws, the cousins, aunts, and uncles that appear throughout the novel. They add richness to the story.

I'm grateful to the town of Gridley, KS. Weary, KS. is based on my attachment to the small Kansas town and my love for the Flint Hills is real.

My online writing group, Write Stuff Novels, has been with me every step of the way. Without their encouragement, critiques, and input the story would not have been developed.

I add Holly Lisle's *How to Think Sideways* to the mix. Her online course handed me the missing pieces in my knowledge. I learned techniques from her that allowed me to finish what I start. I will be forever grateful for her generous sharing of knowledge and experience.

My son, Joshua, is the model for Jake. The relationship between Charly and her son is very much based on life experience. I think anybody that is a full-time caregiver will recognize the honesty in Jake's character. If the reader gets nothing else from the story, I hope they realize that it's the heart of a person that matters, and not their ability.

My journey is not a solitary walk. It's a rich and varied path and I thank you all.

Chapter One
Australia

I took the first hit right between the pot roast and the apple pie.

My husband, Hal, swabbed the last bit of gravy with a piece of bread, popped it into his mouth, and stabbed me with a brilliant, blue-eyed gaze that can still curl my toes. "I have something to tell you."

I automatically scooped up a spoonful of blueberry yogurt and held it to our seventeen-year old son's mouth. Jake obediently opened, and I fed him. He flicked me a quick eye-glance, smiled his thanks, and turned expressive brown eyes back to his father.

"Cut me a piece of that pie," Hal told our eldest son. Russell walked over and handed Hal the plate holding the piece of pie he had just sliced. Even at twenty years old, Russ can still manage a superior eye-roll. Then he went back to slice another piece for himself.

Hal cleared his throat. I felt a stirring of worry. My husband isn't big on conversation. He's the strong, silent type given to one sentence responses, or one-line zingers depending on whether the topic is a serious matter or a joke.

He put another bite of apple pie in his mouth and chewed slowly and methodically. I felt like walking around the table and smacking the back of his head to encourage him to speak faster.

I sighed, knowing from experience that trying to rush Hal would only lead to frustration. I glanced at Jake, saw him staring at the mashed potatoes and gravy, so I loaded up the spoon and offered him another bite.

Hal swallowed; then he looked at me as if he really saw me. After twenty-four years of marriage that doesn't happen as often as it used to.

"Remember the meeting we had at the bank last week?" he asked.

I nodded. "Yes. Mr. Black explained all the investments your mother had. Then he finalized turning her checking and savings accounts over to us."

He nodded, and for a minute I was afraid he'd start eating again, but he didn't. "Remember what I said that night? About how the amount we get from her investments is more than what I earn in a year?"

He seemed oddly hesitant. I sighed and filled Jake's spoon with more yogurt while I waited for Hal to continue.

"I've been thinking about it ever since Ma got sick. How having financial security could change our lives." His voice, always deep, softened, and his eyes went sort of hazy as he spoke. I hadn't seen him like this before. My worry deepened.

He sighed, a big, from his toes sigh, and stabbed me again with eyes so blue and fierce I could hardly meet his gaze. "I quit my job today."

I heard his words. They jolted through me like a lightning bolt. My hand moved before my brain could think, and the spoonful of yogurt moving toward Jake's mouth reversed direction. I stared in horrified silence as one of Hal's eyes disappeared behind a glob of blueberry delight.

Mouths fell open, mine included, as we watched Hal clear the yogurt from his face.

"I'm so sorry." I fought to stop myself from babbling. "I don't know why I did that." I wanted to go to him, but I didn't. His words rang in my ears. I couldn't sort through my emotions. What Hal had done was so out of character for him. But flinging food at him? Whatever had possessed me?

In a strange, surreal way, I saw Russell duck his head. I noticed his shoulders start shaking. Wise child, he kept his laughter silent. Jake wasn't as careful. He didn't understand the portent of his father's words. All he knew was his mother had nailed his father with a spoonful of yogurt. To him, it was funny. He started to laugh. I started to cry.

Through my tears, I watched emotions flit across Hal's face as he stared at us. Then the pupils of his eyes contracted, and his eyes, always blue, became glacial, impossible to meet. He stood so abruptly, his chair fell backward.

"We'll talk about this later." Hal waved a hand at me and left, stunning Russ, Jake, and me into silence.

***

I took the second hit right between reruns of *The Honeymooners* and *Mash*. I'd just returned from settling Jake into bed where he could watch his own TV. He prefers to escape the endless parade of old reruns Hal insists on watching every evening. And I suspect he's glad to get out of his wheelchair and relax tight and tired muscles.

Russ had already left for work. He's a night guard at a local nuclear plant. So when Hal dropped bombshell number two on me, I didn't have to worry about shielding the children.

"Are you able to talk now? Listen to me without getting hysterical?"

My teeth clenched so hard my jaws ached. "I never get hysterical. And yes, I'm ready to hear why you quit your job today without a word of discussion or warning."

He sighed and came over to sit by me on the couch. In an uncharacteristic gesture, he reached out and grasped both my hands. It shamed me to wonder if the hand holding was a protective gesture rather than a loving one.

"Do you remember what I told you when we were dating?"

Braced as I was for talk of him quitting his job, his words disarmed me. "You told me a lot of things when we dated. Can you be more specific?"

His hands tightened on mine, then loosened again. "Where did I talk about going? What was my dream?"

Now he was scaring me. My husband never talked about dreams or goals in our entire married life.

"Think," he urged me. Something powerful was moving in him. Something I couldn't remember ever seeing in him.

I sighed and thought back. Had I even paid that much attention to what he said? Surely I had.

He sighed, a world of sadness sounded in that sigh.

"I'm leaving." He said the words so calmly they didn't register at first. He could have been telling me it was raining outside, so soft his voice.

My insides went cold, and my brain stopped working. "Could you give me a little more information?" The cold, hard knot in my stomach was a blessing. As long as I stayed frozen, I could talk.

"I want to use half of the liquid assets that were transferred from Ma's inheritance. You keep the other half; your monthly expenses can be paid by the income generated from the investments. It's more than what I was making anyway, so you'll be fine."

He leaned toward me, my hands held by his in an unbreakable grip. His eyes burned with an energy and light I hadn't seen in them before. The rock that was my stomach became a stone. Passion burned in Hal. A passion so long absent I hadn't realized it was gone until I saw it now, shining from him like a beacon.

"Who is she?" I asked, not wanting an answer but needing it. Why else would Hal leave me?

"Australia," he responded.

"Who in their right mind would name their daughter Australia?" I asked, stupefied at the idea.

"What are you talking about?" Hal shook my hands again. "I don't know any daughters. I'm going to Australia. The country." He stared at me as if I was the one who had lost my mind.

"You're kidding." I struggled to put his words into some sort of logical order and couldn't do it. "You quit your job; you're going to spend money we could live on for several years on a vacation? You're not asking for a divorce?"

The lunatic actually grinned at me, and a tall, lean man with summer-blue eyes that could look right into my soul strolled through my memory.

"I don't want a divorce. I want a chance to live a dream. I've worked hard every day of my life since I was sixteen years old. Surely you can understand that?"

His grip tightened again. The blue of his eyes shone with a light I'd never seen in them before. "You could come with me. Can't you leave Jake with one of your sisters for a year? One year, Charly. Don't we deserve that?"

We did. Of course we did. I started to cry for the second time that day, and I hate crying. It's such a useless thing to do. And I love my husband with a deep down, gut-wrenching love. But Australia. I couldn't go to there. The very idea of an ocean between Jake and me terrified me.

My heart broke into tiny little pieces. I couldn't follow Hal into this dream. I wished I could. I should have been able to. I didn't want to choose, but I did. And Hal lost. I lost. The only thing I could do was step aside and let Hal go, not cling to him or try to guilt him into staying with us.

I envied him, in a way, the ability to walk away from responsibility. I can't. I don't know how. But then, I'm not sure I want to. I only hope when his year of freedom is up, he'll find his way back home.

Chapter Two
Going Home

I reached up to adjust the rearview mirror. Jake's face came into view. I took my hand off the steering wheel long enough to do a quick finger wave at him. His eyes flew upwards, his signal for yes, but this time I interpreted it as 'back at you.'

"At least you didn't desert me." I spoke out loud and wished I could grab my words back. What normal young man would choose living with his mother over an Australian adventure? In my heart I knew Jake would have preferred traveling with his father and brother.

Guilt gnawed at me. I could have gone with Hal, probably should have, but Jake never had any choice at all. Life is so unfair.

"Traipsing across Australia," I glared at Jake's reflection in the mirror. "And where does your father get off telling me I can't go home? What did he expect me to do while he's off looking at kangaroos?"

Jake ducked his head, hiding his face from me, but I knew he was grinning. Having his father and brother take off for a year didn't seem to faze him at all. Maybe living with cerebral palsy has given him the ability to accept whatever blows life hands out. That's a lesson I don't seem to ever learn. I flop around like a fish on a hook while Jake swims through life with serene faith.

"I don't care what your father said." A frown pulled my eyebrows together. I rubbed my forehead in a conscious effort to smooth it away. "No way am I going to sit in Illinois for a year while he wanders the Outback. If he gets to do what he wants, then so do I."

Hal didn't argue very hard when I put our house on the market once he realized half the sale price would be added to the finances allotted for his big 'tour'. The fact that our house sold as soon as it hit the market seemed to be a sign I was making the right decision.

I fell silent and stared at the scenery flashing by me; aching for my first glimpse of the Flint Hills. Even though I understood Hal's need to see Australia, I couldn't understand his ability to walk away from family for such an extended amount of time.

"I feel better knowing Russ is with him." I caught Jake's eyes in the mirror again, and he looked upward, the speed and height of his gaze telling me louder than words could that he was worried and agitated.

When we broke the news to Russ that our family was going in two different directions for a year, I overheard him mutter, "What the hell does the old man think he'll do in Australia? Wrestle crocodiles? He'll get eaten."

Russ came home the next day and told us he'd given notice. He intended to accompany his father to Australia. The argument that followed changed forever my estimation of my eldest son. He went toe to toe with his father and came out the winner. And he did it with strength, grace, and courage. If we accomplish nothing more in life, Hal and I raised a good man.

Two good men. I examined Jake's reflection in the mirror again. Seventeen years old and small in stature, I doubted if Jake tipped the scale at eighty pounds. Cerebral palsy left him non-verbal and non-ambulatory. He needs help in all areas of his life. But when you look in his eyes, you forget the disability and see his strength of character.

Jake talks with his eyes. They are large, brown, and full of wisdom and humor. He doesn't miss anything. He communicates in subtle and wonderful ways. A large, wonderful soul shines from him. There are few people who don't respond to his beautiful smile.

Looking into Jake's face when Hal and Russ walked away from us almost broke my heart. His eyes held so much pain and sorrow, I wanted to wail. I held it together keeping what felt like a clown smile on my face as Hal and Russ boarded the plane.

I held it together while I wheeled Jake back to the van, maintained my composure while I navigated the traffic out of O'Hare, and didn't fall apart until later that night after I'd gotten Jake settled in his room.

Two weeks later, I was on the road again, minus the dogs. I left Murphy and Molly with a friend who agreed to keep them until I could get relocated. I didn't anticipate a problem buying a house in Weary, Kansas.

More people move away from the small town than to it. And the lack of buyers meant property values were low compared to where I lived. I expected to find a house within a matter of days. My needs weren't exactly normal when I considered the wheelchair and the dogs, but not impossible.

I leaned forward, eager to soak in the view of the Flint Hills of Kansas. June was the perfect month to see them. The black ash from the annual spring burn off has disappeared under fresh green grass and colorful wildflowers. Rolling hills stretch as far as the eye can see.

My imagination can easily picture pioneers crossing the endless expanse of prairie in their covered wagons. Sometimes, I think of the Dalton gang or the James boys riding hell-bent for leather pursued by various posses. There is a timeless quality to these hills that I hope never goes under the advance of civilization.

My soul breathes freer when I'm in the hill country. "I'm almost home," I said again, softly, under my breath. Jake heard, and he grunted in agreement, knowing my eyes were on the hills and not the mirror.

I tore my eyes away from the view. Excitement flowed through me despite my sadness at being separated from my husband and older son. I caught Jake's eyes in the mirror again. "Your dad doesn't get it. My grandparents lived and died in Weary, Kansas. I have aunts, uncles, and cousins spread all over the county. But most of all, I want my sisters and brother. For one year, we're all going to be in the same place. Doesn't he realize how rare an opportunity this is?"

I fell silent, feasting on the beauty of the hills. No, Hal hadn't understood. How could an only child understand how a big family functions? He didn't have the built-in family memories and loyalties that have been ingrained in me since birth.

I'm number five out of eight children, and I guess I'm running too. Not away from life, but toward it. I'm heading to Weary where, for the first time in my memory, all my siblings will be in the same place.

My name is Charlotte Edgewood. And I'm going home.

Chapter Three
Unexpected Side Trip

"It's not my fault," I protested Jake's silent stare of accusation. "I didn't do anything wrong."

Through the window I saw my van, all doors standing wide open. Two officers stood beside it, one of them holding the leash of a nice-looking German Shepherd. I slunk deeper onto the uncomfortable chair and glared at the policeman sitting behind the desk.

"Have you contacted Uncle Claude yet?" I asked him.

He looked at me over the top of his glasses. "If you're referring to Sheriff Claude Russell, then no, we haven't called him in for a routine check."

"There is nothing routine about being pulled over for no reason and brought to the county jail without even being told what I've done."

"You were informed when we pulled you over that your van matches the description of a vehicle used in a felony robbery and abduction of a disabled minor." His eyes slid toward Jake. "We're simply checking things out."

I wanted to say more but was afraid my mouth would get me into trouble, so I pulled my cell phone out of my pocket. The officer raised his eyebrows, and I asked, "I can make a phone call, can't I?"

"Certainly." His tone of polite sarcasm almost matched mine. "You're not under arrest."

I started by calling Mary Lee. She's the eldest in the family and good with practical details. At the very least, she could call Uncle Claude and get his rear over here to vouch for me.

"No answer," I muttered to Jake. He frowned, and his facial expression told me he was worried. He flicked his eyes to the phone and he added a grunt.

So I dialed sister #2, Samantha. The line was busy; bad news because Samantha has been known to chat for thirty minutes with a stranger. Heaven help me if she was talking to a family member.

I glanced out the window again and watched the dog jump into the van and start giving it a thorough sniffing. "Oh, great." I looked at Jake. "He's going to have fun sniffing your overnight bag." Jake frowned and I felt guilty for worrying him.

"What kind of drugs does the dog look for?" I asked the officer.

He glanced up from his magazine and examined me with eyes that had gone from bored and annoyed to sharp and assessing. "What kind are you worried about?"

I pointed toward Jake. "My son is on muscle relaxers and anti-seizure medication. Does any of that affect the dog?"

"If the drugs are in prescription bottles made out to the right person, you shouldn't have any problems."

Jake gave a big sigh and looked slightly less worried. I punched in sister #3's phone number. Phoebe answered on the third ring.

I poured out my troubles to her.

"You're where?" Her shock was gratifying to hear. "I'll come, of course. But Charly, I'm not home. I'm shopping in Emporia, and it will take me over an hour to get to you."

I sighed and told her not to worry; that I was sure Uncle Claude would show up eventually and vouch for me. I glared at the officer when I said that. He flipped a page of his magazine and ignored me.

I didn't want to call my brother. He'd come, but he'd make my life miserable with his teasing. I'd call him last.

"Couldn't you give me Uncle Claude's phone number, and I'll call him myself?" I asked.

The officer sighed and didn't even look up from his magazine as he spoke. "I can't do that, ma'am. Sheriff Russell would chew my ass if I gave out his phone number to just anybody."

"I'm not just anybody," I protested. "I'm his niece."

"So you say." He licked his finger and turned another page.

I dialed sister # 4.

"Josie." I held the phone in a death grip. ""You've got to help me. I'm stuck at the Burlington police station." I stopped my tumbling words because I could feel myself edging toward hysteria.

Josie sympathized with me, but she was stuck at work. There wasn't any way she could get free for three hours.

"Can you at least call Uncle Claude?" I pleaded. "I'm sure he'd come over and straighten this out, but they won't call him, and I don't have his number."

Josie promised she'd get hold of him, and I clicked off the phone. I sat; frustrated and irritable, watching the man read his stupid golf magazine.

"Can I at least look at the phone book?"

"Sure." Without looking up, he opened a drawer, pulled out a thin book, and pushed it toward the edge of the desk. "But if you're hoping to find Sheriff Russell's phone number, he's unlisted."

I scowled and punched in sister #5's number. I knew Roni couldn't help me, but I could gripe to somebody new. I enjoyed my five minute talk with her and hung up.

"Aren't they done yet? The dog has been around the van five times."

"He's very thorough," the man murmured.

I dialed sister #6, Katie. "I'd come, Charly. I will come, but I'm waitressing for Mick today. I can't get free until the lunch crowd goes."

"Can you at least call Uncle Claude? Please?" She promised and I closed the phone.

I started to stand up and sank back down when the officer went on full alert. "I was just going to pace. I'm getting nervous."

I got even more nervous when he put his magazine down. "I'd rather you stay where you are, ma'am."

"Okay." I leaned back and didn't relax until he picked up his magazine.

I sighed and punched in the one number I hadn't wanted to call. Out of eight children, seven were girls. My brother, Buddy, was #4 in the birth order. I came along five years after him. I'd tagged after him during my childhood, and once I heard him introduce me as the brother he never had.

When he built a tree house, probably better described as a tree platform, to get away from me, I spent the summer learning how to climb to it. I followed him onto roof tops and off of them. If our mother had ever caught us hanging from the eaves and free falling, she'd have made us sit on chairs for the rest of our childhood.

I had his number on speed dial. He answered on the first ring.

"Hey, Sis." His cheerful voice tightened my jaw. "I'm on my way. I should be there in ten minutes."

"What?" I was surprised how far my tight jaw could drop. "You're on your way where?"

"I got hold of Uncle Claude. He's on his way to the station." Click, Buddy hung up on me.

"How did he know?" I asked Jake. "How does he always know?"

Jake grinned; his brown eyes sparkled at me. I wished for the umpteenth time that he could talk.

"You're in for it now," I muttered softly, eyeing the officer. I didn't speak loudly enough for him to actually hear me. I didn't want to be noticeably rude, but it felt good to voice my displeasure. I'm a rebel all right. Jake, master of body language, started to giggle, and the man put down his magazine. He felt the change in my attitude, so points to him.

The dog barked, and I glanced out the window to see vehicles arriving.

I recognized Buddy's pickup. I wasn't happy to see he had a passenger. Mary Lee's husband, Logan, was with him. Logan has been a brother-in-law for a lot of years. He's almost as bad a tease as Buddy is. My life sucks.

I didn't recognize the car that pulled in next to Buddy's pickup, but I recognized the man getting out of it. Uncle Claude to the rescue. They stopped to talk and I waited. And waited.

Impatience drove me to my feet, and the officer behind the desk stood up. "Ma'am, I'll have to ask you to sit down."

I glared at him and pointed out the window. "Uncle Claude is here. I want to talk to him right now."

Before the man could move to the door, it opened, and I watched my uncle enter the room. For one brief moment, I saw my father. Claude's eyes were the eyes of my dad. He was heavier, softer than my father had been, but the family resemblance was strong, and I did the one thing I most didn't want to do in front of any of these men.

I burst into tears.

"Stop it." Uncle Claude glared at me. "Don't go blubbering now. I came as soon as I found out. Why my brother had to go and have eight children, I'll never know." His phone rang, interrupting his tirade. He stared at it in disbelief. "Damn it, now you've got your cousins calling me."

He answered the phone and barked into it, "Stop it, right now. You get on the phone and you call everybody and tell them I've got the situation under control. I don't want to get one more phone call about this."

I wiped my eyes, sniffled to stop the snot running, and protested, "I didn't call any cousins. And you should have been here sooner anyway. Nobody would call you even when I asked and asked."

Uncle Claude shot a look at his deputy, and I hid a grin when I saw the man slide the golf magazine under a folder. I was pretty sure my uncle saw it too.

"How long have you been sitting here?" my uncle asked me.

I glanced at my watch. "About an hour, I guess. But it seemed like three."

"An hour? For a routine check?" My uncle looked thoughtful. He stepped to the door and barked, "You men, get in here."

They entered and stood at what I assumed was attention. The dog was the only one I gave points to for proper form. He sat at his handler's left side in a solid, square sit.

"Can any of you explain why my niece has been sitting here for an hour? Why was she brought here in the first place?" he scowled at the men.

The men looked anywhere but at my uncle, and the handler finally cleared his throat. "Sir, we first noticed the suspect when she was stopped at the stop and go light. The van matched the description of a vehicle that was involved in a robbery-kidnapping. We thought it would be a good idea to bring it in and let the dog go over it while we checked out the ownership of the vehicle."

"Bull!" Uncle Claude snapped, and I looked at him in amazement. My uncle is usually easy going and kind. I'd rarely seen him angry. All the phone calls he'd gotten must have really annoyed him. "What you mean is, you have a new dog and wanted to work him. You've seriously inconvenienced Charly, and by doing that you seriously inconvenienced me."

He turned to glare at me. "The next time you sic your family into calling me, I'll lock you up myself on whatever charge I can dream up. Go on, you can leave. I'm sorry you were detained. It won't happen again."

Buddy and Logan stood grinning like idiots. Buddy spoke. "Nice dog, Ben."

The handler grinned and I felt a shock of recognition. I looked more closely at him and noticed he had the same Russell eyes that Uncle Claude had. In fact, probably the same eyes that Buddy and I have.

"Ben?" I choked on the name. "As in Cousin Ben?" How many years had it been since I'd seen Uncle Claude's oldest boy?

His grin widened and I asked him, "What did I ever do to you?"

I thought hard for a moment and remembered the summer he was thirteen and the squirt guns filled with perfume. And the angry, odiferous child who threatened revenge at a time and place when I least expected it.

"Never mind," I said.

I grabbed Jake's wheelchair and headed toward the door. Buddy scrambled to hold it open, and I wheeled through without slowing down.

I called over my shoulder, "Thank you, Uncle Claude," and I ran for freedom.

I loaded Jake into the van, returned to thank Buddy and Logan for coming to my rescue, then headed out of town as fast as I legally could.

Chapter Four
Finding a House

"How was I to know finding a house in Weary would be so hard?" I didn't look at my brother, Buddy. I know better. He could look at me cross-eyed, and I'd laugh so hard I'd drop whatever we were carrying, or worse, have to go change clothes.

"Move it, Sis," Buddy prodded.

I looked at the big vanity mirror, too large for either one of us to carry alone. Where did Samantha find these old pieces of furniture? I grabbed hold and lifted. Being the mother of a disabled child, I lift weight on a daily basis. I didn't see any of my sisters out here hefting furniture with the men. They were inside unpacking boxes. *This is another fine mess I've gotten myself into,* I thought, and made the mistake of saying it out loud because Buddy heard me and started to snicker, which set me off before we'd taken six steps.

"Put it down." I set my end down forcing him to follow suit. I leaned on it and struggled to get my composure back. How my brother can send me back into our childhood dynamics without even saying a word, I don't know. But it happens, and I'll have to remember how to deal with it.

"How long is Logan going to let you stay with them?" Buddy leaned against his end of the mirror.

"I never intended to stay more than a few weeks. I thought I'd come back here, find a house, buy it, and move in. I didn't expect complications." I wiped sweat off my forehead before it dripped into my eyes. "How many people want to buy a house in Weary? I thought half the town would be for sale."

"It is." Buddy reached down to pick up the mirror. "The problem is you need a really big house. You went from needing a two bedroom house for two people to needing one that will house eight people, two dogs, a cat, and a wheelchair."

"This is true." I picked up my end, and we started an awkward march to the front door of the parsonage. "Josie took a job running the school cafeteria. Keira and Téa are still in school. I found out yesterday that Anna lost her job and will have to move back until she finds a new one. Roni's husband, John, took a teaching job in some European town that I can't even pronounce. He'll be gone for a year. Roni applied for librarian in the new library and got it. It doesn't make sense to buy a house for one year for her and Mitchell."

I stopped again, forcing Buddy to once more lower his end of the mirror. We were at the front door anyway, so it seemed like a perfect spot to catch my breath. "I would love to have all of us in one house. I just can't find a house that will hold us all."

"You better find something fast." Logan, husband of my eldest sister, Mary Lee, pushed past us, a big box balanced on his shoulder. "You can't freeload off me forever. I'm going to padlock the fridge."

I narrowed my eyes at him but lacked the energy and imagination to think of a good come-back. He's all bluff, spouting fire and smoke to hide a really big heart. You can tell he's ex-military from his trim haircut to his equally fit body. His attention to health puts us all to shame. But he has a potty-mouth, and you just have to take him the way he is because he sure isn't going to change.

He opened the screen door for us. "Get the lead out. I can't stand around all day waiting for you two."

We hustled. And we continued to work hard all morning. That's one of the nice things about a big family. When one of us needs help, an army shows up. And it's a good-natured, willing army accompanied by lots of laughter and plenty of food.

***

"You're so lucky." I walked into the kitchen, saw an open chair at the table, and grabbed it before Roni could get to it. She made a face at me and altered direction to snag a bar stool.

"Why is that?" Samantha looked surprised. She was making pitchers of drinks, iced tea for the adults and Kool-Aid for the children. A beautiful smile lit her face. I didn't often see her without a beaming face. Even her voice smiles when she talks.

Josie raised her hand. "I know. Because you have a house all ready to move into. When Theo agreed to be the interim pastor, the parsonage came with it. And a nice house it is."

It was. I sighed and reached forward to snag a potato chip out of the bag lying open on the table. Two bedrooms, finished basement, open kitchen and living room, and two full baths. To my eyes, Samantha, Theo, and Blair had landed in clover. No hunting, no haggling, no frustration at having all of your belongings sitting in a storage unit.

Josie, sitting next to the window, pulled the newly hung curtain aside and pointed. "I'd love to see the inside of the house across the street."

"So would I." Phoebe leaned over Josie to look out the window. The rest of us did a mass move to the windows to peer at the big house.

"Too bad it's not for sale." Buddy watched Katie unwrap the platters of sandwiches sent over from the café then grabbed a ham sandwich off the top. As the only boy in the family of girls, he almost always got the first bite. Some things never change.

I hate when he gets my brain spinning. He's done it to me my whole life. He opens his mouth, arouses my curiosity, and then waits for me to react.

It didn't take sixty seconds before I asked, "Who does live there? Do any of you know?"

"It's the old Whittaker house." Mary Lee spoke first. "I don't think the family lives there anymore." She fell silent, and we all stood at the windows, looking at the big house across the street.

"If nobody lives there," Roni spoke up, "do you think they would consider selling it?"

"I don't know." Mary Lee shook her head.

"Well," Katie drawled; her voice holds the same kind of smile that Samantha's does. "I guess we better call one of the aunts to find out. I bet Aunt Ellen would know all about the house."

We made Mary Lee call. Being the eldest she has a huge, overgrown sense of responsibility. I hope she never decides to make us grow up.

We could only hear Mary Lee's side of the conversation, and there wasn't much of that. When her left-hand twitched, we scrambled for pen and paper so she could jot down a name and telephone number.

"Wait a minute," she complained when we started pelting her with questions as soon as she hung up the phone. "Aunt Ellen said she thinks the family would consider renting the house. It's been empty for over five years."

I fought down a wave of irritation. "Why didn't she say anything before this? I've been looking for a house for six weeks. I don't know about renting, though. I need to be able to adapt a house for Jake's wheelchair."

"That may be why she didn't say anything," Samantha spoke. "She knew you wanted to buy a house, and this house doesn't appear to be for sale."

"I love it," Roni spoke up. "After all the years I lived in a little apartment, it would be so nice to be able to spread out."

"We haven't even seen the inside." Josie has learned how to be practical. "It might be full of horrible little rooms with dark, cruddy walls and no closets."

"And spiders." Buddy gave a wicked, teasing laugh, feeding into Josie's spider phobia. She was bitten by a brown recluse when she was little and screams if you even say the word spider. We had a lot of fun when we were little. Josie is a world-class screamer. Today was no exception, and it served Buddy right when she let out a shriek that rivaled the whistle on the daily freight train into his ear.

"Don't forget how expensive it would be to heat." Gloom descended on me. The younger girls may not remember the unheated bedrooms and frost on the inside of the windows. I do.

I don't want to go back to wearing long flannel nightgowns and socks to bed or wake up dreading an early morning dash to the stove. I don't regret growing up that way, but I don't want to live that way ever again. I've earned a few comforts, and I intend to make sure I get them, especially when it comes to staying warm.

We went back to eating our lunch, taking occasional glances out the window at the big, handsome Victorian. Samantha, once the procrastinator in the family finally gave an impatient sigh, reached over, and grabbed the scrap of paper that Mary Lee had written on. She flipped open her cell phone and punched in the number. I tensed up when I realized she was talking to a real person and not a voicemail box.

She flipped her phone shut. I leaned forward, noticing the others did too. "There's someone over there right now. If we want to, we can go look at it this afternoon."

Chapter Five
We Find our House

"We can't all go." I protested and shuddered at the idea of the troop we are marching over in masse. "Whoever is over there would lock the door and hide if he saw us all coming. And getting Jake up the stairs would be a nightmare. I can tell from here that his portable ramp isn't long enough to span the porch steps."

Then I tuned them out because I knew it would take a good fifteen minutes of argument and debate and my opinion wasn't going to count anyway. Whoever really wanted to go would, and nothing I could say would change that. I refilled my iced tea glass, grabbed a lonely cupcake, and nibbled while I waited.

In the end, Josie and Roni said they had to go since it might end up being their home for a year. I had to go because, to be honest, if the house should turn out to be available, I'd be the one taking responsibility for the lease. I knew everybody would chip in equally, but because of the sale of my house in Illinois, I was the one with the most available cash.

Phoebe refused to be left out. She didn't need a reason. Of all my sisters, she's the one who has an even bigger curiosity bump than I do and has way more stubbornness than I've ever possessed, and that's saying a lot.

Theo and Logan weren't letting us out of their sight. Partly it's the good ol' boy mentality thinking that women can't make up their minds about anything, and if they do, it's probably for the wrong reasons. But I suspect it's more a case of self-preservation. We were going to look at a monstrous, big old house. They likely knew who we were going to call if a pipe burst or a toilet back flushed.

So out of the army that turned out for Samantha's move-in day, six of us walked across the street to look at the big Victorian house. I lagged behind, wanting to get a feel for the outside of the house. It sat by itself on what had to be several acres of land, a nice benefit to being the last house on the street.

A big porch sprawled across the front of the house and wrapped around the side. Between the house and a detached three-car garage that was an obvious late-comer to the property, sat a porte-cochere. I'd have to measure it to be sure, but I thought it would allow enough head room to accommodate my raised-roof van.

I stopped at the curb and looked up and up. The house stood three stories tall; a rounded turret graced the right hand corner of the house and big picture windows sat on both sides of the front door. I don't think Josie's fear of a dark house would hold up.

The other's stopped at the bottom of the front steps, and I hurried to catch up with them.

"Look!" Josie pointed to the right. The end of the porch was screened by a white trellis covered with honeysuckle vines.

Roni pointed upwards, and we obediently followed her pointing finger. Her voice sounded a bit thick as she spoke. "Just waiting for a porch swing."

I don't think I was the only one who blinked and swallowed hard to ease a suddenly tight throat. All of us were caught by memories of warm summer nights, locusts humming, and the sweet aroma of honeysuckle in bloom. The creak of the porch swing rang in my ears. The soft murmur of our parent's voices reached from the past and touched me. I wanted this house with a passion just for bringing that memory close again, and I ached with longing for loved ones gone.

Theo and Logan had no patience for our reminiscing. Logan gave us a look only he is capable of and rapped loudly on the front door. We scrambled to position ourselves beside him as the door opened.

I judged the man standing in the doorway to be either side of forty. A charming smile lit his face, but I noticed watchfulness in his eyes, and I wondered if he was a lawyer.

"Come in." He opened the door and ushered us in. The entryway did what it was supposed to do. It welcomed us.

A large, formal dining room opened to the left side of the entry and to the right a big living room. Straight ahead a beautiful staircase, taking up half of a generous hallway, curved gracefully upward to the second floor hallway. The beautiful hard-wood floors and elegant molding hinted of a genteel past. The big old houses we had grown up in had been anything but genteel, and I'm pretty sure none of those houses still remained standing. Most of them were torn down as soon as our family moved out.

"I'm Scott Whitaker." The charming smile was back on his face. The watchfulness I'd seen could well have been my overactive imagination. "Please feel free to wander around. I'll follow along and answer any questions you might have."

Logan and Theo knew us too well. They weren't going to follow us anywhere listening to us 'ooh and ahh'. "If you don't mind," Logan spoke quickly, "why don't you show Theo and me the hot water heater and heating system?"

"Of course." Mr. Whitaker hesitated a moment and then glanced at the five of us standing there. I don't know about the others, but I couldn't have been more anxious to start if I'd been lined up for a relay race and waiting for the starting shot.

I could hear the reluctance in his voice, but what else could he say? "Why don't you just look around while I take these gentlemen down to the basement?"

"That's fine." We waved them away and never gave them another thought.

***

I would have taken the house just for the kitchen. Cabinets everywhere, beautiful stone counter tops. Old-fashioned, yes, but well crafted and in good condition. I wanted to hug the walk-in pantry. Space, glorious space.

We thundered up the servant's stairs to the second floor to find five bedrooms and two bathrooms. The rooms were large with high ceilings. Nowhere did we see the cramped, small rooms that Josie had feared would exist.

The third floor was a wide open room with enough head space to be comfortable. The round tower that provided a cozy nook in the living room and a comfortable corner in the master bedroom provided a wonderful view from the third floor.

"I wonder how cold it gets up here in the winter," I muttered.

Phoebe was examining the windows. "These seem to be thermal replacement windows. They tilt in. No way could they be original to the house."

"I wonder what year they replaced them." Roni was curious.

"There are several radiators up here," Josie pointed out. "If they work, it should be comfortable up here."

We had seen radiators all over the house, so we weren't surprised when Logan and Theo told us the main heating of the house was steam. What did surprise us was that it was relatively new and efficient. Logan told us the kitchen, living room, and the bathrooms were heated by a forced air furnace.

Logan and Theo went off to look at windows, insulation, and other structural stuff that, truth be told, I didn't really want to know about. Logan is known in our family to be fanatically picky about doing things the right way. Theo spent many years of his life doing carpentry work. I trusted them to be honest with us.

Coming back down to the first floor, we followed the hallway to the back part of the house. We had noticed from the outside that there was a one story addition at the back. Here we found an exceptionally large great room, another bathroom, and two smaller rooms.

One room seemed to be set up as an office, but both rooms looked large enough to be used as bedrooms. It was obvious this was a later construction from the original house.

Logan and Theo returned from their tour of the second and third floors.

"What do you think?" Roni is always practical.

"The house is sound." Logan took his hat off and wiped sweat off his face with his arm.

Theo nodded. "Everything is in good working condition. It's remarkably well-kept. There's even a back-up generator in the basement." Theo would notice something like that.

"I don't know." Reluctance pulled at me. I'd never wanted to live in a house as badly as I did this one. But Jake's needs always come first. "Any place we live, I need to be able to make it accessible for Jake. I don't think I'd want to spend that much money on something we rent."

"Rent?" Scott gave a startled jerk. "This house isn't for rent."

"It isn't?" The strength of my disappointment surprised me. The house had charmed all of us, and I knew there probably wasn't another house in Weary that would give us this much room.

"No." Scott shook his head. "We want to sell the house."

"Sell?" I echoed. I'm from Illinois. I know what a house like this would sell for back there.

"Yes. We want to sell it. Most of the family is gone, and the ones who are left don't want anything to do with this house."

His tone of voice should have warned me, but I was struggling with the idea of buying the house. I couldn't bring myself to ask the obvious question.

Logan asked in his no-nonsense, blunt way, "How much?"

Scott Whitaker's answer stunned me. I asked. "Would you mind repeating the price?"

He did, and then I did something that I probably shouldn't have. I took a big breath and said, "I'll take it.

Chapter Six
A Disappearance

"You did what?" Mary Lee's shock wouldn't normally worry me. When Logan was stationed in Thailand for a year, I moved in with her to help out with expense and her children. I learned really fast that my eldest sister and I are very different. I grew accustomed to tuning her out.

Samantha and Katie, adding their shocked voices to hers, sent me mentally scrambling over my actions of the previous hour.

"I had to buy it," I protested. "Logan and Theo said the house was sound. The heating system is in good shape. The roof is okay. There are a couple of acres of land that come with it, and, most importantly, it's big enough for all of us."

"What is Hal going to say?" I wish you could hear Katie's voice. She talks the way she writes with lots of punctuation and capital letters. It's entertaining to listen to, but not when it's directed at me.

"That's the best part." I knew I sounded defensive. I get that way when someone questions my rash, impulsive decisions. "I have half of the sale price from our house in Illinois to use on housing here. The price Mr. Whitaker quoted me is about half what I expected to pay. He's practically giving the house away."

"And that doesn't worry you?" Katie asked.

Frustrated at being questioned, I shook my head. Buying the house made perfect sense to me. Why didn't the others see it that way? "I worry more about freeloading on all of you. We need a house. I wish I'd known about the house two months ago. School starts in three weeks. Life would be a lot simpler if we could all get settled into one place."

Logan hates to sit around. He really hates listening to us bicker. He got fidgety and asked Theo for the keys to the U-Haul. He told Mary Lee he'd be back in time for supper and left to return the truck. Buddy followed to give him a ride home.

Samantha got up and poured a fresh cup of coffee. She handed it to Theo. I settled back and soaked up the feeling of family. Twenty-seven years of marriage hadn't taken the homesickness out of me. I missed my husband and oldest son, and I would have been happiest if they were with me, but right then, looking around the kitchen at various members of my family, I was more contented than I'd been in a long time.

My peace didn't last long. Loud knocking on the front door interrupted. Someone must have answered because I heard deep, rumbling voices, then rapid footsteps coming toward the kitchen.

Samantha's daughter, Blair, poked her head through the doorway and yelled, "Theo, you have company." Then she vanished back toward her bedroom. I think the speed of her disappearance had something to do with her being dressed as a cupcake.

"Where did you say Blair works?" I asked Samantha.

She grinned, and the others tried to stifle giggles. "She took a job with a company that provides specialty promotions. This week she's advertising Dolly's baked goods in Emporia."

Josie spoke. "She told us the job is temporary until she finds something better."

"Was she coming or going just now?" I thought back to the crazy costume she had been wearing. "Wouldn't she just change at the store and not risk being seen dressed as a cupcake?"

Josie raised an eyebrow. "I think there was a problem with a zipper. She was informed that if she tore the costume, she had to buy it. I think Keira and Téa are helping to free her."

I knew my nieces and suspected they would give Blair a lot of grief before they freed her from the cupcake, but maybe I was being too hard on the girls.

Two men I didn't recognize entered the kitchen. Worry rolled off the older gray-haired man. "I'm sorry, Reverend. I hate to bother you while you're moving in, but we've got a problem."

Theo put his coffee cup down and stood up. "Mr. Kelly, isn't it? You're one of the church deacons, aren't you?"

"Yes, sir, I met you when we interviewed you for the job."

The younger man moved restlessly and started to speak; Mr. Kelly held up his hand and silenced him.

"Reverend, this is John Ramsey. I don't know if you've met his wife, Jennifer. She's the church secretary."

Theo shook his head in the negative. "I'm sorry, I haven't met her yet. I wasn't going to open the church office until tomorrow."

"She hasn't talked to you at all?" John's voice cracked. I noticed his eyes were red-rimmed and tired.

"No." Theo looked over at Samantha and she shook her head. For some reason the rest of us did too.

"I don't know what to do." Mr. Ramsey seemed to sink into himself. "I've called everyone I can think of. I've checked everywhere."

Mr. Ramsey's eyes glistened wetly as if he wanted to cry but wouldn't allow himself to. "My wife is missing, Reverend. I last saw her yesterday morning. I've called the hospitals, the police, and her relatives. No one has seen her."

His words made me uncomfortable. I lost my sister Roni once when she was five and I was nine. I will never forget that awful, hollow feeling when you realize an entire person has gone missing. I truly sympathized with Mr. Ramsey.

My family is big on sympathy. If even one person started to tear up, the others would follow. I think Mr. Kelly sensed that because he was quick to get Mr. Ramsey and Theo out of the kitchen and over to the church office. I couldn't blame him.

Samantha steered us away from the subject of the missing secretary by asking for more details about the house. We forgot the missing secretary and talked about the house and how long it would take to finalize the sale. We needed to move as quickly as possible.

Not for me so much, although my welcome with Logan was wearing thin, as it was for Roni and Josie. They had jobs they needed to start, and Josie's girls had school. Mitchell was too young for school, but Jake and I were willing to watch him during the day. While we talked, I kept listening for Theo to come back. What had happened to Mr. Ramsey's wife?

We didn't get a chance to find out. My brother-in-law, wise to the ways of our family, waited until we left. Samantha did tell me later that she would be taking over the duties as church secretary until Jennifer Ramsey showed up.

Chapter Seven
Moving In

Guilt is a harsh master. Two weeks is my limit when visiting somebody. I'd been bumming off Mary Lee and Logan for almost eight weeks. Mary Lee doesn't care. She's never happier than she is having guests in her home. Logan is another matter. I know in my heart that he possesses a kind and generous spirit. I sometimes have a hard time getting through the layers of gruff to find it.

I would have bounced from sister to sister, spreading out the burden, but I couldn't. Josie, Keira, Téa, and Anna were camping at Phoebe's. Roni and Mitchell were staying at Samantha's. We needed our own house so I pushed hard to get legal ownership of the big Victorian house as quickly as I could.

I should have been surprised at the speed my brothers-in-law pitched in to help move us, but I wasn't. Seldom have I seen men so willing to move big items of furniture. By Labor Day our three families were merged into the big house.

Jake and I took the rooms at the back of the first floor addition. I hadn't yet decided how to adapt the house to the wheelchair, and the added-on rooms posed no barrier problems. It had a big, open floor space in the main room, and the back bathroom was more than big enough to accommodate Jake's bathing needs.

For the time being, Jake would be confined to the main floor. Logan and Theo built a ramp onto the side porch so I could bring Jake from the van into the kitchen. The porte-cochere was tall enough to allow me to pull right up to the door, making it much easier to load and unload Jake, especially in inclement weather.

Roni and Mitchell claimed two adjoining rooms on the second floor. Josie moved into the master bedroom. This left two bedrooms empty and created a minor war.

With Anna out of work and living at home, that meant three girls were fighting over the two remaining bedrooms.

***

I'd been fearful that merging three households into one would pose a logistics problem. How many couches does one home need? Will there be room for everything? I found out that a house the size of this one needed every piece of furniture our combined families possessed, and it still looked uncluttered.

The men beat a hasty retreat as soon as the big items were in place. Each family's boxes were placed in the appropriate areas awaiting individual care. Kitchen items were another matter. They were universally used by all, so late afternoon I found myself in the kitchen with Roni, Josie, Jake, Keira, Téa, and Anna.

Look." Josie opened one of Roni's boxes and held a bright purple glass in the air. To our children it appeared to be a dented metal glass, but to us, the ones who remembered, it meant Grandma Lavona, Wednesday nights, and popcorn.

I reached past Josie's shoulder and pulled out a brilliant green glass. "I can't even remember who got what color except for the purple. That..."

"Was Roni's," Josie finished with me.

"Why Wednesday?" Anna came closer to peer into the box at the rest of the metal glasses nested there.

"And why Grandma Lavona?" Keira leaned against the counter, waiting for one of us to explain.

I reached up and placed the green glass on the shelf, setting it next to Roni's purple one. "Grandma Lavona gave them to us. We didn't often get gifts from her. She had a lot of children and very little money, but one Christmas she sent us these glasses. There was one glass for each of us."

Josie continued the story, "Mom would get so mad at us. Every time she'd do dishes, one of us would get thirsty and pull out a clean glass. We always worried about getting somebody else's germs, so we kept getting another clean glass instead of using the one already sitting out. Grandma gave us the metal ones so we each had our own color. It made it a lot easier on Mom when we each started using one glass a day instead of a dozen."

"Wednesday." Keira reminded us. "Why were Wednesday's so important?"

I smiled at my sisters. How do you explain Wednesday to someone who hadn't been there?

"Wednesdays were popcorn and pop night." Josie picked a yellow-gold glass out of the box and placed it on the shelf. She turned around and faced her middle daughter. "Our dad had a truck route. On Wednesdays, his route took him too far away to get back home."

I grinned at the girls. "On those nights, Mom let us have popcorn for supper. She popped enough popcorn to fill a dishpan."

Roni took over. "Wednesday night was the only night we got to drink soda pop. It was always Pepsi Cola. Mom would buy a six pack of Pepsi. They came in big glass bottles back then. She would never have let us get by just eating popcorn and soda if Dad had been home. It was as much a treat for her as it was for us."

I watched Roni put the last glass onto the shelf, pick up the empty box, and move it out of the way, bringing back a full box and setting it on the counter.

Such simple memories. Sometimes, a feeling would steal over me that maybe giving our children the material things we'd gone without was a mistake. Not having a television meant we ran and played outside, usually with a group of neighborhood friends. There wasn't any talk of hyperactivity after we spent our days running, climbing, and wrestling. All that energy got burned off.

No, I decided, looking at the faces of my young nieces and nephew. As wonderful as television, video games, and portable radios were, our children missed out on something equally wonderful and precious. We couldn't go back and give it to them now. Maybe banding together like this for the next year would give us the opportunity to pass down our memories, and they could pass that knowledge on to their own children. Continuity; isn't that what family is all about?

Bored with our memories and afraid we'd put them to work, the girls left the kitchen. Roni sat Mitchell at the kitchen table and gave him a cookie and a cup of milk.

Peace reigned for all of ten minute.

"Mo-om," a wail from the living room full of such anguish that Josie took off a run.

I grinned when Jake flashed his eyes at me then toward the doorway.

"You want to go see what's going on?" His eyes flew skyward, his silent signal for yes.

"Okay." I grabbed the handles of his chair and pushed him toward the living room, enjoying the ease of pushing the wheelchair across hardwood floors.

Seventeen-year old Keira had a mulish look on her face, a mirror image of Téa's face. "I'm not sharing a bedroom with Téa. I want my own room."

I couldn't blame her. They had shared a bedroom their entire lives. And not peaceably, I might add.

Anna didn't look mulish, she looked downright scared. "I can't sleep on the third floor by myself. It's spooky."

I love teasing my nieces. "Tell you what, Anna. You can keep one of my dogs up there with you." I have two. Molly is a big yellow lab. Murphy is a Golden Retriever. I knew that Murphy would go up with her, but as soon as it was bedtime, Anna would have to tie her to make her stay upstairs. "Of course, you won't get a lot of sleep going up and downstairs to let them in and out at night."

"Mom," Anna wailed again. It was clear she didn't appreciate my offer.

"You can leave the light on at night." Roni likes to tease the girls too.

We let the girls bicker for a while, but it was clear Anna was truly frightened.

Why don't all three of you move to the third floor?" I suggested.

"What?" All three faces swiveled toward me. The idea grew in my mind.

"It could be fun. There's lots of room. The extra furniture is up there anyway. It would be like one big apartment." I could see the girls thinking.

"It could work." Roni is the logical sister. "Put your beds at one end. We can get you wardrobes for closets, and they can be positioned between the beds so you'll each have some privacy. The other two thirds of the room can be arranged with the chairs and tables. You'd have lots more room than you would in the bedrooms. Maybe you could talk Blair into moving up there with you. She's really cramped in the little spare room at the parsonage."

It worked. Arranging the third floor kept the girls out of our hair for quite awhile and left us with two extra bedrooms. In a family the size of ours, extra bedrooms are a rare commodity.

Chapter Eight
A Mystery

Our days quickly fell into a routine. Josie and the girls left the house together. The library didn't open until ten so Roni didn't have to rush around. I'm an early riser, getting up between five and six, so preparing breakfast usually fell to me. Jake sleeps as late as he wants; he usually wakes up between eight and nine.

For various reasons I had been home schooling Jake, but I'm not a trained teacher. My biggest strength is that I can communicate with him better than anyone else and I never underestimate him. He has cerebral palsy and his diagnosis is multi-physically disabled and non-verbal with normal intelligence.

I did a happy dance when Phoebe said she would tutor Jake. With Phoebe spending time with Jake, I agreed to watch Mitchell for Roni. It's a real treat for me to be around him. He tickles my funny bone. I'm convinced he's a genius, but that's probably because I've forgotten what it's like to be around a child with normal development.

September flew by with all of us getting used to the house and the new jobs. Roni and I missed our husbands, but the letters, texts, and phone calls assured us they were doing fine. Every time we got a little depressed about being separated from them, Mary Lee reminded us how many times Logan had been stationed overseas. We quickly learned not to complain in front of her.

I enjoyed the Flint Hills in summertime, but fall arrived, and overnight the leaves turned gold, red, and bronze. The cold snap that brought out the color of the foliage was followed by a perfect Indian summer.

The first day of October found me sitting at the kitchen table. Sunlight poured in through the big open windows, throwing a lacy pattern of leaves onto the table and walls. Jake was up and dressed and I was feeding him. Roni and Mitchell sat at the table with us.

"Phoebe's late today." I glanced at the wall clock. Roni had to leave soon.

"What?" Roni looked up and I swallowed a grin. I loved watching her try to convince her three year old son that a hot dog wasn't an appropriate breakfast item.

"Phoebe is usually here by now." I gave Jake another spoonful of yogurt. I've done this so many times the motion is automatic.

Before Roni could reply, the phone rang. Jake jumped and laughed, and Mitchell flew off the chair in a flash. I wasn't far behind him. Luckily, most of the phones in the house were too high for him to reach.

"Hi," I answered and tried to keep Mitchell from climbing up me. Roni laughed at me trying to cope with her energetic son.

"It's me." Phoebe' voice sounded tense. "I'm going to be really late coming in."

"What happened?" My stomach clenched. "Are the kids okay?"

"Oh, yes," Phoebe reassured me. "It's nothing to do with them. Jed was out taking care of the cattle, and he found one dead. It was all ripped up. He doesn't know what caused it. He said he's never seen anything like it. I'm supposed to get hold of the vet and show him where they are. Jed's staying out there. He wants to count the cattle and make sure the rest of them are all right."

"Is he going to use the horses?" I love horses and have owned my own for years, but I've never gotten to work cattle, and so far Jed's managed to avoid my help.

I heard Phoebe swallow a giggle. "I don't think so. If he does, I'll tell him you offered."

I didn't think I'd hold my breath waiting for Jed to call. I probably shouldn't have told him about the time I was sixteen and visiting my cousin, Will. He was barrel racing his mare, Sugar, and when he finished, he asked me if I wanted to go bring a calf in. I was young and confident so I said yes. That's the day I learned a cow horse can turn on a dime and stop even quicker. I hit the ground hard enough to dent it and ended up so saddle sore I couldn't sit down the next day.

I make jokes, but losing a cow isn't fun, and having one brutally killed is definitely not funny. I repeated Phoebe's message to Roni.

"What would kill a cow?" Roni was curious.

"I don't know. A pack of dogs probably could. Coyotes might but I'd think they would be more likely to eat one after it was already dead. I guess we'll have to wait until Phoebe comes in to find out any more details."

Roni left. I finished feeding Jake and Mitchell, but I was thinking about the cow. What bothered me most was Phoebe saying Jed had never seen anything like it. He grew up on a farm, and he'd farmed his whole adult life. He was a hunter as well as a farmer. What was it about the dead carcass that he hadn't seen before?

Chapter Nine
Playing Hooky

With Phoebe coming in late, I knew Jake's schooling fell on my shoulders once again. Not so difficult a task for me now that Phoebe had taken charge. It would be easy enough to follow her lesson plan.

"Outside." Mitchell tugged on my jean-clad leg. Jake's eyes flew rapidly upward, telling me he agreed with his small cousin.

It amazes me how Jake can take a simple move like looking upward and make it mean so many different things. If he looks up slowly and briefly, it means he's not sure or maybe. If you ask if he's hungry or he really wants something, he looks up as high as he can without his eyes rolling to the back of his head. That's what I call a big yes. If his eyes go rapidly up over and over, he's excited. Mitchell was saying please, but Jake was saying yes, yes, yes.

I looked out the window at the perfect fall day and weakened. "You win, you little munchkin." I grabbed Mitchell and swung him high. He giggled as I lowered him. "Go find your jacket and we'll take a walk. I declare a field trip."

"We'll go swing?" Mitchell ran up to me. I got the zipper started for him; then he brushed my hands away to pull it up by himself. His independence amuses me, and from the wide grin and sparkling eyes on Jake's face, I wasn't the only one. Bringing Jake to Kansas, giving him a chance to be around his cousins, has been good for him. From Mitchell's words I was pretty sure he had a destination in mind.

"Maybe." I ruffled his hair. "I want to talk to Aunt Samantha first."

I tossed a poncho over Jake and his chair. The dogs came running, but I didn't think I could handle two big dogs, the wheel chair, and Mitchell.

"Maybe if I put the leash on Mitchell," I muttered to Jake. He laughed and shook his head no.

I laughed with him and told the dogs they had to stay home. I promised to let them out when I got back.

We left by the kitchen door so I could wheel Jake down the ramp. I still hadn't decided how to adapt the rest of the house. An elevator was possible or a stairway lift, but I hated to do anything that would damage the beautiful banister on the staircase or risk scarring the wonderful woodwork throughout the house. I'd have to make a decision one of these days. There really wasn't any reason Jake would have to go upstairs except if he wanted to see it. I hated for him to be left out or isolated if I could do something about it.

I knew Samantha would be at the church, so we went directly to the office.

"Hi." Mitchell ran ahead and got to her first.

Samantha looked from Mitchell to Jake. "Is Phoebe sick today?"

"No." I shook my head. "She called a little while ago, and Jed has a problem with the cattle."

Theo walked in through the door leading to the sanctuary, and I brought them up to date on what I knew. He glanced at the clock, then at Samantha. "I think I'll go out there and see what's going on."

Samantha nodded. "You don't have any appointments until this afternoon. I'll be here to take any phone calls, and file the new music away."

I frowned as I watched Theo leave. "He looks worried. Is anything wrong?"

Samantha sighed and leaned back in her chair. "It's a mess. Mrs. Franklin came by yesterday and asked Theo to make an announcement Sunday about the Halloween haunted house. The party seems to be an annual event here. I guess the church has been offering the haunted house for the past five years as an alternative to trick-or-treating. They thought it would be a way to keep the junior high and high school students occupied so they don't run the streets and get in trouble."

"That sounds like a big job." It also didn't sound like anything I wanted to be involved in, but that's because I try to avoid large crowds of children. I like children. I just don't want to be responsible for them. I carry too big a load on my own and don't need to add to it. "What's the problem?"

"Right after Mrs. Franklin left, Allyson Wright and Trisha Byerly arrived and told Theo that members of the congregation are against the church having anything to do with celebrating a pagan holiday."

"Good grief!" I shook my head. "It doesn't sound like the church is promoting paganism. Children don't think about the origins of Halloween. They think about candy and having fun."

"I know." Samantha rubbed her forehead. "But Theo got phone calls all evening, and he's had a few already this morning."

"For or against?" I was curious.

"Both." I could tell this situation stressed my sister. "It would be easier if they were all for or all against. So far, it seems evenly divided."

"What's Theo going to do?" I didn't envy him his decision. Whatever he decided would turn one-half of the congregation against him. Politics in a small town can be vicious.

"The only thing he can do is make a decision based on what he feels is right, regardless of what anybody else thinks."

"Do you know what that decision will be?" I asked.

"Not for sure." Samantha stood up and moved toward Mitchell. He'd climbed on a chair by Theo's desk, making it easier for him to examine the contents of the desk drawers. She scooped him up and he giggled. It was time to take him to the park and let him run off some little boy energy. "I don't think he likes the idea of a haunted house being held in the church."

We started for the door. Samantha tried to hold Mitchell's hand. He wasn't cooperating.

"Help me push Jake." I stepped back from the chair. Mitchell grinned. More often than not he was told to stay away from Jake's chair. He scampered over to grip the handles. I put my hand on the back of Jake's chair, and together we followed Samantha outside.

"It's hard to believe its October." Samantha stopped and looked upward. "The trees are so beautiful this fall."

I had to agree. "So warm it feels like early summer instead of autumn." For a few moments I allowed myself to really see. So often I walk through life absorbed in my own thoughts, I forget to look. Now I gazed and the colors dazzled my senses. The air glittered, dancing with little sparkles of light. The gold, bronze, and red of the autumn foliage added warmth against the cool blue of the sky.

Mitchell brought me back to earth with an ear-shattering yell. "Uncle Buddy."

"Where?" I looked but all I saw was a man on a riding lawnmower turning the corner and coming toward us.

"That is Buddy," Samantha exclaimed. "What in the world is he doing on the lawnmower?"

Mitchell ran toward Buddy and I chased after him. Samantha took our place behind the chair and pushed Jake.

I grabbed Mitchell just before he reached the lawnmower and scooped him up. He wiggled and squirmed, and Buddy turned the lawnmower off. "Let him go, Sis. He can sit on the mower." Buddy stood up. I lowered Mitchell to the ground. We watched the little boy climb onto the seat and play with the steering wheel.

"What's up?" I gasped, trying to catch my breath.

Buddy gave a disgruntled snort. "You won't believe what happened."

"What?" Samantha pulled the wheelchair to a halt. Jake grinned at his uncle.

"I was getting ready to go bowling last night. When I got in the car, my keys were gone."

I've been around Jake too long. I rolled my eyes. "I told you, you shouldn't leave the keys in your car."

"Did you find them?" Samantha is nicer than I am and genuinely sympathetic.

"No. I looked everywhere but I know I left them in the car. They're gone."

"Did you have to stay home?" I knew the answer to this one. I asked him anyway.

"No way." The look my brother gave me let me know what he thought of my question. "I couldn't get the truck out because I had the car parked behind it." I noticed he didn't mention the old '55 Chevy or the '69 Chevelle that he parked next to them. He knows my opinion of his so-called classic cars. He says they're all there. I think some of the pieces might be in the trunk.

"I had to hot wire the car. I figured I'd find the keys today."

"I take it you didn't find them?" Samantha sounded really concerned.

"No." Buddy's voice sounded as grim as I'd ever heard it. "I looked for the keys, but even if I'd found them, they wouldn't have done me any good. All four of my tires were slashed. There was a word painted on the driver's side window of the car."

"What did it say?" Worry gnawed at my stomach now. I may tease my brother, but I love him, and my family tends to be protective of each other. Losing a key was one thing; slashing tires was vandalism.

"It said, 'Walk.'"

Samantha and I both glanced at the lawn mower. Our brother is a gentle soul, but there is a line you don't cross with him. Once angry, he boils long and hard. If someone slashed his tires and told him to walk, he'd find a way to have wheels under him.

"Why the lawn mower?" I couldn't stand it. "Why didn't you drive the pickup?"

A sheepish look flitted across his face. He didn't reply.

"You didn't!" I choked back a laugh.

"He didn't what?" Samantha looked confused.

"Samantha." Tears of laughter clogged my eyes. "When our brother got home last night, he parked behind the pickup again, didn't you?"

"Yes, I did." No wonder Buddy sounded so disgusted.

We finally calmed down. "I know it's not funny, and now that I think about it, it's probably a good thing you parked there. Whoever wants you to walk probably would have damaged the truck too."

Buddy nodded in agreement. "I checked in the truck, and the keys were gone out of it."

I asked, "So, you're stuck with the lawn mower?"

Buddy sighed. "It looks like it."

Mitchell, bored with the silent lawnmower, went back to trying to push Jake, but the brakes were on.

The problem would keep him busy for a few more minutes.

I snickered again. I can't help it if I'm cursed with an inappropriate sense of humor. "At least no one will think you're strange. Uncle Bugg and Uncle Harry ride around town on lawn mowers all the time. They'll just figure it's a family thing."

The look in Buddy's eyes took me back to the age of twelve. "Thanks a lot, Sis. I don't have time to sit here and talk. I better get busy."

"Me, too," Samantha said. "I can hear the office phone ringing. Bye." She waved and ran for the phone. Watching her run, I doubted if she'd get there in time to answer it. It was probably more haunted house bickering anyway.

"Where are you off to?" Buddy asked.

I waved toward Mitchell and Jake. "I promised to take them for a walk. We'll probably go to the park. Why don't you meet us for lunch at the café?"

"Sounds good." Buddy turned the mower back on. "I'll see you at noon."

He puttered off and I unlocked the wheelchair, noticing Mitchell watch me with intent eyes. I knew putting the brakes on the chair wouldn't deter him ever again. He only has to see something once, and he never forgets it. I'd have to keep an eye on Jake for awhile so Mitchell wouldn't practice on the chair when Jake was in it.

Mitchell reached up to hold my hand. I smiled down at him. He must want to get to the park bad to voluntarily walk beside me. "Let's go, guys. We're off."

Chapter Ten
Showdown at the Café

Watching Mitchell run wild made me glad he was at the park and not tearing up and down the hallways at home. My eyes slid from Mitchell to Jake, and love for my handsome young son squeezed my heart. A beautiful soul lives in his small-framed body; I couldn't help but wonder, sitting in his wheelchair and laughing at his young cousin, what he was feeling inside.

His limitations probably don't affect him like they do me. He's never known what it feels like to be able to move and walk and run, so he probably doesn't even think about it.

He wasn't much older than Mitchell the first time I took him down a slide. I slung him over my shoulder and climbed the ladder one-handed. At the top I carefully sat him between my legs, and holding tight, down we went with Jake laughing all the way. Jake humbles me the way he goes through life, so confident and joyful. He asks for so little and gives back without measure.

Mitchell, running for the slide, pulled me out of my bittersweet memories. I hurried to get behind him on the ladder. Jake laughed.

"I'll do it." Mitchell pushed my hand away.

"That's fine," I assured him, "but I want to go down the slide too. You go first." This was a big fat lie. I've hated slides ever since I suffered an unfortunate accident at the age of sixteen when I made the mistake of going down one while sitting on a potato chip bag, greasy side down. The landing left a lot to be desired. The big mud puddle at the bottom met mine with a jolt that shook my teeth. The worst part of the experience was walking home through town because my brother-in-law refused to let me in his car. Small wonder I'm not fond of slides, but I am fond of my young nephew. I climbed up after him, careful to give him the illusion he was climbing by himself. At the top he took one look down and froze.

I smothered a giggle and said, "Mitchell, I'm a little nervous. Would you mind going down with me?"

His little face when he grinned up at me squeezed my heart. "Sure, Aunt Charly." I didn't look down as I positioned myself behind him. Once again, memories of sitting with Jake flittered through my memory. I guess I'd do anything for Mitchell too.

Hearing Mitchell laugh as we slid down made the whole ordeal worthwhile, but I didn't want to risk having to do it a second time. I glanced at my watch. "Hey, guys, it's almost noon. Would you like to have lunch at the café?"

Jake's eyes flew up. I'm not surprised. I've never known him to refuse food. Mitchell looked at the merry-go-round, and I could see he was torn between eating and playing.

I coaxed, "We're supposed to meet Uncle Buddy, remember?"

"Oh, yeah." His blue eyes sparkled. My sister has brown hair and big dark eyes, but this blond-haired, blue-eyed little boy is his mother all over again.

I turned Jake's chair toward town, and Mitchell crowded in between me and the chair so he could help push. Main street in Weary is only two blocks long, so we didn't have far to walk.

The honking of a car horn made me jump. My sister, Phoebe, pulled into a parking place in front of the café.

I waited until she was beside us to say, "We're eating here today. Did you have a rough morning?"

"Yes." She stopped talking as she caught sight of Buddy coming down the street on the lawn mower. "What is our brother doing now?"

"Wait until we get inside. You won't believe what all happened this morning."

She shook her head and held the door open so I could push Jake through.

Once inside, Jake grinned at Katie's husband, Mick. Mitchell called out in a voice heard by everyone in the café, "Hi, Uncle Mick." Mick looked up and waved, too busy cooking to come talk to us. The café was crowded, but we saw a booth at the back where we could sit and not block an aisle with the wheelchair.

Phoebe grabbed a youth seat and put Mitchell against the wall. It hadn't taken the aunts long to learn it was best to block all possible escape routes from him. Buddy and I locked eyes. He hates to sit in a booth unless he can have the outside position, but I needed that spot. I can only feed Jake if he's sitting to my left. I won the spot but it wasn't a victory. My brother is left-handed, which meant I stood a good chance of being bumped while he ate. And I knew from experience that he would make sure I did.

We gave our orders to Patti, the waitress. While we waited for our food, Buddy told Phoebe about the lost keys and the slashed tires. He added information about a police report that was news to me.

I knew my brother well enough to know he would have preferred handling the problem his own way, but if he wanted the insurance to pay, the report had to be filed.

"Did you have to talk to Uncle Claude?" I didn't envy Buddy that ordeal. As a sheriff, not so bad, but if Claude slid into uncle mode, the ordeal would have been brutal.

"No." He shook his head. "All I had to do was fill out a report. Uncle Claude was out of the office."

I hurried him through the rest of his story; right now I wanted to hear Phoebe's tale. "What about Jed's cows?"

She made a face and shook her head. "I'd rather eat before we talk about that. It's kind of gruesome."

Patti brought our order. As she placed the plates in front of us, one of those odd silences that occasionally occur happened. A woman's shrill voice pierced the silence in decibels that would have rivaled the monthly test of the nuclear alarm system. "I can't believe a church would permit a haunted house anywhere on their premises."

Everyone turned toward her. I leaned forward to see around Jake and saw her looking at our table.

A softer voice responded, and all eyes swiveled toward the younger woman sitting at the same table. "It's a proven fact there is less vandalism by teens and children if they are offered a fun, safe alternative to running the streets."

The older, heavy-set woman pulled her gaze away from our table and turned it on the women seated at the table with her. We could see her visibly quivering with what I could only assume was rage as she replied, "It shouldn't be held in the church. Halloween is an evil day. It's allowing the devil a toehold on hallowed ground."

"Oh, please," the younger woman drawled. "I've never heard such drivel. The children have fun and eat candy. What's evil about that?"

The older woman rose to her feet sending her chair crashing backward. She leaned forward and braced her hands on top of the table. "You dare to call yourself a Christian and don't know where Halloween comes from? It's a pagan holiday and it has no place in a church."

The younger woman rolled her eyes, and the woman sitting next to her giggled. We could almost hear teeth grinding as the older woman grabbed her purse and stormed out of the café.

"Wow!" Buddy made a funny face at Mitchell and Jake. "I'm glad I wasn't standing between her and the door."

"Who was that?" I asked Phoebe. She has lived in Weary for years and taught school for most of those years.

"Allyson Wright." Phoebe made a face but she's too nice to gossip.

"Does she have any children?"

Phoebe nodded. "She has a son and a daughter. The boy is in high school. The daughter must be about twelve now."

"Who are the other women?" I glanced over at the two women who were busy talking and laughing although in tones too low to be heard.

Phoebe frowned. "I know the blond woman. Her name is Ann Richardson. I think the other woman might be Dana Franklin."

Buddy gave me a deliberate poke as he shoveled food into his mouth. I glanced over at him and knew we were thinking the same thing. "I hope Mrs. Wright doesn't head straight for Samantha, but I bet she does." He nodded in agreement.

Jake grunted at me, and I realized I'd been so caught up in the little drama I'd forgotten to feed him. I loaded his spoon with mashed potatoes and gravy and started feeding him while Buddy told Phoebe about our talk with Samantha. Phoebe had left for town before Theo had gotten there, so she hadn't heard about the controversy over the Halloween party.

I listened to them talk while I ate and finished feeding Jake. There are no fast meals in our life. By the time we finished, most of the lunch crowd was gone. Mick finally had time to bring a plate of food over. He sat at the table next to us.

"I heard you had some problems out at the farm." He bit into a big, juicy hamburger while he waited for Phoebe to answer.

"How did you find out so soon?" she asked.

"It's Weary," he grinned at her. "Your neighbor came in for lunch. He said Jed had a cow down. Maybe killed by dogs or coyotes?"

Phoebe rolled her eyes pretty much the way Dana Franklin had. "It wasn't coyotes." She hesitated as she watched Mick eat. "We better wait if you want to finish eating."

Mitchell was done and trying to stand up in the booster seat.

"Hand him over here." Patti reached for him. Phoebe passed Mitchell to the waitress.

"Come on, big guy. Let's go play some music." Mitchell wiggled and Patti set him down. In a flash he was off for the jukebox.

"I don't have a lot of time," Mick told Phoebe. "Go ahead and tell us what happened."

I could tell Phoebe didn't want to talk and was glad Mick was the one pushing her. That meant my curiosity would be satisfied without me being too noticeably nosy.

She sighed and leaned against the back of the booth. "Jed went to check the cattle this morning, the way he does every morning. When he got there, the cattle were huddled in one corner. He could tell they were spooked. He knew by counting them that one was missing, so he came back home for a horse. He thought he could cover the ground quicker on horseback than he could on foot. I followed him back to the pasture.

64

He unloaded the horse from the trailer and took off to look for the cow. That pasture is full of ravines and timber. I thought it would take him awhile. Fifteen minutes later, I saw him heading back with the horse flat out running."

She fell silent, took a drink of water, and eyed Mick chewing on his hamburger. He waved at her and she continued her story. "He found the cow dead with big hunks of meat gone. Someone or something had hacked it up. Jed said he'd never seen a cow so ripped apart."

"If it wasn't coyotes that tore it up, what else could it be?" I wished I hadn't asked when I saw Mick put his sandwich down.

"We don't know." Phoebe's fingers shredded her napkin. "I left Jed waiting for the vet to arrive. He did tell me that it looked like something sharp had been used. It didn't look pulled apart and ripped like it would if an animal had done it."

Mick frowned. "Were there any tracks?"

Phoebe shook her head. "I don't know. I left before Dr. McCarty arrived. There wasn't anything I could do, so I came on into town."

Her story silenced us and left me feeling uneasy. Anytime something unexplained happens, it wakens a feeling we all feel as small children: that fear we have when we know there's a monster under the bed. When we're little we can call for our parents, but now we are the parents, and who can we call to make the scary things go away?

Chapter Eleven
A Visit to the Library

We stopped at the cash register to pay Patti for our lunch. The phone rang and Patti answered it. I saw her wince before she called out, "Mick, Julie's on the phone."

We waited for her to hand the phone to Mick before Phoebe asked, "Anything wrong?" Phoebe knew Mick's part-time cook better than I did.

"Not with Julie." Patti shook her head. ""She got a phone call from the school that her son got hurt during gym. She has to go with him to the doctor. She'll be late getting to work."

"I told her not to come in." Mick hung up the phone. "She's pretty sure her son's leg is broken." He looked over at us, and we could see the concern on his face. Mick's a nice guy who cares about his workers. "Would you let Katie know I'm working until we close at nine? I'll call her when I get a chance, or she can stop in. If I get busy, I might not be able to get to the phone."

"That's fine," I said. "Katie usually stops by after school anyway. Elliott and Lili are enjoying having their cousins around." I was sure the newness would wear off eventually, but right now the cousins were having fun together.

"I'll drop by about four o'clock." Buddy waved at us and headed out the door. We followed him outside and watched as he started up the lawn mower.

"Okay." I couldn't help grinning. He did look silly driving a lawn mower around town.

Phoebe wanted to take Mitchell with her and drive to the house, but he wouldn't cooperate. He wanted to walk so she walked with us.

"Mom." Mitchell planted his feet, refusing to take another step as we approached the entrance to the library.

"I should have known," I muttered. "He is his mother's son." Roni is probably the most devious, determined member of our family. We learned when she was quite young not to argue with her. Mitchell takes after his mother. It's often entertaining for the rest of us to watch a battle of wills when he goes head to head with his mother, but I don't like to participate. It's humiliating to lose to a three year old.

Phoebe, Jake, and I eyed Mitchell, who was standing with one hand on the door looking at us with that big, hard-to-resist grin.

"Do you suppose he planned this whole outing just so he could stop and see his mom?" I took my eyes off Mitchell to look at Phoebe and Jake.

Phoebe shrugged. "I wouldn't put it past him."

Jake dropped his head but I could see his grin. His shoulders shook as he giggled. I had no doubt he'd seen it coming and just hadn't known how to tell me.

Phoebe pulled the door open and held it. "Let's go see your mom, Mitchell."

We didn't even try to slow him down. He wanted his mother, and he'd probably find her quicker than we would. He surprised us when he skidded to a stop right inside the door and bellowed, "**MOM**."

I guess you're never too old to be embarrassed. If my face looked anything like Phoebe's, we were a sight to see. Jake lost it. He laughed so hard everyone within earshot joined in.

Mitchell's yell stopped Roni in mid-sentence, and that's not easy to do. Mitchell saw her and he was off before either Phoebe or I could grab him.

"I feel so old," I moaned to my sister.

"Tell me about it," she muttered back.

As we approached Roni, I noticed the man standing next to her. I tried not to stare, but he wasn't the kind of person you expect to see at the library. He would have looked more at home in the alleys of New York City. Not that I've ever been in a big city alley, but I have a healthy imagination. He looked like I imagine a street person would look.

He had a grim cast to his face. His hair was shaggy and greasy, not styled long but more like he was long overdue for a haircut. He needed a shave and he looked tired.

I leaned on the back of Jake's chair and waited for Roni to finish talking. She was giving him directions.

I turned a bit as he walked past me and watched him leave the building. I spoke. "Those directions sounded like you sent him over to the church."

"I did." Roni bent over and lifted Mitchell up. He wiggled all over, he was so happy to see her. "He's got a pregnant wife and a young son. He's out of work and their car quit running. He asked if there was a church in the area where they might be able to get some aid, so I sent him over to Theo."

I felt sorry for the young family, but I didn't give them much thought. I told Roni about Buddy's missing keys and how he was driving around town on his lawn mower. She laughed. "He's not the only one who does that. I'd feel better if the men riding around town on lawn mowers weren't all related to us."

We understood. Uncle Bugg started riding his lawn mower after losing his license to drive. Whenever he saw a police car, he would drive into someone's yard and start mowing grass. Uncle Harry drove his because it was cheaper than driving his car, and Buddy was driving his because someone had vandalized his car and stolen the keys out of his pickup.

Phoebe repeated her news about the mutilated cow.

"I already heard about that," Roni told us. "A couple of people stopped in. One of them checked out a book on UFO's. She wanted to see if there was any similarity between Jed's cow and some of the stories about alien mutilation."

"Great," Phoebe muttered. "Jed will probably have to padlock the gate to keep people from going out to see where it happened."

"As if that would stop them." I grinned at a mental picture of people climbing between barbed wire or rolling under it. I'd done it often enough as a child. Padlocks wouldn't keep anybody out of a cow pasture.

"I didn't even think about the cow being anything but a freak accident. I should have, especially with Halloween coming up, but I didn't. I guess our brother's adventure distracted me." A small town waits for something strange to happen just to make life a little more exciting.

I gave myself a mental shake. There wasn't anything I could do about Jed's problems. I had my own to deal with.

"What do you think about a family night?" I looked over at Roni. "Mick has to work late, so I think I'll make a big supper and have everybody over. Maybe we can get a game going." It was a given if Mary Lee was there a game of some kind would happen. She's a game fanatic. The children loved having an adult around who would spend time playing with them.

"Sounds good." Roni put Mitchell down. "I should be home by five."

"Okay," I smiled at her and held my hand out to Mitchell. I thought for a minute he was going to turn stubborn, but one look at his mom, Phoebe, and me must have convinced him that fun time was over. He was going home if I had to carry him every step of the way.

And I did. Once we were outside, he wilted, so tired he couldn't stand. I picked him up, Phoebe pushed Jake, and I was thankful Weary was a small town. By the time we got home, Mitchell was asleep.

Phoebe took Jake back to our part of the house where we kept Jake's school materials. He has an eye-gaze computer with speech capability. He's not real good at it yet, but he's trying. My goal when I first started home schooling him was for him to read. I felt if he could only read, the world would be his, but he shook his head no. After playing our usual twenty questions, he made me understand that it wasn't taking information in that he wanted but a way to get information out. He wanted to be able to let us know what he thought and felt. I sincerely hope his dream comes true, and I'm grateful that my sister, better trained in teaching, is willing to help him.

At three thirty Josie came home with her daughters, Keira and Téa. The girls headed upstairs. Josie came into the living room and collapsed.

Katie came in a few minutes later with Elliott and Lili. The kids detoured through the kitchen to scrounge a snack, and then I heard their footsteps pounding up the back stairs.

"What a day." Katie dropped into a recliner. "The kids were bouncing off the walls."

I gave a polite snort. "You were better off at school with twenty students than you would have been here." I brought her and Josie up to date on the news of the day. I even remembered to give Katie Mick's message.

"Gosh," she groaned. "What's going on around here?" She stood up. "I better go call Mick and find out."

I called after her. "Don't worry about supper. I'll fix something here."

"Okay." She waved a hand back at me.

"Will Anna be here tonight?" I asked Josie. Her oldest daughter worked several part-time jobs. I had a hard time keeping track of her schedule.

"As far as I know," Josie stretched. "What are you making for supper?"

Before I had a chance to tell her, the dogs started barking and someone knocked on the front door.

I shushed the dogs and opened the door.

"Hi," I smiled at Samantha. "Since when do you knock on the door?"

She looked confused; then her face cleared and she laughed. "I wasn't thinking. Theo sent me over here to talk to you. I was in business mode."

She came in and the dogs got so excited they wouldn't settle down. "I'll be right back. Josie is in the living room. Katie's on the phone and Phoebe is teaching Jake. Take your pick where you want to be." I headed for the back door with the dogs.

By the time I got back to the living room, Katie, Josie, and Samantha were catching up on the news.

"What's up?" I curled up in the comfortable recliner.

Samantha hesitated. "I don't quite know how to put this."

I had a sudden hunch. "Does it have anything to do with the man Roni sent over to you?"

"Yes." A slight furrow marred Samantha's forehead. "Theo had just gotten back from the farm. He was disturbed about the cow being killed. Mrs. Wright has been calling him every day about the Halloween party. She heard about the cow being killed, and she was positive the cow was mutilated by Satanists. Then this man, Gary Prescott, shows up with his wife and son. He's polite and friendly. His wife looks like she could give birth any day.

"Ted called one of the parishioners and got permission to borrow a camping trailer. They're going to park it by the parsonage for a few weeks while this man gets back on his feet."

"That's really nice." Katie and Samantha talk alike. They both have what I call happy voices. There's a lilt when they speak that makes you want to keep quiet just so they'll keep talking.

"That's only part of it." Samantha sounded nervous and something in me went on alert. I was pretty sure I wouldn't like what I was about to hear. "Theo wants me to ask if you will hire Mr. Prescott to work around here." She hurried on as Josie and I opened our mouths, "At minimum wage. Theo says there are a lot of odd jobs that need done here, and he knows Hal and John won't be around for awhile."

Josie gave a sudden laugh and gave me one of her famous, ornery looks. "Pretty smart. He knows the brothers-in-law will end up having to do whatever needs to be done before winter hits."

I bristled. "I'm quite capable of doing anything that needs done."

Three pairs of eyes rolled at me. Okay, I may be capable, but I'm not known for speed. It just annoys me when men think women are helpless or, worse yet, fools.

"He mentioned the rain gutters." Samantha is a master manipulator. She knows how to work me, anyway. A vision of the roof-line floated through my head. Lots of roof and lots of gutters, and a good number of those roof lines had a severe slant to them.

"Okay," I muttered. I may admit defeat but I don't have to like it.

"That's fine," Katie jumped in, "but you don't know anything about this man. He could be a serial killer. Do you really want a stranger working around your house?" I don't know why but it always surprises me when my youngest sister is practical.

Samantha responded, "He gave Theo references to call and they checked out."

I sighed and glanced at Josie. "What do you think?"

She made a face. "I think someone needs to clean the gutters, and I don't want it to be me."

"Neither do I." A memory of a hot summer day flashed through my mind. I know what hot tar on bare feet feels like, and I ached for my mother, who had threatened to call the fire department when I couldn't get off the roof. I pushed the memory away. It wasn't the roof episode that upset me, but the reminder that Mom was gone.

Josie added, "We do have a lot of work that needs done, but can we afford it?"

Samantha jumped in again. "It will only be for two weeks. Theo gave him a time limit."

Josie and I did some figuring. We made a phone call to Roni, and a few minutes later, we came to an agreement.

"Call Theo and tell him that we'll hire Mr. Prescott for two weeks at minimum wage. We'll make out a list of jobs that need done. If he works out and we have enough jobs, we'll negotiate for a longer time. He can start tomorrow."

Chapter Twelve
See What the Storm Brought

I slapped a lid on the pan of eggs gently simmering on the stove and turned the burner off under them. The residual heat of the water would finish cooking them to perfection. The bang of the kitchen door swinging open startled me. I heard my brother call out his usual exuberant greeting to the dogs. I turned and smiled at the sight of them meeting him, tails wagging, tongues lolling: pure love on four legs. The neat thing is, that's how children react to my big brother too. I think little kids and dogs recognize a kindred spirit.

Buddy's arrival created noise and chaos loud enough to be heard in the back part of the house. Knowing my son like I do, I figured tutoring would be over. Jake will always choose to be in the middle of a crowd, so I wasn't surprised when Phoebe wheeled him into the big kitchen. The smile on his face bloomed into an ear to ear grin when Buddy greeted him. I turned back to the stove, grabbed the pan of eggs, and carried them to the sink to run cold water over them.

Josie vanished into the walk-in pantry and emerged carrying the old meat grinder. Some families have silver tea sets as family heirlooms. Not us. A dull gray, prone-to-rust meat grinder and a fragile-bladed old butcher knife we fondly call Old Faithful are keepsakes for us.

I doubt if anybody outside our family would understand how excited we were when we discovered one end of the kitchen counter had a built in block of wood for the express purpose of tightening down one of these old-fashioned meat grinders. Finding that feature in the kitchen felt like a sign had been given to us that we were meant to be in this house, using this kitchen. Josie assembled the grinder with familiar ease, and soon the aroma of onions, pickles, and bologna being put through the blades filled the kitchen.

Roni came through the door at 5:15. Mitchell met her in much the same manner the dogs had greeted Buddy. Mary Lee called to tell us that she would be there by six, and that Logan wasn't interested in family night. He preferred the café, and I knew he'd soon have a game of penny pitch going. I would bet money that Theo would choose the café too. When Samantha came back alone, I gave myself a mental dollar for guessing right.

Mary Lee came in bringing Aunt Ellen with her. "Harry said he'd eat at the café," Aunt Ellen said. It looked like family night for us was turning into men's night out at the café.

I felt the eggs and decided they were cool enough to handle. The shells came away in big strips. I passed the tender, glistening globes to Josie so she could add them to the meat mixture. "Are you going to desert us?" I asked my brother. You never know with Buddy.

He might choose to stay and enjoy visiting with us, or he might decide to go play cards with the men.

I watched his face while he thought. I guessed he would eat with us and then take off for the café. Then I saw his eyes glance toward the window, and he hesitated. "I think I'll stay here."

I couldn't help laughing. "You mean you don't want to show up at the café riding your trusty lawnmower?"

He looked disgusted. "I've answered enough questions for one day. You'd think no one had ever seen a man riding a lawn mower before."

Mary Lee, mixing mayonnaise into the ground-up lunch meat, looked up. "I was in the bank when you pulled up to the drive-through window."

Josie choked but before she could tease Buddy, Anna and Blair blew in through the kitchen door. Blair looked pretty and animated with her dark auburn hair windblown and her cheeks flushed pink.

Anna's face looked as stormy as the weather. I didn't have to ask her what was wrong. Nothing could have kept her silent. "Do you know what kind of place Blair works for?"

"Yes," Josie answered with understandable caution. "Why?"

"She said I could work there too. They have a big turnover and now I know why."

"Why?" Josie responded again but she started to grin. We all did, because we knew what kind of work Blair did for a living.

"Do you know what I have to wear tomorrow?" Anna glared daggers at her grinning cousin. "She gets to wear a pretty fairy costume." A loud crack of thunder boomed and lightning flashed. "And I got to be a troll."

Blair laughed. We all did at the look on Anna's face. I know I couldn't help it. Anna has big, tragic eyes, and she's just too cute, even as upset as she was now.

"It's getting bad out there." Blair brushed her hair back from her face. She was right. In true Kansas fashion, the pretty fall day had turned nasty. Black clouds roiled in the sky, and we heard a faint growl of thunder.

A louder rumble reached our ears. The sound of footsteps running as children came pouring down the stairs. Elliott, Lili, Téa, and Keira burst into the kitchen.

"Is supper ready?" Elliott is a master at misdirection. He didn't want us to know the storm made him nervous.

Téa didn't care what anyone thought. Her eyes reminded me of a lemur, wide and dark and frightened. "The third floor is too close to the storm."

"I agree." Keira, oldest of the four, wasn't braver. "The rain and the wind sounded like it was right there with us.

"Are there any leaks?" I had reason to be concerned. When you grew up in a big family and not much money, the houses you lived in weren't always very nice. I know how to put pots and pans underneath leaks to catch the water. I still remember what it sounded like to hear the ping, ping of drips hitting metal.

I saw them look at each other and realized they wouldn't notice a leak unless they happened to be standing directly underneath one.

"You better go check," I told them. Again, four pairs of eyes swiveled toward each other. A loud crack of thunder cemented their decision. The only way I would get them back upstairs would be to tie them hand and foot and physically carry them. Not a task I was up to. I turned to my brother.

"Why don't you go look, Buddy? We're busy cooking. Make yourself useful."

"Me?" Buddy looked at me with mournful, puppy-dog eyes.

"Oh, for Pete's sake," I muttered. Annoyance rippled through me, but I didn't want to go upstairs either. I wondered if we could put enough of a guilt trip on Mary Lee and get her to go.

Lightening crackled, bright enough to be noticeable in the kitchen. Thunder rumbled on its heels. Closer now. Louder.

Mary Lee's hand moved faster as she mixed the meat mixture." "Supper's ready," she sang out.

You could almost see a visible relaxing of all of us. The roof could wait. It wasn't raining that hard yet.

We heard a clatter on the porch and the dogs barked. Seconds later, the old-fashioned front-door bell rang. Keira and Elliott raced each other to answer the door. Minutes later they appeared back in the kitchen followed by four more children.

Extra mouths to feed at meal time are not a problem in our family. We grew up cooking for an army because Mom never knew how many of us would be home for a meal, or who we'd bring home with us. She taught us well. None of us, except Mary Lee who has frugal down to an art, can make a small amount of food.

Josie, without being told, pulled more meat from the fridge and started grinding. I peeled a few more eggs. Phoebe pulled another loaf of bread out of the freezer. Samantha disappeared into the pantry for more cans of shoestring potatoes and bags of chips.

"It's not fancy but it tastes good," she sang out.

We put everything on the kitchen table, including paper plates and glasses. We opened a bag of ice and filled glasses while everyone fixed their own plates. It may not sound like much of a meal, but ground-up lunch meat, better known in our family as goop, continues to be comfort food eating at its best.

Aunt Ellen wasn't shy about asking for introductions from the newcomers. Of us all, she would recognize what family they were from. Unfortunately, I recognized one of the families myself.

The tall boy with dark, curly hair was Duncan Wright. We'd seen his mother in action that very day at the cafe. His sister, Karen, was Téa's age. The pretty blond girl with vivid green eyes was Sara Graham. Her freckled-faced, red-haired brother, Jimmy, was a quiet, shy classmate of Elliott's.

"What are you doing out when it's going to storm?" Josie asked.

"It wasn't raining when we left home." Duncan piled his plate high with food. I bet he never got this kind food at home. Allyson Wright didn't seem to be a ground-up bologna kind of person. "We were taking a walk when it blew up. We were near here so thought we'd stop in. We didn't mean to crash supper."

His eyes slid toward Keira, and I thought he was probably glad to have an excuse to stop by. We filled our plates and headed into the living room. In our family growing up, we'd gotten used to grabbing a chair anywhere we could find one, and that didn't always include sitting at a table.

It didn't take long for the kids to get jumpy. Giggles started. Whispers and pokes. Teasing that brought on louder laughing. I love my nieces and nephew, but I wasn't used to the restless activity or the noise level. Jake and I had lived in solitary quietness. I didn't know what to do about the problem other than retreat to my part of the house.

Aunt Ellen had no such problem. She's good at making suggestions. She's really good at making those suggestions sound exciting and fun. One by one she listed some indoor games. The kids were bored enough to take her ideas and run with them.

Growing up in a family of eight, we always had someone to play with. It wasn't until we were grown that we realized that Mom's policy of everyone playing in our yard meant she could keep an eye on us and know where we were at all times.

Back then, it just meant fun: red light-green light, mother may I, tag, hide and seek, and statue. Add jacks, hopscotch, and jump rope to the list. At least before television entered the picture. One by one, TV's invaded the homes, and the big group of kids that played in our yard dwindled. I felt a momentary sadness at the memory. The games that were so familiar in my youth are new to our children.

With a big, three story house to play in, it seemed inevitable they would choose to play hide and seek. And it was even more inevitable that they would choose to go down instead of up. The second floor was acceptable to them, but they refused to go near the third floor. We put the living room and dining room off-limits. Once the food was put away, I knew a game of Trivial Pursuit wouldn't be far behind. With Mary Lee there, playing games was inevitable.

We munched food and talked, all the while listening to shrieks, giggles, and the pounding of feet. Once in awhile the phone would ring, and we would assure parents their kids were fine, they weren't making a nuisance of themselves, and we'd be glad to give them rides home so they wouldn't have to walk in the rain and the dark.

We did have a rousing game of Trivial Pursuit. I wasn't on the wining team. I blamed my poor showing on too many sports questions. Before my brother could twit me about not knowing what RBI stood for, we noticed the noise level from the younger faction changed. It was too quiet, the kind of quiet that every parent recognizes as a danger signal.

Josie and I rose at the same time, but Katie beat us to the basement door. "Elliott? What's going on down there?"

We stood behind Katie, each of us craning to look over her shoulders. Sarah appeared at the bottom of the stairs. "We found something, Mrs. Emerson. Duncan, Elliott, and Keira are trying to get to it."

"What is it?" Josie sounded anxious.

"Don't worry." Duncan's voice sounded muffled. "We almost have it."

"Do you need help?" Buddy came up behind me.

We heard a thump. "No, we got it." Several voices spoke together. "We'll bring it up."

We backed away from the doorway and watched as they pushed and pulled the object up the stairs. It was big, about six feet long and four feet high.

We kept backing up to give them room to get it through the door and into the kitchen. They carried it past us into the dining room and leaned the sign, for that's what it was, against the dining room table.

"I found it." Elliott's face lit up with excitement. "I was hiding behind some boxes, and I looked up and saw this stored up by the ceiling. I saw the writing on it. When I saw what it said, I figured you'd want to see it."

He was wrong. I didn't want to see it. I wished I'd never laid eyes on it.

"Mom." Anna nudged Josie with her elbow. "What does it mean?"

No one spoke, but we all read it.

Samantha, the eternal optimist, spoke. "Maybe it doesn't mean anything."

"We couldn't be that lucky," I muttered.

The sign, leaning against the table, seemed to grow before my eyes until it filled the whole room. In big, black letters, I read:

WHITAKER FUNERAL HOME

Chapter Thirteen
Shadow from the Past

Standing silent, deep in thought, staring at the big black letters on the sign, I didn't notice Aunt Ellen move with slow, quiet steps to the living room. I did hear my brother snicker. "Oh, stuff it," I growled at him.

"What?" He raised his eyebrows at me and gazed at me with wide-eyed innocence. He makes me mad when he pretends ignorance, but deep down I wish I had the knack. Sounding innocent comes easy to my brother.

"What do you think it means?" Mary Lee's voice pulled me back to awareness. She never hesitates to confront a problem, figuring the quicker you take care of a problem the faster it goes away. I'd just as soon not know a problem exists.

I slanted my eyes over at her. "I think it means this house used to be a funeral home."

Roni not only looks like our eldest sister, Mary Lee, she possesses the same ability to go right to the heart of a matter. Her big, dark eyes bored into me, causing my insides to squirm. "Did you know about this?"

I glared at her. "Do you think I would have bought the house if I'd known? I'll probably need therapy to get over this." That statement might be a slight exaggeration. As desperate as we had been for a house big enough to hold all of us, it's possible I would have bought the house anyway. But I would have burned the sign before anyone else saw it.

"It could be worse." Josie started to snicker along with Buddy. "At least it's not a house of prostitution."

This wasn't such a strange comment for her to make. Back in our high school days, our Dad really did take us to look at a house he wanted to buy. It was Josie who found out the porch light of that particular house used to sport a red light bulb and what the meaning of that red light meant. Dad decided, having a houseful of daughters, buying the notorious house wasn't a good idea.

"You're being silly." Samantha sounded impatient. She's better at dealing with the idea of the hereafter than I am. Maybe it's because her husband is a minister and funerals are part of his work. "There's nothing wrong with funeral parlors."

An indignant snort escaped before I could stop it. "There is if you're living in one."

Anna's eyes widened in alarm as the meaning of my words sank in. "We're living where dead people were?"

That did it. Lili clutched Katie in a death grip. Elliott wasn't much braver. Katie looked like she had six legs and three heads as she walked to the living room. With her son and daughter clinging so close, she bypassed the recliner and headed straight for the couch.

One by one, we trailed after her. As I sank to the floor, an unexpected feeling of déjà vu swept through me. Growing up, we never had enough chairs in the living room for everybody. A few of us always ended up sitting on the floor. As I looked around, the years peeled away and in my ears rang the words dibs, no re-dibs: the magic formula that would mean the cushy seat you had would still be yours when you returned to it. Family. As uncomfortable as I was with the present situation, I was glad that my brother and sisters were sharing it with me. Somehow, that made the present situation easier.

I leaned back against the edge of the chocolate-colored recliner, my gaze moving from one face to the next. Aunt Ellen hunched lower and raised her magazine higher, hiding her face from my gaze.

The babble of children's voices created a buzz of white noise.

Mary Lee, always the first to address a problem, spoke. "Did you know about this?" she asked our aunt.

Aunt Ellen peered over the top of the magazine. "Know about what?"

Josie, Roni, and I rolled our eyes at each other. I know we should be more adult than this but we aren't.

"Did you know this house used to be a funeral parlor?" Mary Lee gave a genteel version of an eye roll.

"Well, yes." Aunt Ellen seemed reluctant to speak. "That's why the house is in such good condition."

"Why didn't you tell us?" I asked her.

Aunt Ellen gave a soft snort and defended herself. "I thought the house was for rent. After you bought it, it seemed better if you didn't know. I've seen you at funerals." She frowned at me and my insides squirmed again. I'm a soppy, hysterical mess at funerals. Everybody in the family knew about my problem dealing with death.

She looked at all of us sitting around the room. "Besides, where else in town would you find a house big enough for all of you?"

She had a point. Even without the four friends, we were a crowd, and we weren't even all here. I sighed and looked through the doorway to the dining room where the sign leaned against the table. We couldn't change what the house had been. The house wasn't different just because we learned something about it that we hadn't known before. We'd been happy with it before we knew. There wasn't any reason we shouldn't be happy with it now.

The jangle of the phone startled me. Roni answered it.

"That was your mom," she told Duncan and Karen as she hung up the phone. "She wants you home. She said Sarah and Jimmy should come with you."

They groaned. Duncan grinned at us. "She would call the minute we start having fun." They could afford to enjoy the situation. They didn't have to live here.

"I'll give you a ride." Mary Lee stood up.

Aunt Ellen closed her magazine and laid it on the end table. ""You can take me home too. It's way past my bedtime."

"Do you have room for me?" Phoebe asked. "My car is still parked in front of the café. You can drop me off and I'll drive it back here."

They left and the house seemed quieter. "Let's get the food put away." Josie spoke.

"I'll help." I hauled myself to my feet.

Katie started to rise but fell back when Lili grabbed one arm and Elliott the other. "I think I'll stay here with the kids."

I gave her a nod. "Jake can stay here with you. If there's nothing on TV, maybe you can put a movie on."

I didn't even want to look at the sign as I walked past it toward the kitchen and said so. Buddy and Samantha pushed it out onto the porch and laid it flat so the wind wouldn't blow it over.

Phoebe, back from getting her car, came in through the kitchen entrance. She shook her head, sending raindrops flying. "Mary Lee decided to stay at Aunt Ellen's. If anybody can get more information from her, she can."

Before she could say anything else, we heard Elliott yell. "Mom!" The panic in his voice brought Josie, Phoebe, and me to the living room.

"What?" Katie is used to Elliott's theatrics.

"We left the lights on in the basement."

Katie laughed. "Well, go down and turn them off."

"No way." Elliot shook his head. I could tell by the stubborn set to his jaw this was one argument my little sister would lose.

"You were playing down there." Katie always tries to reason with Elliott. "It's no different now than it was then."

"Yes, it is," Elliott said.

"Lili," Katie called, "go with your wimpy brother to turn off the basement lights."

Lili gave her mother a horrified look. "You've got to be kidding."

"Buddy!" Katie can bellow when she needs to. "Show your niece and nephew there's nothing to be afraid of."

Buddy's face mirrored Lili's. "Me? You want me to go down to the basement to turn off the lights?"

Katie threw her hands up in the air. "You work in a cemetery."

"But, Katie." Buddy spoke in a calm, reasonable voice. "I don't go there at night or when there's a thunderstorm."

"What does that have to do with anything?" Katie seemed genuinely puzzled.

"Forget it," Roni told her. "We'll just leave the lights on for right now."

"Unless you want to go turn it off," Josie piped up.

We burst out laughing at the look on Katie's face.

Our long, long day was winding down. One by one, people left for home. With the rain coming down, Buddy hitched a ride with Phoebe.

Thunder rumbled. Lightning still flickered across the sky. We settled in the living room. For once, the kids chose to say in the same room with us. Not because they wanted our company. They didn't want to be alone, and most definitely, they didn't want to go upstairs.

"Put on a nice comedy," I told Elliott. "We need something that will make us laugh."

One by one, Elliott held up DVD boxes for Jake to see. Jake would give them a quick glance and shake his head in denial. I watched them, amused and pleased that Elliott took the time to ask Jake what he wanted to watch.

"How many do I have to hold up?" Elliott scowled at me. "He's said no to eight movies."

I laughed. "He knows which one he wants. Look at his eyes."

All of us looked at Jake. He was staring with unwavering intentness at the shelf of DVD's. The intensity and directness of his gaze always impresses me. I'm so attuned to his eyes that it surprises me when someone else misses what he's saying.

For a moment, all of us were caught up trying to decipher his want. Blair, Keira, Anna, Téa, Elliott, Lili, Josie, and Roni are all trying to read him. Mitchell, the youngest of the small group, walked to the shelf and reached up as high as he could. "He wants this one." And he was right. Jake's eyes flew upwards in a big yes.

I gazed at Mitchell with wondering eyes; only three years old, and already so in tune with his cousin. His brain was still fresh and new, unhampered by the restrictions that happen as we grow up. "How did you know?" I asked him.

He gave me a blue-eyed gaze as silent and unfathomable as Jake's non-verbal silence. Then he shrugged. "I just know." And I had to agree with him. Sometimes, we just know. I can't be any clearer than that.

A loud crack of thunder boomed. Girls screamed, everyone jumped, and the lights went out. Jake started crying. He's afraid of the dark. I can only imagine how terrible it would feel to have the one part of his body that he can rely on, his eyes, blinded. Without the light, he feels totally helpless. I made my way over to him as soon as I could so he'd know where I was.

Mitchell immediately joined in, shouting for his mother. Pandemonium reigned, and it all would have been funny if it happened to somebody else.

"Hang on," I shouted over the noise. "Don't anybody move. I know where the flashlights are. Just stay put."

Josie felt her way over to us so she could stay by Jake. Roni found Mitchell. I figured Blair, Anna, Keira, and Téa probably had a death grip on each other. One of them was doing a lot of yelping and whimpering. It might have been all of them considering the amount and pitch of noise they emitted.

Working from memory, I felt my way through the dining room to the kitchen. I knew which drawer I had stowed the flashlight in. I kept hoping the lights would come back on and I wouldn't need the flashlight, but they didn't. The dark was thick, and I was grateful for the intermittent lightning flashes that helped me navigate through the kitchen.

Thank goodness the batteries were good. I used the feeble light of the flashlight to search for matches and candles. With my hands full, I turned to move with slow, searching steps toward the dining room. Out of the corner of my eye, I saw a flicker of movement darker than the night. The dogs, I thought.

Then a force slammed into me sending me and the objects I held flying and the flashlight spinning in a crazy circle. I lay on the floor, frozen, and tried to make sense of what had just happened. The beam of the flashlight, feeble and dim in the big kitchen, lit up the gaping black hole of the open basement door. I did the only sensible thing I could think of. I screamed.

A chorus of answering screams sounded from the living room. Fear for the people I loved broke through the fear holding me frozen on the floor. Reaching out, I grabbed the flashlight and stood up, working my way through the dark dining room into the entry hall, and then to the living room.

Josie grabbed me. "What happened?"

"I don't know." Another flash of lightning lit up the room, and we all saw the dark space leading to the porch. "Who opened the front door?"

"Nobody." Roni spoke. She was trying to calm Mitchell, who was clinging to her like a cocklebur. She couldn't get him pulled loose. "I think the wind blew it open."

"I don't think so," I muttered. "Come with me." I grabbed Josie. I don't know why it's less scary with two, but it is. We inched our way toward the front door. As I closed it against the storm-pushed wind, I could see Samantha's house across the street all lit up. We stood there a moment staring at that wonderful light.

"I don't like this." Josie spoke softly in my ear. "We seem to be the only house without light. Do you think we got hit by lightning?"

"I wish." My stomach dropped to the vicinity of my toes. "I think it's worse than that. I think we're going to have to go down to the basement whether we want to or not."

Chapter Fourteen
What Evil Lurks

I shut the front door, closing out the storm. Leaning my head against the solid, old-fashioned door, I stared through its oval glass toward Samantha's house where a warm glow poured from her windows. I sighed and longed for even a piece of that light.

Josie grabbed my arm in a tight grip pulling me upright. "What do you mean we have to go down to the basement?"

"Think about it," I hissed at her. Between the wind, the rumble of thunder, and the intermittent shrieks coming from the girls, I didn't think there was much danger of being overheard.

"All the other houses on our block have lights. If we don't, it probably has something to do with the fuse box."

Josie pondered my words. "Are you sure the fuse box is in the basement? Couldn't it be upstairs?"

"I wish," I muttered, "but when Steven Whitaker gave us the grand tour he made sure we noticed the fuse box. He seemed real proud the wiring had been updated and the old fuse box replaced with a breaker box. The box is in the basement over by the outside entrance."

The basement stairs opened to the back of the house, a common feature in older houses, and one I preferred. I'm paranoid in basements that only have one way out, but right then I felt like this house had too many exits, and I wished I could remember if any of them were locked.

It felt odd to be talking to a nearly faceless body. The dim light from the flashlight in the living room barely reached the entryway, and only the lightning flashes allowed me to see Josie's face. I was concentrating so hard on the breaker box in the basement that at first I didn't notice the knock. The sound came again. I turned toward the door.

A brilliant flash of lightning ripped the sky. I saw a dark shadow standing on the porch with only glass between us. I opened my mouth in a soundless shriek. A moment later, I stood in the center of the living room with no memory of how I got there, Josie still beside me.

We huddled and I watched in wide-eyed terror as the front door swung open and the dark shape moved into the entryway. Jake wailed louder. Out of the corner of my eyes, I saw Roni standing between the sofa and the recliner. Mitchell clung to her, his arms wrapped tightly around her neck.

I didn't know where the girls were. They could have been hiding behind the couch for all I knew. I could hear them, each one emitting whimpers and shrieks. I'm pretty sure Blair was using language her mother wouldn't approve of. I tried to call out, but my voice didn't want to work. All I managed was a raspy croak.

I felt, rather than saw, the dogs head for the dark shape blocking the front doorway. Where had they been ten minutes ago when I'd needed them? A minute later I heard a well-known voice say, "Molly, how are you, old girl? Murphy, how did you get so wet?"

Shuddering relief almost sent me to my knees. I knew that voice. It's disgusting how those dogs slobber over Buddy. They're convinced he comes to the house just to see them.

"What's going on?" Buddy asked as he stumbled toward us.

I let Josie and Roni explain the recent events to him while I tried to calm Jake down. Now that Buddy was here, I felt better. I called the dogs over and told them to lie down and stay. Then, despite loud complaints, I took the flashlight and went back to the kitchen to retrieve the kerosene lamp.

I placed it on the dining room table and lit it. As we gathered around the table, I gazed at the faces just visible in the dim light and took comfort. A flash of understanding filled me as I felt a stirring inside at what fire must have meant to early man. Light eased a primal fear, chased away the bogeyman. Unfortunately, for me, it didn't chase him far enough.

An uneasy sensation crawled through my stomach as I looked toward the dark kitchen. "We need more light." I spoke in a firm voice. I don't know why. No one here was going to argue with me.

"Maybe we should go over to Samantha's." This gem came from Josie.

"Yeah!" Anna, Keira, and Téa endorsed her plan with enthusiasm.

"I'm going home," Blair declared and stood up.

I glared at them. "If you all leave, I'll never forgive you." They fell silent, even Jake and Mitchell. Blair wavered and for a minute. I was sure she'd bolt, but she came back to the table and sat down.

"I have more flashlights. I'll go get them." I picked up the flashlight. No complaints this time since the kerosene lamp lit the room. I made my way toward my bedroom. It was scary but not as frightening as it would be when I had to go down to the basement. My part of the house was familiar, and the dogs went with me. I knew they would alert me to anything that didn't belong. For most of my married life, I'd lived in the country. Losing electricity wasn't an uncommon experience. I had several large battery-operated lights, including one that would light up an entire room.

I found it first and felt my tense muscles relax as the light reached out and lit up a big area around me, pushing back the wall of darkness.

I held onto that light when I returned to the dining room. I handed flashlights to Josie and Buddy.

"We need to go check the fuse box." I looked directly at my brother. As the eldest one here, in my mind he was supposed to take on the responsibility. Besides being the eldest, he was the only man here.

He raised his hands in the air. "Uh-uh. This is your house."

I frowned at him. "Just what brought you back here, anyway? I'm going to have to dye my hair again because I think you turned it white."

It was hard to tell in that dim light, but I think he looked a little sheepish. "I was going to see if I could stay here for awhile. My trailer's been flooded."

"How?" Roni thinks quicker than the rest of us. "There isn't any water source near your trailer."

"Yes, there is." I could tell from the grim tone of his voice that our easy-going brother was angry, a rare occurrence indeed. "Someone used the kitchen and bathroom faucets. Everything is soaked, the furniture and beds. It's a mess. It will take forever to dry out."

Beneath the anger and disgust, I could hear bewilderment. Buddy couldn't understand why someone would do that to him. To be honest, neither could I. My brother is a kind and gentle soul. I couldn't imagine him doing anything that would cause someone to vandalize his home.

I'd be sympathetic tomorrow. Tonight, I needed him. "You mean, you want us to give you free room and board, and you won't even go downstairs to check a fuse box?"

"I won't go by myself," he protested.

"You don't have to," I reassured him. "Josie and I will be there too."

"What?" Josie yelped. "Why me?"

"You live here, don't you?"

"Well, yes." She spoke regretfully, no doubt wishing she lived anywhere but here.

"Roni can't." I waved toward Roni where she stood with Mitchell still clinging to her like a little monkey. "She can stay with the kids." I could see the girls sag with relief. I knew better than to expect them to go with me. I'd have to tie and gag them if I wanted them anywhere near the basement. It wasn't worth the effort.

"With the three of us going and each of us carrying a light, we should be able to go right to the breaker box."

***

I will never figure out why walking in the dark is so much harder than in the light. I felt like I was taking baby steps as we inched our way through the kitchen toward the open basement door.

"Wait a minute," I muttered. I stopped by the pantry and with utmost caution pushed the swinging door wide. Three flashlights focused on the interior. It was just a pantry. I don't know what I expected to see. I rummaged in a box and pulled out a handful of dog biscuits.

I turned back toward the basement, and we continued our slow inching.

I kissed to the dogs. "Here, pups. Come." They knew I had treats, and even in the dim light I could see their tails wagging and their eager, expectant faces. I love my dogs.

I stood at the top of the basement steps, Josie and Buddy at my shoulder, and I did something I'm not proud of. I tossed the biscuits into the black hole. "Go get them." I spoke with false enthusiasm. "Go find."

With no hesitation they vanished down the dark stairs.

"Okay," I told Buddy and Josie. "Let's go before they start back up."

I started down the stairs, concentrating on the dogs. I could see them at the bottom sniffing for the biscuits, each one concerned that the other would find them all.

Three things happened all at once. The dogs froze, the hair on their necks raised, and low growls came from their throats. I realized that Buddy and Josie still stood at the top of the stairs. And all the lights came flooding back on.

I froze, standing there on that bottom step, and prepared to die. If I heard my dear brother and sister shut the kitchen door, I knew my heart would stop.

The barking of the dogs covered the sound of pounding steps coming down the basement stairs. I yelped as Josie grabbed my arms. "I'm sorry. I'm sorry."

"Sorry, Sis," Buddy apologized. "That joke backfired."

The dogs barked again and we waited, staring into the gloom beyond the light. I needed to start breathing again or pass out. The dogs moved to stand between me and the outside exit.

For some strange, inexplicable reason, as I stood there, I felt my fear slide away from me. Maybe it's true that a person can only feel fear to a certain degree, then it overloads their senses, and the fear vanishes. Or maybe it was just the lights were back on and I no longer feared what hid in the shadows. We made our way to the breaker box. To my eyes it looked completely normal.

"Look." Josie stood between Buddy and me and our eyes followed her pointing finger. On the floor and the steps leading up to the outside door, we could see wet spots. The dogs were at the top of the stairs sniffing at the door. We climbed the stairs and checked the door. It was securely locked.

I spoke absently, my mind busy wrestling with the puzzle about the lights and the door. "I think tomorrow we're going to check all the doors and windows and call somebody to come and change the locks."

We checked the basement out while we were down there. I think we all knew it was empty.

Calling the dogs, we went back upstairs. Roni had convinced Mitchell to sit in a chair, and he was busy eating a pile of chips she had placed in front of him. Josie's girls were still huddled close together. Their big brown eyes looked even bigger. I could tell they were still spooked. Jake had stopped crying, but his eyes followed me. He didn't want me out of his sight again.

"Was it a problem with the fuse box?" Roni spoke.

"Sort of." Buddy's face held an uncharacteristic seriousness.

"Don't you know?" Roni pushed for details and facts. She's never comfortable with suppositions.

Buddy glanced at the girls and hesitated. I knew he didn't want to make the girls more nervous than they already were. I left it to Josie. They were her daughters; it was her decision what they should be told.

Her eyes widened when she saw us looking at her. "The lights came back on while we were on the stairs. The breaker box looks fine."

"What made them come back on?" Anna asked the question, but I don't think she really wanted an answer. I think she wanted reassurance.

"Who can understand electricity?" Josie gave her eldest daughter the innocent, helpless look she does so well. "The lights are back on, that's all I care about."

Keira frowned. "I hope this doesn't happen every time there's a thunderstorm. I didn't like it at all."

Buddy gave her an evil grin. "Just be glad it didn't happen while you all were playing in the basement."

They obliged him by giving shrieks that can only come from teenage girls. I felt a chill run through my body. Chances are whatever or whoever caused the lights to go out had been in the basement while the kids were playing.

Trying to sound casual, I asked. "Did any of you notice anything odd while you were downstairs?"

They shook their heads in denial. I dropped the subject. The last thing I needed was to put fear in their heads.

Now that the lights were back on, Buddy returned to his reason for showing up. "Do I get to stay here tonight?"

"I don't see why not." Roni answered him. Josie and I were in agreement. After the recent episode, I would have invited half the town to stay over if I could have.

Anna and Keira looked at each other in alarm. "Wait a minute." Anna sidled over by her mother. "He can't have the extra bedroom."

Keira's head nodded up and down like the bobble-head doll on the dash of Anna's car.

"Why not?" Josie looked honestly puzzled.

"Because," Anna used three syllables, "we need it." She pointed to Keira and Téa.

Josie still looked perplexed and I hate to admit it, but I started to giggle.

"What are you laughing for?" Josie shot me an annoyed glance.

I forced an answer past the laughter that gripped my throat. "Remember when we were little and Mom's friend, Juanita, took us to the drive-in movie?"

Her eyes widened and she choked. "Oh, yeah. She thought she was taking us to a funny movie and it turned out to be *Horrors in the Black Museum*. All four of us climbed in bed with Mom that night. Thank goodness, it was a Wednesday night and Dad wasn't home. She was so mad at us and Juanita."

We cracked up. My nieces were not amused. Roni had been really small. I'm not sure if she remembers it as vividly as Josie and I did.

By now I was laughing so hard I had to wipe tears from my eyes. I gasped. "I slept with my neck covered clear through high school."

Josie and I couldn't seem to get ourselves under control. Buddy got annoyed. "Well, do I get to stay here or not?"

"Sure you can," I managed to sputter. "But what the girls are saying is they dibs the bedrooms and you get their room."

We watched Buddy's eyes widen as he realized the implication of my words.

"The third floor. All by myself?" The look on his face, the sound of his voice, finished us. We couldn't help it. We laughed. Even Jake and Mitchell joined in.

Chapter Fifteen
A Typical Saturday Morning

I awoke to a day washed clean by last night's storm.

"Thank goodness it's Saturday." I breezed into Jake's bedroom and started pulling the covers off him. I'm so used to getting him up every morning, I don't even think about it anymore. When I do stop and actually ponder about it, I feel like one-half of a Siamese twin that isn't bodily connected. But most times when I help him with his daily grooming, I do it with the same familiarity I use when brushing my own hair.

He grinned at me and then flicked his gaze away to stare at a shelf on his wall. I followed his gaze to the mantle clock and understood the intensity of his gaze. Tears prickled my eyes, and I gave a few rapid blinks to clear them. Winding his clock on Saturdays had been his father's chore.

I had no reason to cry for my husband. The last phone call from Hal had been full of excitement. He and our son, Russ, were having the vacation of a lifetime. I didn't begrudge him his adventure. I pushed the twinge of guilt I felt at not going with him aside. Of all the emotions, guilt bites at me hardest.

Jake grunted, and I shoved my uncomfortable thoughts away. Once he caught my gaze, he turned his eyes back to the clock. I laughed. "Okay, you win. I'll wind your clock." I couldn't blame Jake for being insistent about this chore. The gentle bonging of the clock allowed him to know what time it was even in the dark.

Saturday morning also means breakfast at the café. By the time I got Jake dressed and in his chair, the breakfast crowd would thin out, and my family would start filling up the booths and tables.

The house was empty by the time we left the house. I stood a moment under the porte-cochere and breathed in the crispness of a perfect autumn day. Indian summer at its finest, although last night's storm had greatly diminished the bright fall foliage. I felt energized, and we made the walk from home to the café in less time than it would have taken me to load Jake in the van, lock down the wheel chair, and locate a parking place that would allow me enough room to lower the lift.

With practiced ease I swung Jake's chair to the side and pulled the cafe door open. Holding the door open with one foot, I reached back to grab the arm of his chair and pulled him forward until I could get behind him to push him into the room. I paused inside the door and breathed in the scents of bacon, sausage, and cinnamon rolls.

Jake let out a grunt and his right hand jerked and flailed. That hand gets him in a lot of trouble. It floats and hangs in the air, and he's goosed more than one startled stranger. From the big smile on his face, I knew he was waving. He'd seen his Uncle Jed and Aunt Phoebe sitting at the lunch counter. Samantha and Theo, as well as various other family members, were moving around the buffet table, so Jake could have been waving at any or all of them.

"Hi." I stopped to greet my brother-in-law, Jed. "We don't usually see you here. You're usually hard at work by the time we all get around to eating."

Jed grinned at us. He's a tall, thin, good-looking man. "I won't be here long. I have to make a feed run."

Phoebe made a face at Jake. He laughed back at her. She spoke. "I thought I'd give Jake some extra time today since yesterday was so crazy."

"That sounds good. Thanks." I waved toward the tables. "I'm going to find a place where we won't be in anybody's way. I'll talk to you once I get us settled."

Finding a good place to park a wheelchair at a restaurant or café isn't always easy. I headed for my favorite spot at the back of the room. We had been coming for Saturday morning breakfast long enough the breakfast regulars tended to leave the back booth open for us.

I knew what Jake wanted to eat, but I asked him anyway. "Biscuits and gravy? Scrambled eggs?" With each suggestion, his grin widened as he shook his head no. He knew I was just going through the motions. As I mentioned the foods on the buffet table, his eyes flicked from me to the breakfast buffet. Back and forth until he finally lost patience with me and zeroed in on the food he wanted. I laughed. Without fail, his breakfast of choice is pancakes.

"Keep an eye on the table, Monk, and I'll fix you a plate." He's well used to the nicknames I call him. Monk is short for monkey; sometimes he's Squirt and sometimes Punkin. Needless to say, he's not happy if I call him Punkin in public. Sometimes I forget that he's seventeen and not seven. He's small, barely weighing eighty pounds. His face is smooth and handsome, and sometimes it seems like he never ages at all.

Wasting no time at the breakfast buffet, I fixed Jake a short stack. Mick came around the end of the lunch counter to hand me a full cruet of maple syrup. It takes a lot of syrup to get the pancakes down, and Jake has been known to eat maple syrup on his scrambled eggs. I don't argue with him. I just fix his plate the way he wants it and try not to think about what it tastes like.

Phoebe and Jed moved their plates to our table and I was glad. I couldn't wait to grill Jed about the dead cow.

"Did Dr. McCarty think the cow was killed by an animal?"

Jed hesitated before replying, "He's pretty sure it wasn't. The cow was slaughtered. Someone used a sharp object to cut it up, but Doc said it wasn't done with a meat saw or knife."

Samantha, leaning down to put her plate on the table, froze. "If you're going to keep talking about the cow, I better go sit somewhere else."

"I can wait." I pushed the empty chair out with my foot. "I can find out details some other time."

"What's going on at the church?" I asked her.

Samantha sighed, "There's still no news about Jennifer. Her husband says she didn't take anything with her except her purse."

"Did she say anything to Rev. Thomas before she left?" I asked.

Samantha looked troubled. "Rev. Thomas left so abruptly he was gone before Theo had a chance to talk to him. Several of the parishioners mentioned how upset he was for several weeks before he left. They were worried he might have had health issues."

"Was there a problem at the church?" Roni joined us. Behind her I could see Josie and her daughters filling their plates at the buffet.

I made a face at Roni's plate. If I ate like she did, I'd never have to worry about gaining weight. She says she doesn't think about food and sometimes forgets to eat.

Samantha came as close to a snort as is possible for her. "The only problem we've had is the Halloween party. The phone has been ringing off the wall all week. Half of the congregation wants the party and the other half are screaming that it's the devil's day and the church will be contaminated. Then the pro-half say it's been held at the church for the last five years, and if it's held at the church, they can counteract any pagan influence."

Theo, sitting at the counter with the men, heard what Samantha told us. He turned toward us and added, "Jed's dead cow hasn't helped. The people who are protesting the party started calling up again saying it's a satanic cult and the cow was a sacrifice."

"What are you going to do about it?" Mick asked as he set a fresh decanter of coffee on the counter.

Theo added fresh coffee to his cup. He thinks before he speaks, unlike the rest of us. "I'll make an announcement tomorrow at church. I shouldn't say anything more until then."

"Oh, shoot." Josie, leaning over to put her plate on the table stopped, grinned at Theo, and quipped. "That means we'll all have to be there."

We laughed because we knew she was joking. Most of us don't miss church. Most of us sing in the choir. Family pretty much makes up the whole choir.

"Did you hear about our adventure last night?" I could tell by the way Buddy's face lit up with an evil grin that he was gearing up for a classic performance. My brother loves to entertain, and the bigger the audience, the greater the show.

"Did something happen after we left?" Phoebe should have known better. As Buddy talked the storm grew louder, the darkness blacker, and fear greater. Our fear, of course. He was Superman, able to leap tall buildings and protect the innocent, helpless females and children. If I'd been really mean, I'd have mentioned that this brave fearless knight spent the night on the couch and even tried to convince the dogs to stay with him. Murphy stayed by me but Molly obliged him. He didn't even have to use the leash.

"I don't think it's funny." I had to speak loud to be heard over the laughter of my dear family. "You weren't the one who got knocked down."

Logan, bless his heart, seemed concerned. "Do you think you had an intruder in the house?"

"I don't know what to think. It was pitch black. All I can say for sure is there was movement, and I went flying."

"Were the dogs in the house?" I hate it when Theo is practical.

"Yes." Jake made a noise to get my attention. He made eye contact with me; then he looked at his pancakes, the syrup, and back to the pancakes. I automatically poured more syrup, mashed it into the pancake, and gave him a bite. "They were both in the house, but I'm pretty sure they were in the living room."

I knew I'd lost them with that comment. My dogs are big. Molly weighs close to a hundred pounds. Murphy isn't far behind her. They don't always watch where they're going, and both of them have tripped me more than once. "I know it wasn't the dogs. It didn't feel," I groped for the words, "hairy enough."

Josie, sitting at the next table with the girls, tried to be helpful. "What about the water on the steps? Where did that come from?"

Keira and Anna lifted their heads at this comment. They aren't usually up this early on a Saturday, and their eyes were still heavy with sleep. It was only the thought of being alone in a former funeral parlor that had roused them from their sleep and energized them enough to show up at a Saturday breakfast.

"That could have been from Duncan," Keira mumbled.

"What?" Josie leaned forward. Keira swallowed her food and forced herself to speak. "I said that could have been caused by Duncan. He found a big rock in the basement, so he went up the stairs and opened the door so he could throw the rock outside."

"That's right." Anna nodded. "Murphy thought he was going outside, so she went running out into the back yard."

"Did she come back in?" I was trying to figure out how much water would have been dragged back in.

The girls sat silently. It was almost painful watching their brains trying to function before noon.

A shy smile tilted Téa's mouth and she shook her head. "No, she didn't. Duncan didn't want to get wet, so he came back in without her. I saw him let her in later from the kitchen. He didn't want you to know he let her out without checking to see if the back gate was shut."

"At least now I know how Murphy got so wet. Both dogs were in the house when we went down to the basement." Lost in thought, I reached for the apple juice and gave Jake a drink.

Roni has the determination of a pit bull. She's not easily distracted from a subject. "That doesn't mean the water couldn't have come from an intruder." I watched my four brothers-in-law shake their heads in unison. Logan, Mick, Theo, and Jed weren't buying the intruder story.

"It was stormy. It's understandable that you all were nervous." This gem of wisdom came from Mick.

"The house is old. It wouldn't be unusual for the lights to flicker." I glared at Theo. I didn't want logic; I needed reassurance.

In a voice that should have frozen the coffee in his cup, I told him, "There was no flicker. It was pitch dark for at least fifteen minutes."

Jed smiled. He has a nice smile. I almost softened. Then he spoke. "You all were spooked by that funeral sign, and you did have the dogs in the house. They would have known if there was an intruder."

Before I could respond to his comment, Logan spoke. "That's what happens when you have a house full of women."

Chapter Sixteen
What Else can go wrong?

Before I could choke down my mouthful of food to answer my dear brother-in-law, Buddy stepped in to rescue Logan from my wrath. My brother knows me too well, and he likes Logan.

"Logan, I've been meaning to talk to you." My brother walked over to the coffee pot to refill his cup. He ignored the frowns of seven sisters who know he shouldn't drink caffeine.

"What about?" Logan turned a wary eye on Buddy and with good reason. Ever since he's become mayor of our small town, he's been swamped with requests and complaints.

A charming, innocent grin lit up my brother's face. The kind of expression all of his sisters distrust. Thank goodness he was focused on Logan. I wasn't the only sister watching with intent interest.

Buddy, coffee cup filled, stopped by Logan's chair. "I wanted to ask where you came up with enough money to buy sod for the cemetery and who did you hire to put it in?"

Logan frowned at Buddy, an expression he's especially good at. "What the hell are you talking about?"

The charming, teasing grin vanished. Buddy sat down next to Logan at the counter. "I'm talking about the new sod that's been laid on the grave of Clarissa Whitaker. I don't know why there's new sod. The grave looked fine when I mowed the grass last week."

We seldom see Logan at a loss for words. He stared at Buddy and then shook his head. "I didn't authorize anything to be done at the cemetery. Wouldn't that be paid for by the family?"

Buddy shook his head. "The only Whitaker I've seen around town is Old Ansel. He's everywhere. I bet if someone went outside right now, he'd either be sitting where he could see my lawnmower or peeking in the window to see if I'm still in here."

Of course, as soon as he said that, a whole roomful of eyes, including mine, turned toward the front of the café just in time to see a face jerk out of sight at the edge of the window.

"See?" Buddy shrugged. My brother's a tolerant man who likes most people. "I don't think it was Ansel who paid for the sod. He doesn't seem to have enough money to live on, let alone buy grass for a grave."

"What relation is he to the person buried there?" Samantha is one of the most compassionate people I know.

"I don't know." Buddy shrugged again. "All I know is on top of Clarissa Whitaker's grave is a patch of pretty new grass. Last week it was thick, established grass, and this week it's brand new sod."

114

Logan sat frowning then abruptly stood up. "Come on, let's go take a look."

"What?" Buddy's jaw dropped, and he looked over at the food left on his plate.

"Let's go," Logan jerked his head toward the door. "I don't have all day, and I don't intend to spend any of it wandering around looking for a grave. You can show me where it's at. Let's go," he repeated.

Theo wiped his mouth. "Wait up. I'll come too."

In the end Buddy, Logan, Theo, and Jed went to view the grave at the cemetery. Isn't curiosity a strange emotion? I understand it well. It's an inherited family trait.

Roni, Phoebe, Josie, and I, along with assorted children, walked home. I enjoyed the warmth of the day knowing it wouldn't last much longer. I've known Kansas weather to drop thirty degrees in fifteen minutes. For right now, I'd soak up the sunshine and pretend that winter wouldn't come this year.

From the café, if you look just right, you can catch a glimpse of our house. I couldn't help that my feelings toward the house were different. I knew nothing had changed, but a house that had felt warm and welcoming yesterday now frightened me. I know that's not logical, but right then emotion held the upper hand. The fact that it had been a funeral home shouldn't have made any difference, but it did. My steps dragged.

"Who's that?" Phoebe noticed the man first. He sat on the porch swing moving back and forth in a gentle motion.

I didn't recognize him and said so.

Roni is the logical sister. She leaps to conclusions with speed and accuracy. "Looks like our handyman has arrived."

"What do we do with him?" Josie smiled, and I admired the way she could talk without moving her lips.

The man stood up and came down the steps as we approached the porch. We stood there, silent and awkward, not knowing what to say. He cleared his throat, shifted his feet, and it occurred to me that he felt more uncomfortable than we did.

"My name's Gary Prescott. Your sister, Samantha, said you could use some part-time help?"

Roni took charge. She's better at handling people and situations. "That's right. We just moved in and there's a lot of work that needs done. Theo told us the gutters need cleaned out, and there's a lot of yard work."

Gary Prescott flashed a very attractive smile. I noticed he looked a lot cleaner and more relaxed than he had at the library. His dark-brown hair was too long, but combed neatly away from his face, and I noticed he had very attractive, hazel eyes. "Do you have a ladder and tools to do the work?"

I'd lived in the country for years and over time had acquired numerous items of outdoor equipment. I stepped away from Jake's chair. "If you guys will take Jake in the house for me, I'll show Mr. Prescott where everything is stored." Phoebe took my place behind the chair. She would push him around to the kitchen entrance, the only door with a ramp.

116

"Come with me." I led Mr. Prescott toward the backyard.

"How big an area do you have here?" Gary sounded casual, but when I glanced at him, I saw his eyes moving restlessly, taking in every detail of the yard. I felt a stab of uneasiness and then shoved my feelings aside. I know better than anybody how big an imagination I possess.

"The house sits on approximately two and a half acres. Because we're on the edge of town, it looks like more than that. I'd like to buy the twenty acres in back of us."

"Whatever for?" He sounded alarmed.

I grinned. " Don't worry. You won't have any more work piled on you. I own a couple of horses. Right now, I'm keeping them out at Phoebe and Jed's farm. I'd like to have them closer."

"Oh." He didn't say anything else.

I closed the gate behind us as we entered the backyard, careful to stay on the sidewalk and avoid the mud left from the rains of the night before. On a whim I went over to the basement door and scanned the ground.

"Well, well," I muttered and stooped down. "What have we here?"

I couldn't actually see footprints, but something had messed up the ground by the door. Close by was a big rock. I picked it up and placed it in the depression by the door.

"What are you doing?" Gary crouched down next to me.

"What would happen if that rock was here and somebody tried to open the door from the inside?" I glanced at him.

He gazed at me a moment, then looked down where I'd placed the rock. He reached down and put some pressure on it from the direction the door would open. The rock wedged against the edge of the sidewalk. "I think the door would be stuck." He sounded thoughtful.

I nodded in agreement. "That's what I think too." I stood up, stiff from crouching, and suppressed a groan. "I think Murphy must have dropped this rock here last night." I didn't explain to him about Golden Retrievers and how they carry objects in their mouth. It didn't occur to me he would need to know. Truth be told, I was overwhelmed by the knowledge that last night we had an intruder. Even more disturbing to me was the realization that the intruder had, most likely, been in the basement while the children were playing.

I finished showing Mr. Prescott where the tools were located. He seemed to think the riding lawnmower would need some routine maintenance before he could mow the grass, so I left him to it.

Returning to the house, I took the long way heading away from the kitchen entrance, taking careful note of the different jobs we needed to bring to Mr. Prescott's attention. I climbed the steps onto the big front porch, opened the front door, and walked into chaos.

I'm used to the crowd my family makes. Growing up in a family of eight children, a crowd is inevitable, but a crowd made by family members has a different feel than a crowd containing strangers

118

In addition to family, I counted six almost strangers. I recognized Duncan and Karen Wright and Sara and Jenny Graham from the evening before. An oblong box was tucked beneath Duncan's arm. I noticed this before Roni caught my attention.

"This is Betty Richardson and Dana Franklin." Roni spoke louder than normal so she could be heard over the chatter of the children.

I could feel my forehead wrinkle as I stared at the two women. A niggling sense of familiarity teased my mind. "Oh." Memory clicked. "I saw you at the café yesterday."

Dana's snapping dark eyes darted toward the Wright children. "That's right." She spoke with caution. "I remember."

A flutter of sympathy stirred in me. It seemed obvious to me that she didn't want Duncan and Karen to know about her public argument with their mother.

Betty cleared her throat and spoke in a clipped, nervous tone. "We stopped over at the parsonage first. No one was home, but a lady, I think she said her name was Gayle, called out to us from a camper parked in their driveway. She must have heard us knocking on the door. She told us that Mrs. Rogers was over here. I hope you don't mind us stopping by without calling first?"

I experienced one of those strange moments when my mind seemed to split. I was listening to Betty and Dana but also hearing the conversation of the young people. Duncan spoke, his voice low and persuasive. "Come on, don't be scared. Let's go upstairs. It's only a game, and there's a group of us. What could go wrong?"

If my attention hadn't been divided, I would have questioned him on the spot. Every red flag I owned flapped open at the tone of his voice, but Dana captured my attention, and the moment was lost.

Josie moved toward the children. I assumed she would take care of the situation. They were, after all, her children. I dismissed them from my mind and tried to concentrate on the two women.

Betty seemed nervous and timid and trying hard not to show it. Dana radiated restless energy that, in a strange way, seemed aggressive. It didn't surprise me when she took control of the conversation.

She spoke to Samantha, but her eyes jumped from Roni, to Josie, and then to me. "I talked to you before about the Halloween party."

"I remember." Samantha nodded at the two women then spoke to the young people. "If you're going to play a game, you need to go somewhere else, either into the dining room, the kitchen, or upstairs."

Duncan spoke first, "Let's go upstairs. There's more room up there, and we won't be in anybody's way." Seven pairs of eyes riveted on his face. "The sun is shining." He beamed at them. "No thunder, no lightning, and no rain."

Elliott grinned. He has a charming, ornery grin. "Last one there's a rotten egg." And he was off, followed by a thunder of feet, and the room emptied of children.

I saw Betty and Dana visibly relax. Whatever they wanted to say, they hadn't wanted to talk about it in front of the children.

"Now," Samantha beamed at them. I wish I possessed even a tenth of her people skills. "What did you need to talk about? Would you like to go back over to the church office?"

"No, no." Dana shook her head. "I think it's better to talk about it here. Betty and I think we have a solution to the Halloween party controversy that's been causing so much friction in the church."

"Well, if you do, I'd love to hear about it." I thought Samantha would hug Dana right on the spot, she sounded so relieved.

"Would you like something to drink? Coffee or tea?" Without being told, I headed to the kitchen for the big pitcher of sun tea that we keep in the refrigerator. I added glasses of ice and put everything on a tray. It felt nice to be doing something so simple. I hummed as I arranged the tray. I added a plate of small crackers and cheese and a few cookies and sweets.

I lifted the heavy tray. One advantage, I thought, of pushing a wheelchair around. It does make the arms strong. As I entered the living room, I caught the last few words that Dana spoke

I stopped, stunned and shocked. How could she be smiling? She spoke again, "Betty and I thought the perfect solution to the Halloween party was to have it here. What could be more perfect than a haunted house in an old funeral parlor?"

The tray rattled, tea sloshed, and ice cubes clinked, but my white-knuckled grip on the tray held tight. My mouth moved, but my words were drowned out by Roni and Josie giving excited acceptance.

Carefully, I set the tray onto the coffee table. I tried to stop the flow of excited conversation. "Wait. Stop. We can't have the haunted house here."

I might as well have been spitting into the wind. I tried again. "No party. Absolutely not. We're not even really moved in yet."

My sisters, Betty, and Dana reminded me of a football huddle. I tried tapping Samantha on the shoulder. She brushed me aside as if I were a pesky fly.

That did it. I stepped back, put my fingers in my mouth, and let out a whistle that would have brought my horses in off a twenty-acre pasture.

"What was that for?" Roni glared at me.

I glared back. "I get a say-so in this too. I don't want the party here." The idea of who knows how many children, a lot of teenagers running around the house was enough to turn my auburn- tinted hair white.

For persuasion, Samantha goes right for the conscience. "It's a perfect solution for the church. Everyone would be in agreement with this idea. We'd still be providing a safe alternative to trick-or-treating, and it wouldn't be on church grounds. The phone calls to the office would stop. Theo wouldn't be caught in the middle like he is now."

"I agree having a party away from the church is a good idea." And I did think it would be more peaceful if the congregation would stop arguing and bringing those arguments to service on Sunday. "But I don't agree it should be here."

Josie used nostalgia. "Remember all the great Halloween parties we had as kids? They were so much fun. Wouldn't you like for our kids to enjoy that? We could bring Halloween back the way it used to be, the way it should be."

Again, I agreed in theory, but memories are tricky things. Sometimes we only remember the fun things and forget all the work that went with them. "We did have a lot of fun, but I wonder what Mom would say right now? She's the one who had to put up with the noise, the screaming, and the mess. We're the ones who will end up with all the work, and I don't have time for it."

"We'll all pitch in." Roni is practical, and she usually finds a solution to any problem, but my problem was more than mess and clutter and noise. It involved disruption of my peace and a gut feeling that I would end up with more of the work than I wanted which, right now, was none at all.

Dana and Betty were quick to add their comments. They sensed a hole in my armor. Betty spoke first, eager to reassure me. "We have a party committee. The candy is bought and we already have the decorations. All we need is a definite location."

Dana spoke up, her voice firm and determined. She smelled victory and she pushed in for the final blow to my arguments. "You won't have to do a thing. The party committee will handle any detail that comes up. We'll provide all the chaperones and the food. You won't have to do anything except let us use your basement."

With Josie and Roni on their side, I knew no matter what objection I had, it would be outvoted. I threw up my hands and admitted defeat. "All right, I give up, but I still think this is a really bad idea."

Betty and Dana didn't wait. They left at what I can only describe as a gallop. I figured the party committee would be meeting in force in a matter of minutes. In fact, I saw Dana put her cell phone to her ear the minute she cleared the front door.

I sighed, preparing to give my sisters an ear-full, when a piercing shriek erupted from the nether regions of the house.

"What was that?" Samantha hasn't been in a house with young people for awhile. The sound startled her. I, however, had been living with my nieces for weeks already and was well acquainted with the different shrill yelps they are capable of.

Josie, Roni, and I locked gazes and nodded in agreement. "It's Téa," we spoke in unison.

We cocked our heads, listening to the distant thumping of feet. Once one child panics and runs, it doesn't take long for the others to join in. It took more than one child to create the noise coming towards us. Faint at first, the clatter started on the third floor and descended to the second level. We moved to the hallway to get a clear view from the bottom stairway and listened as the footsteps, running now, pounded along the second-floor hallway.

Téa led the pack as they pelted down the stairs. She jumped the last two steps and grabbed her mother around the waist.

"Mo-om," she wailed and buried her face against Josie's shoulder.

Josie raised her eyebrows at us and shrugged as she patted Téa's shoulder.

I could tell that Téa was terrified, but the faces of the other children were harder to read. The younger ones looked apprehensive. The older children looked downright guilty. Keira and Duncan wouldn't make eye contact with any of us.

I admit I have a suspicious nature. Being a middle child and the one born right after the only boy in the family has taught me a good deal of caution. I looked at all the children, but my gaze landed on Duncan. He held something under his arm. He must have felt my gaze on him because he gave a small slide to his left, putting Keira between me and whatever he was holding.

I tried to look casual as I slid to my left. With equal casualness, Duncan took another step, keeping Keira between us. That did it. I wanted to know what he was hiding. Before he could bolt for the door, I moved close and grabbed the box he didn't want me to see.

I made a sound that rivaled Téa's earlier shriek and held the box up by my fingertips. "This is bad, really, really bad. Take it." I would have dropped the box like a hot potato except I feared the contents would spill all over the floor.

Duncan took one look at me, grabbed the box, and bolted for the front door with Jenny, Karen, and Sara close on his heels.

I wiped my hand on my pants leg, trying to get the feel of the box off.

Samantha stared at me with wide eyes. "What was that all about?"

I ignored her. I wanted to get to the kitchen and wash my hands with soap and hot water. Josie and Roni stared at each other. They knew my problem. They didn't agree with it, but they knew why I was feeling as spooked as Téa looked.

Josie gave me a look, a combination of disdain and irony. "Don't you ever twit me about spiders again because your fear is just as irrational as mine is."

Samantha still looked bewildered. "What fear? What was that box Duncan had?"

"That," Roni spoke up, "was a Ouija board."

I glowered at Josie, "You let them play it here in an old funeral parlor? What were you thinking?"

"That it's just a game." Josie shrugged again.

Another wail erupted from Téa, and she burrowed in closer to Josie. My sister looked helpless as she patted Téa.

Gloom settled over me. "It's never just a game. And now we've got a Halloween party going on here. Ouija boards and funeral parlors? What next? It's going to be nothing but trouble, I'm warning you right now."

Roni made a face at me; then she smiled. She tends to put a positive spin on things. "But, remember what Dana said? It won't be any work. They'll take care everything."

Chapter Seventeen
Another Mystery

Monday morning found me standing at the kitchen sink in as black a mood as I'm capable of. "Don't worry; you won't have to do a thing." I slammed a dirty bowl onto the top shelf of the dishwasher then plunged my hands back into the hot soapy water where last night's dishes soaked.

"We have a committee. We have decorations." I grabbed a handful of silverware, rinsed the soap off under the slow stream of hot tap water, and placed them in the basket.

"Will you give it a rest?" Roni got up from the kitchen table and brought her breakfast dishes to the sink. "So you had to answer a few phone calls. Big deal."

"A few?" I turned to glare at her. "I'd like to know what you consider a lot." I took her dirty dishes and put them into the sink to soak. "The phone rings off the wall, and I spent two hours yesterday running back and forth from the shed to the basement looking for tools. They may have had all the decorations, but they sure didn't bring any hammers with them."

Josie gave a snort of laughter, and I switched my glare to her. She held up her hands. "You wouldn't have had to spend two hours hunting for the tools if they'd been put away where they belonged. It's not the committee's fault you're disorganized."

This was true but I didn't want to admit it. When I get in a mood, I'd rather just stay in it without being bothered by logic. Roni walked over to Mitchell and wiped his face clean before she picked up his breakfast dishes.

I turned back to the sink. Movement caught my eye, and I shrieked at the upside-down devil's mask looking in at me through the window above the sink. It took a moment to still my racing heart before I yelled. "Elliott, if your mom catches you hanging off the edge of the roof like that, she'll ground you for a week. What are you doing out so early anyway?"

Elliott pulled himself up onto the roof, reversed ends, and hung over the side for a minute before he dropped to the ground. I could remember doing the same thing at his age.

Two minutes later the side door swung open, and my nephew came breezing into the kitchen. The big grin on his face stopped my tirade before it began. How can I be mad at such a cute face? The sight of the ugly mask in his hand changed my mind. "You know, I'm getting really tired of hearing girls shriek six times a day. You better watch out or they'll figure out a way to get even, and believe me, girls can be really dangerous. Just ask your Uncle Buddy."

"Ask me what?" Buddy isn't an early riser. He headed straight for the coffee pot. Josie, Roni, and I aren't coffee drinkers, but with Buddy here, I'd brewed a pot for him. No way would I tell him it was decaf. What he doesn't know won't hurt him.

He sat down at the table, said good morning to Mitchell in his best Donald Duck voice, and sipped his coffee. "I was sleeping so nice when I heard somebody scream. You all look okay."

I shook my head and turned back to finish loading the dishwasher. Roni answered him. "The screamer was Charly. The cause was Elliott. He's been going around wearing horrible masks and popping up in windows. Out of closets. From behind bushes. He's caught every one of us at least once in the last two weeks."

I looked back to see Buddy looking at Elliott over the top of his coffee cup with an unaccustomed serious look on his face. "Don't pull that on me. I've had too many scares this week. I could have a heart attack and die on the spot."

Elliott looked at Buddy, a slight frown wrinkling his brow, unsure whether his uncle was joking or not. I hoped Elliott didn't try to scare Buddy because I knew from experience that my brother was quite capable of dropping to the ground and pretending to be dead. Come to think of it, it would serve Elliott right to have someone scare him for a change.

The shrill ringing of the phone interrupted my pleasant daydream. I groaned. "I'm not getting that. I refuse to answer one more phone call."

Josie picked up the phone. From the way she rolled her eyes, I knew it was another committee member with a problem.

I moved to the stove and put some bacon on to fry. All of us girls had grown up feeding our brother. Making him breakfast felt very normal. I heard the front door open and knew from the happy hello it was Samantha. I yelled at her that we were in the kitchen and added a few more strips of bacon to the skillet.

"How's it going?" As grumpy as my brother is in the morning, Samantha is cheerful. She sat down at the kitchen table, and I enjoyed seeing her bright and smiling face next to our brother's sleepy one.

"We're all fine." Roni grinned at me. Her fast response stopped me from reciting my list of complaints again.

"I'm not." Buddy got up to refill his coffee cup. "It's going to take several days for my trailer to dry out. I had to hire someone to come in and use a vacuum to suck up the water from the furniture and mattress. I'm not even sure the mattress can be saved. I might end up having to buy a new one. Whoever trashed it did a thorough job."

Josie hung up the phone. "You know you can stay here. Although you would be more comfortable sleeping in the girl's room instead of on the living room couch."

He raised his eyebrows at her. "They still won't sleep on the third floor? The thunderstorm is long gone."

"I know." Josie gave me a quick look and then turned back to Buddy. "They're spooked about finding out the house used to be a funeral parlor."

Buddy sat quiet for a few minutes, sipping his hot coffee. "Can I take Molly up with me?" He knew Molly would stay with him. Murphy wouldn't. Once bedtime rolled around the Golden Retriever would hunt for me.

I answered before Josie could. "Sure, you can sleep with the dog. She likes it up there. You're welcome to stay here as long as you need to." I didn't add that I would feel better having him here. I'd rather have my teeth pulled than admit to my brother I was spooked in my own house.

Elliott decided he needed a second breakfast, so I fed him and Buddy. Samantha declined the bacon and eggs but accepted toast. It made me happy to be back among my family. I'd been gone for too many years. I sat down and just looked at them. I'd be glad when my husband and son returned from Australia, but for right then, for that moment in time, contentment flooded me.

A sharp knock on the kitchen door startled me, sending my peaceful mood fleeing. The door opened and Logan walked in. That did surprise me. I couldn't remember a time when Logan had come over without Mary Lee, and never at 7:30 in the morning. He didn't look like himself, either. He looked flustered, not a look that sits well on his face.

He caught Buddy's eye. "Put the bacon and egg on your toast. Let's go."

Buddy gaped at him. "Go where?" But even while he was talking, his hands were busy making a sandwich. He knew Logan well enough to know he better grab the food or risk going without.

Logan eyed Buddy's sandwich, paused a moment, and then reached over to pluck two pieces of toast off the plate in front of Samantha. He grabbed bacon from the platter and made himself a sandwich before he spoke. "There's trouble at the cemetery."

Buddy stood up and moved to the cabinet holding the cups and glasses. Opening the cupboard, he pulled out his plastic travel cup. He poured the coffee from his mug into it and topped the cup off from the pot. "Vandals? Did they knock over some headstones?

"No." Logan shook his head, eyeing the now full coffee mug in Buddy's hand. "Is there another one of those?"

Buddy rummaged in the cupboard, and Logan continued talking. "It's worse than vandalism. One of the graves has been opened. The coffin is a rotted mess at the bottom of the grave, and the body is gone."

Oh, puke. I did what I always do when I get upset. I headed for a drink. In my case, that means a cold diet soda. Something exciting happens in Weary, and it has to take place in the cemetery.

I don't handle going into any cemetery, especially the one in Weary. It holds too many memories. My parents are buried there.

I shook off my thoughts. I had to or end up in tears. Maybe I could find out what happened without going out there. "Logan." I tried to sound casual but from the looks my sisters threw at me, I knew I'd failed. "Was it anybody we know? Do you have any idea who did it?"

Buddy handed Logan a container of coffee. Logan threw me an impatient look as he opened the door to leave. "We're not releasing any information yet. It's strictly on a need to know basis." He followed Buddy through the door and pulled it shut behind him with a loud bang.

I glared at the door, wishing the door was Logan so he'd see how annoyed I was. I turned to stare at my sisters. "But, I really need to know."

Roni snorted. Josie laughed. And Samantha said, "You could always go check it out. I can stay here until either you get back or Phoebe shows up."

I hesitated. The idea tempted me, but to do that I'd have to actually go into the cemetery, and I only did that for a funeral. My eyes landed on Elliott. Whatever I was going to say evaporated. I knew that look. I'd seen it often in the eyes of my own son as well as various nieces and nephews. He was going to bolt for freedom, and this little story would spread through the school like wildfire.

"Why are you over here so early? Don't you have school this morning?"

He snagged the last piece of the bacon from the platter and grinned at me. "There's no school today. No water. They have to get the pipes fixed before we can go back."

"Oh, great," Josie muttered. "I better go tell the girls. They'll probably go right back to bed."

Roni laughed, "If they're even stirring yet."

This was true. Getting the girls up and moving in the mornings usually took all of us. We even, at times, sent the dogs jumping onto the beds to roust them out. Having ninety pounds of dog land on their middle, followed by wet, sloppy dog kisses, usually brought them shrieking to their feet. After a few dog episodes, the girls only needed a warning of dog germs on the way to get them up and moving.

Josie left the kitchen, running up the back stairs, to go check on her daughters. Roni went to the phone to call Katie. She replaced the phone and yelled up the stairs. "Josie, it's only the grade school; the junior high school is fine. Keira still has to go to school. Téa stays home."

We heard an anguished cry from Keira and a faint yippee from Téa. A moment later, Josie came back downstairs. "That means I still go to work. That must be why I didn't get a phone call. Most of my work is done at the high school."

"Elliott." I snagged his collar as he moved past me toward the door. "This isn't something you go blabbing about. Your uncle said it's on a need to know basis."

He looked at me with innocent blue eyes. "I know, Aunt Charly. I won't tell anyone who doesn't need to know." And he was off, leaving me, once again, with my mouth hanging open. I knew, oh, too well, what that last sentence meant because every friend that Elliott had would need to know. Just like I did.

Grumpy didn't even begin to describe my feelings now. Roni and Josie needed to leave. Téa had gone back to bed, and Keira flew down the back stairs to the kitchen. She put a pop tart in the toaster and fidgeted, waiting for it to pop up. She would ride to school with Josie and eat her breakfast on the way.

Samantha took the last of the breakfast dishes to the sink, and we found room for them in the dishwasher. Before Roni left she put a coloring book and crayons in front of Mitchell. That would keep him occupied for a few minutes.

"At last." I grabbed a clean glass from the cupboard, filled it to the brim with ice, and went into the pantry to return with another dict cola. Samantha frowned at me. I defended myself. "It's no different than you drinking a cup of coffee." It was because the coffee Samantha got out of the pot was decaf and my Diet Coke wasn't, but I didn't bring that up.

I sat down next to Mitchell, praised his coloring, and turned my eyes back to Samantha, who sat down across the table from us. "What brought you over so early this morning? Is everything all right?"

She got up and vanished into the pantry. She knew where the real goodies were hidden. She returned with a piece of fresh apple pie. Mitchell's eyes lit up, and I sighed, left the table, and brought him back a small piece. There wasn't any use arguing with him. He's a true son of Roni, and no one that I knew of had ever won an argument with her except Dad, and those battles were legendary in our memories.

Samantha loves sweets about as much as any person I've ever known. She took a big bite of pie and chewed. I fought my impatience. Maybe I should get something to eat. I'd cooked breakfast for everybody, but I hadn't gotten to eat any of it. But it wouldn't be pie for me. My choice for breakfast was a bag of potato chips and some onion dip. I know, it's not a good breakfast, but chips and dip can make any day brighter.

Mitchell's eyes lit up at that too, so I put them between us. Samantha knew better than to scold me, not when she was sitting there eating apple pie. What can I say? We're an undisciplined family who grew up with really bad eating habits.

Samantha swallowed her bite of pie and started talking. "There was a phone call this morning for Theo. The connection was bad. It kept cutting out. Theo could only understand a word here and there. He heard the words, 'I'm sorry. It was a mistake.' Then he heard nothing but static. He kept trying to tell the caller to call back and try for a better connection."

She sipped her coffee, and impatience tugged at me again. How many times can curiosity be aroused and left unsatisfied before it causes irreparable harm to a person?

Samantha started talking again. "Finally, the phone line cleared up again. He heard the man talking to someone else. The man yelled, 'No, don't do that.' Then the caller spoke again and said, 'I'm sorry you were left holding the bag.'"

Theo tried once again to explain that the phone was full of static and would he repeat his name. The caller apologized and said, 'It's me,' then more static, 'son,' and then the caller hung up. Theo waited but the man didn't call back"

I'd forgotten all about the chips while listening to Samantha talk. My brain scrambled to put all the pieces together. "Theo heard the word, 'son'. Maybe that was part of his name, like Ericson or Johnson."

Samantha nodded in agreement. "Probably, but those are common names. Theo doesn't know who called or what he wanted. It's very frustrating."

I pulled a big chip out of the sack and put an obscene amount of dip on it. Mitchell imitated my action, complete with cream cheese mustache. I grinned and wiped his face clean, all the while mulling over Theo's mysterious phone call.

This was all I needed, another mystery to think about. This one didn't seem like anything I could help with. I snagged another chip, drank a little more soda, and pondered everything that had happened.

The minister of the church had mysteriously left his job. The church secretary was missing. Someone had stolen the keys to Buddy's car and vandalized his mobile home. One of Jed's cows had been brutally killed and mutilated. A mysterious patch of grass had appeared on top of a grave in the cemetery. An unknown intruder had been in our basement. Old Ansel was following Buddy around like a shadow. A grave had been opened and the bones stolen. And somehow, an entire haunted house was being built in our basement. All these things and we hadn't even been in the house a full two months.

Chapter Eighteen
I Didn't Want to Do It

My mornings start early, but everybody clears out fast leaving me with a few hours of peace and quiet. Since we've merged three families together in this big house, my routine has undergone some changes. Mitchell usually joins me in my early hours, but he's easy to distract, and he makes me laugh. The day goes better when it's started with laughter.

No laughter this morning. I glanced at the clock and frowned. Seven forty-five AM and I'd been presented with three puzzles: the grave in the cemetery, Samantha's report of the mysterious phone call, and the water problems at the grade school.

If I had to identify the biggest motivating factor in my life, it would be curiosity. It drives me, and once aroused, it won't leave me alone. I felt its prod now, poking me with an unrelenting need for answers.

The water problem at school was most likely a coincidence and not related to the vandalism of Buddy's trailer. If I was wrong, then the whole town had a bigger problem than I could solve. I stood up and moved restlessly around the kitchen. Thanks to so many sisters around, the room was uncharacteristically clean and tidy. If I didn't get myself distracted, and fast, I'd find myself wandering around in the Weary Cemetery and getting yelled at by the mayor.

The fact that I'd been yelled at, stuffed in a car trunk, and tickled to the point of no return for most of my younger life has pretty much desensitized me to Logan's displeasure, so I wasn't worried about barging into official town business. What held me back was my reluctance to wander among the tombstones. Nothing has desensitized me to them.

I leaned against the counter watching Samantha help Mitchell color and wished I could turn my brain off before my mental jumble of thoughts succeeded in giving me a headache.

The kitchen door swung open, and Phoebe came in like a breeze of fresh air. A gust of wind came in with her, swirling her hair and turning her cheeks rosy pink. A bright smile lit her face as Mitchell launched himself off the kitchen chair and ran to her. All kids love Phoebe. It's a gift with her. Mitchell pulled her over to the table to see his colorful creations.

"What's up?" That dratted curiosity bit me again. "You're here early."

"Not a lot," she reassured us. "Jed got up early. He wanted to check on the cattle again to make sure we hadn't lost any more. Since he was off early, I decided to come on over."

Samantha laughed, "In other words, you were bored?"

Phoebe batted her lashes, all innocence. "There seems to be a lot more going on here than anywhere else in town."

"Tell me about it." I sank onto a chair and reached for more chips. Just thinking about the Halloween haunted house being constructed in our basement sent me into a spiral of doom. "You have no idea what an inconvenience this party is turning out to be."

Samantha looked distressed, and I felt a pang of guilt: a small pang, but there, none-the-less. I consumed a day's calories and then some while listening to Samantha catch Phoebe up on the morning's events. I started on the next day's allotment when Phoebe took the bag of chips away from me.

I was feeling a bit ill from the ones I'd already consumed or I would have fussed a bit, but I let her take them and store them out of sight in the pantry. It's nice to have family around that doesn't hesitate to help you do what needs to be done, especially when my own will power was at such low ebb.

Before she could start scolding me, we heard the front door open, and a cheery voice called, "Yoo-hoo."

I buried my face in my hands and groaned. "Oh, no. I can't bear it this early in the morning." I peeked through my fingers at Samantha and Phoebe, trying to gauge their mood and how willing they would be to help me.

The voice came again, a bit closer now. "Is anybody home?"

I hissed. "That's Dana Franklin. She's here early. They don't usually start showing up until ten. I forgot to unlock the outside basement door."

Panic flickered in my stomach. "It's too early for me to deal with Dana."

"It can't be that bad." Samantha sounded worried. It was, after all, her fault that I had to deal with half the women from the church. Actually, make that all of them. One half came trooping through the house looking for tools or the bathroom. The other half called the house or stopped me on the street to voice their displeasure. No matter where we were or who we talked to, I always ended up hearing how bad it was to have a haunted house in the basement of an old mortuary. As if I didn't already know that and agree with it.

I glared at Samantha and hissed again. A little louder, still careful to make sure Dana didn't hear me, "The only thing worse than seeing Dana in the morning is having Ann Richardson show up. Dana is pushy, but Ann is needy. She pesters the heck out of me."

"Yoo-hoo." We heard her calling again. Then we heard the sound of toenails clicking on the hardwood floors. The dogs had better manners than I did. They were running to greet her.

"Nice doggies." Dana's voice rose an octave, and I could hear her voice quaver.

I sighed. "If she only knew, those dogs are the biggest babies in the world." I eyed Samantha again and made one of those snap decisions I'm so fond of. "Tell you what." I stood up. "You deal with Dana and the haunted house crew."

I swung my gaze to Phoebe. "And you deal with Mitchell. I'll be back in time to get Jake up. I can't stand not knowing what's going on at the cemetery.

I'm ducking out the back door. I'll be back by nine to get Jake up."

I grabbed the van keys off the key rack, snatched my cell phone off the counter, and put it in my pocket. I could hear Dana moving with little baby-steps as she edged past the dogs. She would be in the kitchen in a matter of seconds.

"Where are you going?" Phoebe looked bewildered. Samantha gazed toward the dining room door. No alarm showed on her face. She likes people. I, on the other hand, wanted freedom. I intended to make my escape before Dana saw me. I opened the back door, ready to bolt at the first sight of her. "I'm going to the cemetery. With any luck, Logan and Buddy will still be there."

"And without luck?" Phoebe cocked her head at me.

I didn't want to think about what I'd do if they had left the cemetery. "Without luck I'll be driving around in the cemetery wishing I was back here dealing with Dana."

I escaped just as Dana entered the kitchen.

In minutes, I arrived at the gates of the Weary Cemetery. Actually, I could have been anywhere in Weary in a matter of minutes. The business section of town is only two blocks long.

The cemetery sits on the south end of town just outside the city limits. It's a pretty spot, peaceful and serene. But not for me; once I drove through those gates, my peace would be shattered.

I sat frowning, staring through the open gates leading into the cemetery. Maybe I should just reverse the van and go home. Then I remembered Dana's voice calling y*oo-hoo*. I put my foot on the accelerator. I didn't get far.

A uniformed officer stepped from behind the big stone pillar that flanked each side of the road entering the cemetery. He held up a hand, stopping me, and approached the window. I put the van in neutral. I should have realized there would be law enforcement involved. I powered down the driver's side window. "Yes, sir? Is there a problem?"

He tipped his hat at me and I recognized him. I'd spent several hours staring at him during my enforced visit to the county jail. "Ma'am? Nobody is allowed in the cemetery right now. You'll have to leave."

I could tell from his tone of voice and my past experience with him, I wouldn't be able to wheedle my way past him. "Could you tell me why?" I prodded.

"No, ma'am. Just back your van up and come back tomorrow." He tipped his hat again and retreated to stand in the middle of the road, effectively blocking my entry.

I backed up the van, driving with care since the eyes of the law were upon me. But I had no intention of going home. I'd be the first person to admit that I have an obstinate side to my nature. I had overcome my dislike of the cemetery and, by golly, I was going to get inside.

Aunt Ellen and Uncle Harry live on the south side of Weary. I could literally see their house from the cemetery entrance, so I parked in their driveway and walked back. I avoided the front area and followed the fence around to the side.

Once there, I gave a mental thank you to my brother for my climbing skills. He spent his grade school years trying to get away from me. I spent mine tagging after him, so climbing a tree and clambering over a wrought-iron fence seemed easy enough to do.

The tree proved no barrier to my determination. It wasn't until I was on the limb overhanging the six-foot iron fence that my courage left me. How was I supposed to get from the limb to the fence? And once on the fence, how was I supposed to climb down it? Six feet doesn't seem so bad when you're on the ground looking up. It looked a lot taller from the top looking down.

As a child, hanging off the side of the roof like Elliott had done that morning was a piece of cake. Balancing on an iron fence? Not so much.

Before I could retreat, the branch I was sitting on shuddered. I heard a creak that scared me more than the six foot drop from the top of the fence did. The last thing I needed was a broken branch dropping me onto one of the metal spikes topping the fence. As carefully as I could, I swung off. Keeping one hand on the branch, I balanced on the top of the fence.

Reaching down, I tried to find a way to safely descend. My foot slipped. A memory of my brother calling me Grace flitted through my head. The branch I had a death grip on failed me, and I plummeted toward the ground

My rear hit the fence, sending exquisite pain all the way to my teeth. I found myself suspended by the seat of my pants, dangling halfway between the top of the fence and the ground below. The last thing I wanted was to be rescued by the officer. Humiliation doesn't sit well with me, so I twisted and turned until my pants ripped. With a speed reminiscent of a long-ago potato chip bag slide, I fell flat on my face and ate dirt.

I struggled to my feet, the process taking far longer than it should have. I didn't remember falls hurting this much when I was a child. I felt a breeze, followed by pain. Reaching back I fingered the big, three-corner tear in the seat of my jeans. My butt cheek wasn't hanging out but close enough I didn't want to turn my back on anybody. No blood. Thank goodness.

I spat dirt out of my mouth and brushed myself off as best I could, feeling a sense of familiarity as I did so. How many times in my life had I ripped my clothes, skinned my knees, lost buttons, and destroyed zippers? I guess the trials of being a tomboy never leave you.

I gave the fence one last frowning look only now realizing I wouldn't be able to leave by the same route. My choices were few. I'd have to find my brother or stand here and risk getting caught by the deputy. Or I'd have to hide out here until everybody left, which to me was a fate worse than....never mind. I don't want to talk about death while standing in a cemetery.

I gave one last swipe at my knees and straightened up. That's when my curiosity came back and bit me in my already traumatized rear. I wanted to find out what was going on. To do that, I needed to walk through the cemetery. And here I stood with grave after grave in front of me. I had no choice. Walk or get caught. Neither of those choices felt good.

"And my brother mows here," I muttered as I picked my way around the tombstones and mausoleums. "He drives right over the top of them." I understood there wasn't any way I could be disturbing anyone's final slumber, but it made me uncomfortable anyway.

I took my eyes off my feet to scan the area ahead of me. The big gust of air that whooshed out of me when I caught sight of Logan's pickup startled me. Relief. I hadn't missed them after all.

A glance in the other direction told me I needed to hurry. The deputy was looking my way. It took all my remaining will power to walk toward Buddy and Logan as if I belonged there. Out of the corner of my eye, I saw the deputy start toward me, but a car arriving at the gate distracted him. As soon as his attention was off me, I broke into a jog.

Logan and Buddy stood shoulder to shoulder, peering into the hole. I couldn't see past them, so I spoke. "What does it look like?"

I thought for a minute, I'd have to go get the deputy. Buddy and Logan jumped so high, I feared they were in danger of falling in.

Logan cussed a blue streak, but he cusses all the time, so I tuned him out. Buddy, on the other hand, scared me. He clutched at his chest. He's had open heart surgery before, and I thought he was having the big one. Once he saw me, he changed the clutch to a wipe, and tried to be nonchalant.

"Sis, where did you come from?" His eyes narrowed. "And how did you get here?"

I gave him the most innocent smile I'm capable of. "I walked. How else would I get here?"

Logan cussed again. "I thought the police were keeping everyone out of here."

I gave him a big smile. "I'm not just anyone. I'm related to the mayor."

Logan looked disgusted and turned his attention back to the grave. Buddy knows me better. He gave me a good once over, the kind of look he used to give me when we were kids, and he knew I'd been up to something. That's the bad part about families. They read you too well.

I could see the wheels turning, so I tried to distract him. "What does it look like in there?"

He reached out and brushed my face.

I stepped back. "What?"

"Dirt," he said. Then he looked down, and a slow smile spread over his face. "A lot of dirt."

Logan looked up, caught by Buddy's comment. "What did you say?"

Buddy started to snicker. I don't like being laughed at. I ignored him.

"Look at her," Buddy told Logan. "I think our dear sister came over the fence. It's a cinch she landed in the dirt somewhere."

Logan looked closer at me, and I feared they were in danger of going into the grave again. The only thing that held me back was the knowledge that they were tall enough, and strong enough, to get out without help. And I knew I wasn't fast enough to outrun them when they did.

Buddy stepped back. I did too. I shouldn't have because it brought the suspicious look back to his face. I tried to be as nonchalant as he'd been earlier as I backed away from them to get to the opposite side of the grave without exposing my backside.

The deputy came huffing up. "I'm sorry, Mr. Daniels. I guess one got through."

One what? Indignation rose in me, but I kept my mouth shut.

Logan sighed. "That's all right. I know her. We'll take care of it."

I didn't like the way Logan said that, and for once, I was glad the deputy was handy. They couldn't do anything too bad to me, not with the law as a witness.

Their voices receded from my consciousness. I stepped closer to the grave and finally had a clear view into the hole.

Most of the casket remains seemed to by lying beside the grave in the big pile of dirt left by the backhoe. Only splintered pieces remained in a hole big enough to hold three caskets. Whoever had dug the grave either hadn't known how to use a backhoe, or they simply didn't care how big a hole they dug. Lucky nobody had been buried beside her. That made me wonder too.

I did what I always do when I'm confronted with a puzzle. I became absorbed with possibilities. Why would someone steal a body? Where would they put it? And how did they accomplish it without being seen?

Deep in thought, the soft voice behind me startled me. "Ma'am?"

Startled, I turned around to see the deputy standing behind me.

"I'm sorry to bother you, ma'am." He lowered his voice. "But did you know your pants are ripped?"

Chapter Nineteen
A Small Victory

I clapped a hand to my nether regions, grabbed the hanging flap of denim, and spoke through clenched teeth. "Yes, sir, I did know that. Thank you for reminding me."

Buddy's shoulders shook, and I knew he was laughing again. Logan stood staring into the grave. From the way his mouth moved, I'm glad I couldn't hear what he said.

A smothered curse from the deputy caught my attention. "Would you look at that?" He stepped out from behind me. I kept hold of the cloth anyway. "If that don't beat all." He stopped next to Logan and pointed about six feet to the right of the front gate. Our eyes followed his pointing finger.

Ansel Whitaker peered at us from above the stone wall that ran along the front of the cemetery. My stomach flip-flopped at the eerie sight of his head, seeming to perch on the wall without benefit of a body. I wished I hadn't been standing at the front of the line when they passed out imaginations.

I shuffled around the headstone, grateful for once that I knew where the grave was and was in no danger of stepping on it. I stood next to Buddy. "Why would Ansel be peeking over the wall at us?"

He never took his eyes off Ansel. "Maybe he knows something about the open grave."

The deputy perked up at his comment and took off for the front gate at a respectable trot. I could have told him not to bother. Ansel popped up a little higher, eyeballed the deputy moving toward him, and vanished. A minute later we saw a bicycle shoot past the front gate, Ansel standing on the pedals and pumping hard. For an old man, he could really move. The deputy didn't have a chance of finding Ansel if he chose not to be found.

I sighed, let go of the torn cloth, and turned toward Buddy and Logan. "Now." I could hear the stubbornness in my own voice. "Tell me what happened. That's a really big hole for a grave, isn't it?"

I think Buddy would have spun me a whopper. Logan would have ignored me except for the fact they were in a hurry. In my present mood, I'd not only waste their time, but enjoy doing it.

Logan started talking. "The grave was opened sometime last night using equipment already here in the cemetery. Mr. Robbins intended to dig a new grave today. He moved the backhoe over yesterday, but it was late. He didn't have time to get the hole dug. He thought the equipment would be safe here."

"This grave is by itself. Apparently, the lots bought by her family were never used. The person digging the hole wasn't worried about neatness."

Logan waved his hand toward the backhoe. "The police think whoever did this came prepared. They must have placed the bones in a blanket. Just rolled it right up and took the body away." He shook his head, disbelief plain to see on his face.

Logan continued, "The grave was that of a young girl, Elizabeth Jordan. She lived here in Weary back in the1930's."

A mournful wave of sadness swept over me, a familiar ache that always hits me when I'm in a cemetery. I moved a few steps to the side so I could read the inscription on the headstone. Elizabeth Jordan. Beloved daughter. b. July 26th 1920-d. Oct.31, 1936. *Wouldn't you know it?* I thought to myself. I'm haunted by Halloween; I have a spook house being built in my basement, a nephew who delights in wearing scary masks so he can scare the living daylights out of anybody who happens to be around, and this poor girl died on Halloween.

My peripheral vision caught sight of Buddy and Logan moving toward Logan's truck. I ran after them. "Hey, if you're leaving, I need a ride to my van."

"Sorry." Logan climbed behind the wheel, slammed the driver's side door, and grinned at me. How one man can look so darn ornery all the time is beyond me. "We're in a hurry. You got here by yourself; you can get back by yourself."

Buddy slammed the door on the passenger side. I tried again. "I can't go walking through town like this." I waved toward my rear. "It's embarrassing."

Logan shook his head, "Can't help you." He turned the key and the engine started right off. One thing about my brother-in-law, he keeps all his possessions in top notch running order.

He shifted gears, preparing to take off. Though I stood by the driver's window, I saw Buddy lean forward and rummage around. He sat up and said something to Logan in a soft voice.

"Tell you what." Logan shifted back to park. "I'll help you out here." He turned toward Buddy. I heard a soft, tearing sound. He turned back to me and handed me something through the window.

It was a long piece of gray duct tape. "Gee, thanks." I'm no fool, I took the tape, but visions of another brother-in-law and a backside full of mud flashed through my mind. I'd had to walk a lot further that day, and I'd only been sixteen. The embarrassment factor is bigger at sixteen.

He leaned out the window and leered at me. "Do you need help putting that on?"

"No." I snapped, and flashed him what I hoped was a mean look; I'm never sure how threatening I actually look. "I can manage just fine." I tore the long strip into two manageable pieces and with a minimum of twisting was able to tape the loose flap into place.

I straightened back up and glared at Logan and Buddy. "Just remember this, Logan Daniels."

He turned away from me, shifting the truck into gear again. I raised my voice so he could hear me over the sound of the truck engine. "The next family get-together, and there will be one soon, is going to be at your house. I'll make sure of that."

He froze, and sensing victory, I continued my threat. "Every sister, every spouse, every niece and nephew, every new baby, every aunt, uncle and cousin I can round up." I paused for effect and leaned in close to the window. "Every one of them will be at your house."

He sat for a moment in deep thought and then slammed the gear back into park. "Shit!" He shook his head. Then he swiveled a look at me and said, "Get in, and make it quick. I don't have all day."

He didn't have to say it twice. I bolted around to the passenger side, made Buddy move over, and climbed in. Victory never tasted so sweet.

Chapter Twenty
Victory is Fleeting

"You can let me out here," I told Logan.

His knuckles whitened on the steering wheel, and he leaned around Buddy to peer at me. The look on his face brought back childhood memories of me trying to outrun him and get to Mom before he got to me. Even at my present level of maturity, the look made me nervous. "Here?"

"Yes." I opened the door and hopped out onto the road, grateful the passenger side was closer to the house than the driver's side. "Here is fine."

He spoke through clenched teeth. "You parked at Ellen and Harry's?"

I saw him glance out the window and knew exactly what he saw. The front gate of the cemetery a mere block behind us.

"It seemed the right thing to do at the time." I shut the door and spoke through the open window. "I appreciate the ride."

"What ride? There was no ride. It was blackmail, pure and simple, and," he said, the look on his face curdling my stomach, "you owe me." He pointed a finger at me. "Christmas is at your house."

I jumped back as he took off, saving my toes by inches.

Christmas. Well, I'd sort of counted on that anyway, but better to let him think he'd won the round. It was safer that way. You never knew what Logan could think up.

Thinking about Christmas made me smile. It's a holiday full of laughter and music. Logan might hate the invasion, but I was starved for a full family gathering. If Logan had been thinking, he'd never have believed my threat back at the cemetery for one minute, but one-upping my eldest brother-in-law happens rarely, and it felt good.

I couldn't pick up my van without stopping in to say hi to Aunt Ellen and Uncle Harry. Ellen is my mother's youngest sister. I feel as at home in her house as I do in my own.

I gave a quick rap on the front door and then poked my head in. "Yoo-hoo, it's just me. Anybody home?"

Aunt Ellen called out a welcome, and I went on in to find her, Uncle Harry, and my cousin, Jessi.

"No school for you either?" I asked Jessi.

"No." she shook her head. "The grade school is closed until the water pipes can be fixed. The whole system is antiquated and needs replaced. I don't expect them to open until next Monday."

"Was the leak from normal causes?" I was cautious. So many odd things had happened in town, I wouldn't have been surprised to find out we had a mad practical joker going around causing havoc.

156

"Yes, thank goodness." Jessi walked into the kitchen area and started preparing lunch for her parents. "How are things at your house?"

Visions of Christmas flew from my head as the reality of Halloween rushed back.

"Other than Elliott popping up at unexpected times in unexpected places wearing horrendous masks and the dear church ladies driving me crazy? Things are just peachy at my house."

I rummaged for a cutting board and knife and started chopping onions while Jessi browned hamburger.

Uncle Harry got up, grabbed his hat off the coat rack, and stood by the kitchen door. "Did you hear about the dead squirrels?"

I shook my head.

He added, "And Patti Selleck's dog was found lying dead in their yard. Lots of weird things going on since Jed lost his cow."

I didn't give the disdainful snort I would have if I'd been talking to one of my siblings. I respect Uncle Harry too much for that.

Jessi said the words I wanted to. "Pop, there's nothing mysterious about any of it. The dead squirrel was road kill. And Patti's dog was at least seventeen years old. He most likely died of natural causes."

Uncle Harry quivered. "I've lived in Weary all my life, and I never saw so many strange things happen in so short a time. Don't tell me its natural causes."

With that, he left the house, leaving me with my mouth hanging open, which was a mistake because I inhaled onion fumes and my eyes started watering.

Jessi laughed, "You've chopped enough onions anyway. I'll get this casserole thrown together and in the oven. Mom won't have to do a thing. Thank you for helping."

As I grabbed a paper towel to wipe my eyes, the mantel clock chimed nine o'clock.

"Darn it. I promised Phoebe I'd get back by nine to get Jake up. I better head out, but I sure enjoyed the visit."

I dropped a kiss on Aunt Ellen's cheek and started for the door only to find myself captured by color. The sun shining through the windows, sparkling and dancing through Uncle Harry's colored bottles, hypnotized me. Red, amber, green, and blue, the sunlit bottles flooded the walls and floor with brilliant color. Jessi walked up behind me, bringing me back from fairyland.

"I know you're in a hurry." I could hear laughter in her voice. "But Mom wants to know why you're wearing duct tape on your rear?"

I gasped and clapped a hand to the seat of my pants. "I meant to keep my back to you all. I was hoping no one would see it." I gave one more glance at the pretty bottles, looked at my watch, and gave up. I was late anyway; a few more minutes wouldn't make any difference.

I explained my misadventure in the cemetery. Aunt Ellen and Jessi laughed. I started out only to be stopped at the window again. Only this time it wasn't pretty colors and sunlight that halted me in my tracks. Through the window I could see a battered old pick-up truck. I leaned closer to the window to make sure I was seeing right: trees to each side, a garage in front, and Uncle Harry's truck parked right smack dab behind my van.

"Jessi?" I looked over my shoulder at her. "Is there another set of keys for Uncle Harry's truck?"

She stood up and came to stand beside me. "He always leaves the keys in the ignition."

"I hope so." I waved at Aunt Ellen and took off at a trot with Jessi right behind me. Curiosity is a big hereditary trait in our family, and Jessi's share may equal mine. We stood shoulder to shoulder, peering through the driver's side window.

"I don't see any keys." My stomach slid to my ankles.

Jessi opened the door to get a better look. She checked the visor and, bending over, looked under the seat. "I'm sorry," she apologized as she stood up. "I've never known Pop to take them before. He always leaves them in the ignition. Who, in Weary, would steal his truck?"

She stepped back and examined the truck from hood to tailgate. "Who in their right mind would want it?"

I had to agree with her. It ran okay, but it wasn't anything to look at. Chances are it was something Uncle Harry had picked up cheap, tinkered with it enough to get it running, and called it a bargain.

I heard an engine start up, followed by a sharp horn blast. Jessi and I turned around. Logan pulled out from behind Uncle Harry's barn. He had a big grin on his face as he waved at us. I could see Uncle Harry sitting in the middle and Buddy riding shotgun.

From the way my brother's shoulders shook, I knew he was laughing again. Over the top of the truck, I could see his hand, holding a big roll of gray duct tape, waving at me.

I slapped a hand to my rear and ran for the truck. Maybe Logan would let me ride in the truck bed, but it wasn't to be. With another honk of his horn, Logan's grin widened, and he took off, leaving me in a cloud of dust.

"I can't believe Uncle Harry would do this to me," I told Jessi as she came up beside me. "I'm not a bit surprised at Logan and Buddy, but I thought better of Uncle Harry."

"I guess you shouldn't have twitted him about the dead dog," Jessi told me.

I rolled my eyes at her and didn't bother to remind her that it hadn't been me who'd argued with him. It wouldn't do to disagree with someone I was going to ask a favor from. "I don't suppose you could run me home, could you?"

"I would," she said, starting back toward the house, "but I don't have my car here. It's getting an oil change at the garage. Pop picked me up after I dropped it off. He'll take me back later to pick it up."

I looked at my watch again, wincing when I saw I was already fifteen minutes past the time I'd told Phoebe I'd be home. Thanks to my dear brother-in-law, I was going to have to walk home. I wondered who really thought this little prank up. Had it been Logan? Or was it Buddy? If my brother was responsible for it, I'd get even with him later. He had to show up sometime to sleep.

Chapter Twenty One
The Party Grows

Walking through town proved every bit as embarrassing as I'd thought it would be. Every block I walked I imagined the tear getting bigger with the duct tape shining like pure silver. At least my shoes matched. A few weeks earlier, in a rush to run errands, I slid my feet into shoes as I walked out the door and didn't realize until I got home that one shoe was white and one navy blue.

I hit the front walk at a full gallop. All I wanted was to get indoors, shower, and change my clothes. The sight of tombstones littering the front yard brought me to a screeching halt and wiped my tape-covered rear right out of my head.

"What in the world?" I spun around in a slow circle, taking in the sight of tombstones, jack-o-lanterns, and cobwebs. My eyes drifted up to the first branch of the big oak tree where some creative soul had hung an effigy, complete with hangman's noose. It hadn't been one of the girls who climbed that big tree. I suspected the culprit responsible was the same one who had hung off the edge of my kitchen eaves.

"Oh, no," I groaned out loud. "Now we've not only got a spook house in the basement and living in a retired funeral home. They built an entire cemetery right in our own front yard."

As awful and gruesome as it looked to me, the little child that still lived inside me appreciated the aesthetics of it. The quality of the spook house went up a few notches just from the spookiness of our front yard.

What little fight I had left drained out of me. I dragged myself up the front steps and crossed the porch to the front door. A grinning skeleton met me. Someone had taped it to the glass on the inside of the door. No doubt it would glow in the dark.

An eerie screech and howl met me as I opened the door. I was so dispirited, I didn't even flinch. A ghost could have popped out and said boo right then, and I would probably have said, "Nice to meet you."

Phoebe appeared at the end of the hallway. A look of relief spread over her face. "Your son is really mad at you."

"So what else is new?" I muttered. "You should hear what happened to me this morning." And I dumped the whole story on her.

***

Phoebe was right when she said Jake was upset with me. I cringed at the look in his eyes. If it's true that the loss of one ability increases another, then Jake, not being able to speak, has developed a powerful gaze. I defy anyone to have those dark eyes turned on them and not feel it to their bones.

162

No matter where I moved, his eyes followed me, including to the closet where I grabbed a plain t-shirt and gray sweat pants. He grunted at me. That meant I had to make eye contact with him and face his accusing glare. I looked over to see him looking at the purple shirt in my hands. He shook his head no; then he shifted his gaze back to the closet to stare at the red t-shirt bearing the words *Be Vewy Vewy Quiet*, that his cousin, Nita, had appliquéd for him.

With as much speed as I could muster, I took care of his personal needs and dressed him. I moved the wheelchair into position. I slipped one hand under Jake's head and another behind his back. One. Two. Three. I lifted him to a sitting position. As I changed my hand positions, I gave him an apologetic hug. Then, with right hand behind his shoulders and the left under his knees, I lifted him up and moved to the wheelchair. I have made this move so many times over the years, I don't even think about it anymore. It's part of life and as normal to me as breathing.

Phoebe and Samantha were in the kitchen when I wheeled Jake in. I pushed his chair into his customary spot and noticed my sisters had cleaned up the breakfast clutter. Another wave of guilt washed over me, along with love and gratitude, emphasis on the gratitude. Housework is my least favorite thing to do.

"Thanks. You guys are the best. Where's Mitchell?" I pulled open the refrigerator and pulled out a container of yogurt. Jake doesn't like to eat as soon as he gets up. He'd rather wait a few hours, but he needs food to get his medication down. Yogurt and pudding are his foods of choice to hide the crushed pills in.

"He went back to sleep." Phoebe made a funny face. Jake smiled at her. "He'll wake up soon, I'm sure."

I grabbed a roll of paper towels and started tucking them into his shirt. Jake was still mad at me, but he knew I was the only way he would get breakfast. He gave that small grunt that always catches my attention. I glanced at him and saw him licking his lips then looking toward the pantry door. "I'm sorry," I apologized to him. "I forgot to get you something to drink. Just a second."

I finished getting his medicine poured out and the small pill put into the little plastic pill-crusher, then headed to the pantry where we kept the soda.

Phoebe and Samantha were seated at the table when I emerged from the pantry. They aren't as good at the dagger-glare as Jake is. Well, Samantha isn't. Phoebe comes close. She looked with disapproval at the can of root beer in my hand. Sometimes Jake prefers juice and sometimes he asks for soda.

"I'm sorry." I gave a helpless shrug to Phoebe. "He's old enough to know what he wants." And I knew from experience he would let unwanted liquid dribble from his mouth without swallowing if I offered him something he didn't want. I'd lived with Jake seventeen years to learn that my job as care-giver didn't include making decisions for him.

I poured his drink into a plastic cup. He has a bite reflex that goes right through glass. And bone. Getting a finger near his teeth was risking a great deal of pain and possible dismemberment.

I could hear the pounding of hammers and the soft murmur of voices coming from below. Even with the basement door shut, the noise was continuous.

"Do I even want to know what's going on down there?" I spooned some yogurt into Jake's mouth and glanced over at my sisters. Samantha avoided my eyes. Phoebe just shrugged.

I wiped Jake's mouth off and offered him a sip of soda, "What's with the tombstones and dead body in the front yard? No one said anything about decorating the front yard."

Phoebe stood up and moved toward the pantry. "You can thank Elliott. He's become the number one consultant for the Halloween decorating committee." She disappeared through the swinging door reappearing a minute later with a box of Cheez-Its. She gave another little shrug at my accusing look. "It's not chocolate, but it'll do."

I grunted and spooned another bite of yogurt into Jake's mouth. "If you want chocolate, you'll have to wait for Roni to do the shopping."

Phoebe sat down at the table and slid the box toward Samantha, who didn't hesitate to grab a handful of the tasty cheese crackers. A wave of love swept through me. Bad habits are so much easier to bear when they're shared.

I wiped Jake's chin and offered him another drink. He smiled at me, a sweet beautiful smile, and I knew he'd forgiven me for being late. I always feel better when Jake and I are in harmony.

I set the glass down. "Now, tell me about Elliott and our front yard."

"You know Elliott." Phoebe spoke first. "He got this brilliant idea of using the history of the house as part of the party theme. There aren't a lot of people left in Weary who remember this house was the Whitaker Funeral Parlor in the 1930's."

My stomach slid to my toes, a feeling I was getting all too familiar with. I had a feeling I wasn't going to like where this story was going. "Didn't anyone tell him that was a good thing? That maybe we didn't want people to know that about this house?"

Samantha was looking everywhere but at me, a sure sign she was hiding something. I asked her, "What did you do?"

"Nothing much," she protested. "A few weeks ago, he stopped by the church office to ask me about the haunted house. I explained to him about the controversy and told him who the women in charge were. He thought the house being a mortuary would make a really good haunted house."

She grabbed a Cheez-It and took her time nibbling on it.

"You mean the haunted house being held here started with Elliott? And I'm just now finding this out?"

I gave Jake a few more bites of yogurt while I waited for her to tell me the rest of the story.

Samantha looked uncomfortable. "He said he wished he could find out more about the house, but he didn't know how to go about it." She stopped talking again. A sudden thought struck me. I looked up at her and narrowed my eyes.

"You didn't by any chance tell him to decorate the front yard?"

"No, I didn't," she protested. "He came up with the idea all by himself, but I did suggest he go talk to Aunt Ellen and Aunt Lila to see if they knew who was still alive and living here in town. I didn't know Elliott was serious. I thought he was bored."

Jake grunted at me. I looked over and saw him staring at the root beer. Without thought, I picked it up and gave him another drink. My concentration was on Samantha. "Elliott and boredom didn't send warning flares off?" I shook my head in disbelief. "Tell me the rest of it. What did he do?"

Samantha winced as a loud clang came from the basement and a muffled curse from one of the dear church ladies. "Nothing much. He wrote down the names of the people still living here in town that remembered when this house was a funeral parlor. Then he called them up and made appointments to interview them."

"You have to admire his ingenuity and enthusiasm," Phoebe broke in. "There aren't many kids his age who would have the ability to do that, go up to strangers and ask them questions."

"Well," I muttered, "nerve has never been one of Elliott's problems. I'm not sure it's a good idea to let his imagination run loose right now. He's been popping up wearing scary masks where you least expect him. I think he's made every girl in the house scream at least once daily, including me this morning."

I glanced through the wide double doorway between the kitchen and dining room. I could see, through the big picture window, the fake tombstones. The body swung gently from the branch of the oak tree.

It was gruesome beyond belief, and I wished the yard could be full of reindeer and elves. I wanted Halloween gone.

With a gloomy heart, I reached for the box of Cheez-Its and realized I was lining right up beside Allyson Wright, leader of the anti-Halloween party group. And I was in the minority around here. For a split second, a tiny part of me wished I was slogging alongside Hal and Russ through the wilds of Australia.

Chapter Twenty Two
Peaceful Interlude

A sharp rap on the kitchen door startled me out of my dark thoughts. The door immediately opening after the rap told me it was a family member. "Anybody home?" Katie stepped through the kitchen door, bringing in a swirl of autumn leaves with her.

"We're here." Samantha called out but she didn't need to. Katie was already in the kitchen, Elliott and Lili at her heels.

"Hi." Katie's usual cheery smile was in place. "The kids said they wanted to help get ready for the haunted house. Elliott seems to think the ladies won't get it scary enough, so I told him I'd drive them over. There's nothing I can get done with the grade school shut down. If I stay home, I'll just clean house, and that's no fun."

She would too. My sister, Katie, is the only person I know who would bleach mop the basement out of boredom. Well, Mary Lee might. She and Katie have birthdays the same week. Mary Lee is the oldest and Katie is the youngest with twenty years spanning them, but they both are organized, spotlessly clean,

169

and punctual. When something needs to get done, either of those sisters would be the ones I'd call.

I shook the visions of Katie and bleach water out of my mind and turned my attention to Elliott. "Weren't you here already this morning? I seem to remember you hanging upside down outside the kitchen window and scaring the liver out of me. Never mind," I interrupted him before he could speak. "I'd rather find out about the front yard."

"Sure thing, Aunt Charly." He flashed a charming smile at me, the one that always disarms me. "But I need to get downstairs. I have something that Mrs. Franklin really needs. I told her I'd bring it right over." For the first time I noticed the big brown sack he held in his arms. Before I could ask what was in it, he vanished through the basement door with Lili at his heels.

"Well," I leaned back in my chair and goggled at Katie. "What was that all about?"

She laughed. "You know Elliott. The kids have had their heads together all week coming up with ideas for the haunted house. I've never see them so excited about a holiday."

I frowned at her. "Have you seen our front yard?"

"Yes, isn't it wonderful? The kids worked really hard to get it just right. Elliott actually interviewed a bunch of people. I'm so proud of him."

I goggled at her again and tried to think of a way to ask her if they could just take it all down. Then a horrible thing happened. I remembered what it felt like to be twelve and looking forward to Halloween. I remembered the smell of homemade cookies and the fun we had making popcorn balls and caramel apples. Even worse, I remembered how much fun Mom had making costumes.

"Rats," I muttered to Jake and gave him another drink. "I think I'm stuck." He just grinned at me with a grin that would have rivaled Elliott's.

Katie spoke. "Elliott even interviewed old Evan Whitaker. He's 90 years old and still lives here in town. He lives in that big house behind the library. Ansel Whitaker lives with him. They have a lady that keeps house and takes care of both of them."

That caught my attention. "Ansel has been following Buddy around town. Buddy doesn't know why, but every time he turns around, he sees Ansel peeking at him from somewhere. Sometimes it's through a window. This morning it was over the fence at the cemetery."

What was Buddy doing at the cemetery?" Katie was curious. "Did someone put sod down again?"

"Worse than that, someone took sod up." Phoebe pushed the box of Cheez-Its toward Katie. "Logan stopped by this morning to pick up Buddy. Someone robbed a grave last night."

Katie's mouth dropped open, giving us an unpleasant view of orange cracker. "You're kidding. Which grave? Was it a relative?"

"Not one of ours." I reached over for a handful of crackers before the box was empty. "It was a girl's grave. Her name was Elizabeth Jordan. Someone used the backhoe to open up a really big hole. They had to have a box or a blanket or something to remove the bones." I looked at the orange crackers in my hand,

and a wave of nausea hit me. I thought my sisters might object if I dropped the crackers back into the box, so I laid them on the table and saw three other hands do the same thing.

None of us liked thinking about open graves and a casket full of bones and food at the same time. I continued my story. "The cemetery isn't very far from town, but it has a stone wall across the front of it and tall wrought iron fencing around the other three sides. Add to that a line of trees growing around the perimeter, and it makes seeing into the cemetery a bit difficult."

Not to mention hard to get into if you didn't go in by the front gate. "I seem to remember the front gates are closed at night, but I don't think they're locked." I glanced over at Samantha and raised my eyebrow in a silent question.

She raised her hands in the air and shrugged. "I don't know. They can be locked, but that's a question you need to ask Buddy."

Jake grunted at me again. I looked over at him to see him staring at Phoebe. From the intensity of his gaze and the way he held his eyes on her without blinking, I knew he had something he wanted to know that only she knew the answer to. I puzzled about it for a minute and then asked him, "Are you wanting to know if you're having class today?"

His eyes flew up in a rapid yes sign. Then he looked over at the clock hanging on the wall, a clock that was fast approaching eleven. "Oh, you're worried you'll run out of time."

His eyes flew up again.

"Do you want to work today?" Phoebe was curious.

His eyes flew up, but this time he added a big smile to his face. Sometimes I forget how eager he is to learn. His patience and sweetness of nature always amaze me when I think of how frustrating it must be trapped in a body that won't do what he tells it to. Then I realized I was looking at it from a viewpoint of person with normal ability.

Jake has never known what it feels like to be able to reach out and touch something just because he wants to feel it. Never known what it's like to open his mouth and ask for anything, so his understanding of normal is different than mine. For him, life is a series of joys.

A loud knock on the door stopped my mental musings. When the door didn't immediately open after the knock, I knew it wasn't a family member. At least whoever was out there knew to come to the kitchen door instead of the front door. People who knew us well could pretty much count on finding us around the kitchen table.

I opened the door to see Gary Prescott standing there, hat in hand. "Morning, ma'am, I wondered what you wanted me to do today."

That floored me. I'm still not used to being in charge, but I guess, the way things work in our family, I was the eldest living here, and Josie and Roni weren't here anyway. I rubbed my hand on my pant leg and felt the edge of the silver duct tape. I hadn't gotten around to changing out of my torn jeans. I took a small slide sideways and hoped Mr. Prescott wasn't very observant. From the muffled giggles behind me, I knew my sisters were.

"I guess getting the yard in shape would be enough work for a day or two. The grass needs cut before winter hits, and whatever flower beds are out there need taken care of. If there are any dead tree limbs that need cut off, go ahead and trim them out. The tools and the lawnmower are in the shed out back."

"There's a fruit cellar in the back yard." I started to step outside to point out the hump in the ground that identified where the fruit cellar was located but remembered the state of my jeans and stayed where I was. "I'd appreciate it if you opened it up and made sure it's not full of snakes. I don't think anything could get in there," but," I added, giving him a helpless look, one that usually works on men, "you know how women are. Just the thought of a snake makes me nervous, especially with so many kids around."

He smiled, making me wonder if every male around knows how to use a smile or if I was just as susceptible to smiles as most men are to the helpless female act.

"That's fine, ma'am. I'll make sure everything outside is shipshape and snake free." He placed his hat back on his head and moved toward the backyard. I watched a minute and then shook my head, wishing I had a little of that energy for myself.

I closed the door and moved back toward the kitchen table. Four grinning faces stopped me.

"What?" I protested. "Is there some joke that I don't know about?"

"Nope." Katie popped a Cheez-it into her mouth. "I just want the story about the duct tape."

I froze and once again slapped my hand to my rear. "I already told the story today; I'm not going to tell it again. Ask Phoebe about it while I take a shower and change my clothes."

I winced as another loud bang came from the basement, "And then I'm going to find something to do that doesn't have to be done here. I'm going somewhere else. Anywhere else. I whirled around toward the dining room door. "Because this place is a madhouse."

Chapter Twenty Three
Face to Face with Ansel Whitaker

I took the fastest shower of my life and then pulled on a pair of clean, hole-free jeans, topping them with my favorite sweat shirt. I breezed back into the kitchen twenty minutes later.

I knew from Katie's grin, Samantha's frown, and Phoebe's eye roll that I could have chosen a better outfit, but I didn't see much point in it.

Considering my morning, you can see why. I've spent much of my life with ripped hems, safety pins where buttons used to be, and stains from unexpected sources landing on my clothes. I've even gotten splattered by bird droppings more often than the average person should. So it doesn't make sense for me to spend a lot of time dressing up. I don't have the energy to fight bad karma.

"Are either of you leaving right away?" I asked Katie and Samantha. "If you are, can I catch a ride with you?"

"I'm going." Katie grinned at me and reached for a last handful of Cheez-Its. "I can give you a ride. I only stopped by to drop Lili and Elliott off. With the school shut down, I don't have anything else to do."

"I'm free for a while." Samantha stood up. "Theo is working on a sermon. He said he'd answer the phone if it rang. I'll tag along, if you don't mind."

I let out a sigh of relief that surprised me. The prospect of a few hours away from home with two of my sisters was just what I needed. I smiled at Jake, "I'll be back in time to feed you some lunch. Work hard for Aunt Phoebe." He gave me a big grin and raised his eyes upward in a yes.

"Don't worry about us," Phoebe spoke up. A loud rapping of a hammer floated up to us. She blinked her eyes. "We'll be fine. If it gets too noisy, we'll take a walk to the library."

"Don't be surprised if you run into us there." I grabbed my purse and headed for the kitchen door. I wanted to bolt before anybody else needed anything from me. "We'll probably stop in and talk to Roni." And with that, I made my second escape of the morning. I hoped it turned out better than the first one had.

***

"Where do you want to go?" Katie asked.

We were seated in Katie's Bronco, and, true to family age hierarchy, Samantha rode shotgun. We learned the rules before we could talk.

I sat there a moment in silence. I didn't want to get my van yet, partly because I didn't want to give up the time with Katie and Samantha, but I also suspected that Logan would still have Uncle Harry.

"Let's go past Buddy's trailer and see if it's drying out yet. I can't believe it could be as big a mess as he said. I think he just wanted home cooked meals and company." I had good reason to mistrust our brother. Growing up, he'd taken great pleasure in feeding me whoppers that I usually gobbled up hook, line, and sinker.

We could have walked to Buddy's in about the same time it took to drive. It was easy to tell which trailer belonged to him. It's the mobile home surrounded by all the "classic cars" parked around it. These cars are usually rusty with flat tires and no interiors. Back in high school he traded so many vehicles we thought he'd have to apply for a dealer's license.

Katie didn't even attempt to park in the driveway. With all the vehicles only a bicycle could find space. I shook my head, knowing it didn't do any good to get upset with Buddy. The cars make him happy, and a happy brother is a good thing to have.

"Is the door locked?" Samantha sounded worried. We picked our way across the yard cluttered with car parts and tools.

"Of course not." At least I didn't think it would be. "Why would he lock the door after the damage is already done?"

Katie reached the front door first, grabbed the handle, and turned it. She grinned back at us. Of all my sisters, Katie is the best natured. "You're right. It's open."

We tumbled into the living room of Buddy's trailer and stood there, stunned into silence.

"I can't believe it," I complained out loud. "Now I'm going to have to apologize to him for all the thoughts I had. This is a real mess."

***

The smell hit us first. Even though he had fans blowing and windows open, you could smell the mildew. It was a humid jungle inside the mobile home.

"I had no idea." Seeing the damage saddened me. I walked toward the back bedroom.

"Oh, my." Katie spoke. She and Samantha crowded behind me. "There is no way he'll be able to salvage that mattress."

His mattress stood upright against the wall. I knew Mary Lee and several women from the church had been here and vacuumed as much liquid as they could out of the mattress and carpets, but it wasn't enough. The fans weren't capable of drying out the mattress fast enough. I didn't think the mattress would ever be usable again.

"This is really awful." Samantha poked the soggy mattress. "It looks like he'll be staying at your house for awhile."

"Looks like it," I agreed. I forgave him for the duct tape and the teasing. When family needs family, we're there for each other. "Who would do such a horrible thing?"

"And why?" Samantha shook her head. "I'll never figure people out."

***

The damage inside the trailer stunned us into silence, and keeping three of us quiet is no mean feat.

"Where should we go next?" Katie looked over her shoulder at me. "Do you want to go get your van?"

I shook my head at her. "I still don't think Uncle Harry will be home. I'd bet a pretty penny Logan has asked Uncle Harry to ride around with him for the entire day. Let's stop by the library. I need something new to read."

We stepped inside the door and Roni waved at us. A group of grade school girls clustered around her desk.

"I'll see you guys later." I edged toward the non-fiction section. "I'm getting out of sight before the kids decide to ask me about the haunted house."

"Coward." Katie made a face at me but I didn't care. She had no idea how topsy-turvy my life had gotten since word had gotten out about our house. Samantha waved me off. There's nothing she'd rather do than talk, and it didn't matter who she talked to. Little girls or grownups, she can chatter with the best of them.

And there's nothing better I like to do than get lost among the books. Wandering through the non-fiction section of a library is like a treasure hunt. I never know what I'm going to find. Whether it's a cook book or biography, a how-to book or history, something always catches my eye.

I feel an attachment to the books on the shelf. Some of them are old favorites that carry me back to my childhood. Some of them tickle my imagination or trigger my curiosity. My troubles floated away and I wandered the stacks, lost in a cloud of pure satisfaction.

My contentment didn't last long. My nose began to twitch. I gave it an absent rub. A whiff of something bad made me cough. A soft, furtive shuffle reached my ears and drew me out of my reverie. I held my place in *Superstitions of the Ozarks* and glanced around. I saw nothing, so I turned my attention back to the passage I was reading and wondered why so many superstitions were just plain creepy. Then, for the second time that day, I had the liver scared out of me.

A hand landed on my shoulder in a painfully tight grip. I yelped loud enough to wake the dead, but nobody came to look, so I must not have yelled as loud as I thought.

I whipped my head around before I thought and found myself eyeball to eyeball with Ansel Whitaker. And found it funny how habit sticks with a person even under the most distressing of times. We were in the library, and even after being scared out of a year's growth, I found myself whispering. "What are you doing?"

He whispered back, "I saw you there: in the cem'tary. It's bad there. You should stay home."

If I thought his body odor bad, his halitosis was worse. It's hard to whisper when you aren't breathing but I managed. "I wanted to find out what happened. There are some real strange happenings in town."

He nodded his head up and down, and a funny thing happened. The grizzled old man stalking my brother faded away. In the face of the old man, I saw the eyes of a bewildered young boy. My fear fled, leaving behind compassion.

I needed to breathe and didn't quite know how to step away from him without insulting him. I'd been raised to never, ever hurt someone else feelings so I stood my ground. I took as shallow and unobtrusive a breath as I could. "Mr. Whitaker? Why are you following my brother?"

It seemed an innocent question to ask, but his eyes bulged. His already tight grip clenched even tighter. His nostrils flared and spittle flew out of his mouth. I prayed it missed me, but I knew as soon as I could do so without him seeing me, I was going to head to the bathroom for a thorough face washing.

He shook me. "It's bad, bad. Tell him to stay away from the cem'tary. He can't find out. It's dangerous. I seen it." His eyes grew wild and he forgot to whisper. "I seen it, I tell you."

He leaned closer, so close his nose almost touched mine. I wondered if I'd be able to smell him after I passed out. "You tell him to stay out of the cem'tary." He gave me one final shake and vanished, leaving me fanning the air with the open book and gasping for air like a goldfish I'd once put in a tree to fly. When I finally recovered, I looked up to see Samantha, Roni, and Katie staring at me with wide eyes full of unspoken questions.

Chapter Twenty Four
In the Library

"It's not me." It wasn't the unison step backward my sisters performed that upset me. It was the hands they clapped over their noses that hurt my feelings. "I took a shower and put on clean clothes right before I left the house. Samantha and Katie both know that."

"I know it's not you." Roni's voice was muffled by her hand. She grabbed the sleeve of my shirt and pulled me away from the shelves into fresher air. She dropped her hand and gave a cautious sniff. "Ansel comes in here a lot. He likes to read although his favorite books to check out are Hardy Boys mysteries. He's mentally challenged. I'd place his mental age about ten years old, maybe twelve.

"When the cleanliness problem gets too much, someone contacts Evan Whitaker and lets him know that Ansel is getting a little ripe. He makes sure Ansel cleans up, and it's okay for a couple more months."

"Evan Whitaker? Didn't you mention an Evan Whitaker this morning?" I asked Katie.

"Yes." I love to hear Katie talk. It's almost as much fun as watching her talk. She has sparkling eyes, a big, flashing smile, and a laugh you can hear in her voice. "Elliott interviewed him. Evan Whitaker lived in your house when it was still a funeral parlor. His father was the undertaker. Elliott thought it would be interesting to ask about the history of the house.

She continued, "He's Ansel Whitaker's guardian. Ansel is a younger cousin. Evan took responsibility when Ansel's parents died. I thought that was really good of him to do that. Ansel wouldn't know what to do anywhere else. Weary is the only home he's ever known. The townspeople keep an eye on him. They understand his limitations."

"That was a nice thing to do," Samantha agreed

Samantha always sees the good in people and isn't bashful about telling them. I was pretty sure she'd find time to fix cookies or a pie or something equally yummy and take it over to Evan Whitaker. While there, she would make sure he was all right and probably come away with enough information on Evan, Ansel, and their entire family to write a biography. People talk to her. It makes it hard to go anywhere with her. We tend to lose her. She stops to talk; we don't notice and keep on walking. Then we finally miss her and end up backtracking until we find her.

"Good." Roni gave Samantha a big grin. "While you're there, you can tell Evan that Ansel needs a bath. That will save me having to make the call."

We laughed at the look of horror on Samantha's face, but we knew she would do it. We also knew that it would be done with kindness and compassion. It's a gift with her and one we take full advantage of whenever possible.

Relief sounded in Roni's voice. "It would really help me out if you'd do that. We want the library to be accessible to everybody, but people tend to stay away when Ansel comes in. There's even been talk about banning people from using the library if they create a problem for others. I'd hate to see that happen."

"Mo-om." Roni winced when she heard the voice of her young son. I swallowed a giggle. I don't know how such a small boy can have such a loud voice, but Mitchell manages it.

We looked toward the front door and saw him holding it open for Phoebe and Jake. His little body quivered with excitement. Even at this distance, I could see his eyes sparkling with excitement.

As soon as Phoebe had Jake through the door, Mitchell let go of it and ran toward his mother. He held his arms up to her. She scooped him up in a big hug. "What are you doing here? I thought Phoebe was teaching you at the same time she tutors Jake."

"It was too noisy." Mitchell returned her hug. Then he wiggled to be let down. "The church ladies were arguing."

"Where is Elliott?" Katie raised her eyebrows at Phoebe.

Phoebe responded with suspicious promptness. "Elliott is right in the middle of the argument."

"Oh, no." Concern clouded Katie's eyes. "Should I go get him?"

"No." Phoebe shook her head. "I'm sure he's fine. The argument concerns a prop he brought over."

"Oh, no." It was my turn to groan. "The paper sack? I knew I should have looked in it."

"The paper sack." Phoebe nodded her head in agreement. I could tell she was having trouble controlling her laughter.

I braced myself for news I was sure I wasn't going to like. "What was in the bag?"

Phoebe blinked her lashes and looked innocent. "I believe the shriek I heard coming from the basement contained the words, 'A skull, a skull. My God, he's brought us a skull.'"

I sighed. I would have yelled, but it seemed like the church ladies had beat me to it. "Where did Elliott get a skull?" I felt guilty, but for one fleeting moment I pictured my young nephew driving a back hoe and digging up a grave. But the whole skeleton had gone missing, and I was pretty sure Elliott didn't know how to use the back hoe.

"Don't get excited." Katie's voice brought my imagination to a full halt. "Elliott got the skull at school. He asked the science teacher if they could borrow it for the spook house. It's not real."

From the accusing look she threw at me, I was pretty sure she'd known where my thoughts had wandered. I can't help it if her son is an inventive child. There isn't much he isn't capable of.

His imagination rivals mine, and that's going some.

Phoebe continued, "Between Mitchell disappearing to the basement every time I turned around and Jake laughing until he couldn't breathe, I decided to take them to the café for lunch. I stopped in so Mitchell could see his mom. Do you want to go for lunch with us?"

"Sure." She didn't have to ask me twice. I wasn't going near home until the church ladies left. They usually disappeared to their own homes between three and four so they could feed their own families.

"I'm in," Katie agreed.

"Me too. As long as Theo is willing to man the phones at the church office, I'm staying out." Samantha looked so happy. Even though she'd started the whole haunted house in my basement mess, I knew she was getting enough phone calls from the anti-party segment of the church that it was stretching her considerable peace-making skills. Even Samantha has limits.

"I'd love to go," Roni added, but I won't get off for lunch until two. You'll have to go without me." She laughed at the pout on Mitchell's face. He's only three, but he has an amazingly expressive face.

Tell you what." She stooped down to his level. "When I get off this evening, I'll take you out for an ice cream cone."

The pout vanished, and he gave his mom another exuberant hug. "All right. I want chocolate."

"All right," Roni laughed back at him, "you get chocolate." She stood back up and glanced back at the desk. "I need to get busy. I'll see you guys this evening."

I moved behind Jake's wheelchair. I've pushed it so many years that it doesn't feel natural to walk alone any more. Phoebe held the door for us, and we filed out onto the main street of Weary. The café was across the street and a block over.

We saw Buddy's lawnmower parked in front of the café. Only in Weary would he get away with that. My eyes sharpened as I saw Logan's truck parked next to it. Maybe I'd get the truck key from Uncle Harry.

The trick would be to get to Uncle Harry without Logan around. Logan was capable of keeping me on foot for a week, but Uncle Harry is a soft touch. Where there's a will, there's a way. With any luck I'd have my van freed before supper.

Chapter Twenty Five
The Plot Thickens

The blackboard on the wall caught my eye as I entered the café. Every day, Mick posts the daily specials. Once in awhile, my sister, Katie, puts her creative mind to work and adds something humorous. Today, it just listed burritos with side dishes of refried beans and Spanish rice.

Everything Mick cooks is good, but his burritos are spectacular. He brought some to a family gathering once, and I almost foundered. I hoped the lunch crowd hadn't cleaned him out.

A quick glance around the cafe showed me the main lunch crowd had left, leaving mostly family. Buddy, Logan, and Uncle Harry sat on stools at the counter. Jessi and Aunt Ellen were parked in a booth.

"Aren't you going to get the truck key from Uncle Harry?" Katie whispered to me.

"Yes," I whispered back, "but I don't want to ask him in front of Logan. Maybe one of you could distract him for me?" I wasn't surprised when all of them, including Jake and Mitchell, shook their heads back and forth. Logan is a nice guy, but you don't want to try and pull anything on him. If I'd remembered that, my van might not be sitting hostage at Ellen and Harry's house.

Mitchell, running ahead of us, drove my van problem out of my mind. He slid into the last booth at the back.

"Is a booth okay?" Phoebe looked concerned.

"Its fine," I assured her. "Jake and I can sit at the empty table next to it. I don't think we'd all fit in one booth anyway."

Samantha slid into the booth by Mitchell. Phoebe and Katie sat at the table with Jake and me. I watched Uncle Harry, all the while running different scenarios through my head that might result in freedom for my van. Katie waved at Jessi and Aunt Ellen. "Psst," she hissed at me. "Jessi is trying to get your attention."

I tore my eyes away from the men sitting at the bar and locked eyes with my cousin. She opened the fingers of one hand, and I glimpsed a set of keys. She nodded her head toward her dad, and then nodded yes at me. I raised my hand in a universal sign meaning okay and blessed my cousin. She'd come through for me.

With that problem taken care of, I leaned back and turned my attention to food. Jake had already made up his mind. He wouldn't even look at the menu I held up. His eyes were glued to the blackboard.

"I take it you want some of Uncle Mick's beans and burritos?"

He swung his eyes to me, and a big grin lit up his face. His eyes flew upwards in a yes, then another, and another. "Okay." I started laughing. "I heard you the first time." He may be non-verbal, but his quiet responses are very loud.

The door swung open and another group of men entered. I recognized Dr. McCarty. He's the only veterinarian in the area. Jed and Theo followed him in. They filled up the remaining stools at the counter.

Aunt Ellen and Jessi stood up, grabbed their plates, and moved toward us. Aunt Ellen slid into the booth across from Samantha and Mitchell. Jessi sat down at the table with us.

"I thought you were fixing lunch when I stopped by this morning?" I'd certainly chopped enough onions for her.

Jessi shrugged. "So we'll have it for supper. Mom and I thought you could use some help." Her eyes crinkled as she grinned at me. That's one of the best things about my family. Aunts and uncles are second parents and cousins feel like siblings. If I could bottle the feeling up and sell it, I would.

"Uh, oh," Samantha yelped and slid down on her seat. A useless move, since anybody walking into the café could look right into her booth.

Mitchell looked anxious. "What's wrong, Aunt Sammi?" He reached out and patted her on the arm.

We all watched her with interest. Samantha is our sister who takes everything in stride. To see her upset or rattled doesn't happen often. She grabbed the menu and held it open in front of her face. I could see her lips moving, so I leaned closer to hear what she was saying.

"Don't let her see me. Don't let her see me." She repeated in a soft mantra.

"Who?" I looked at the others. They all shrugged. We heard the bell above the door jingle. When I saw who entered the café, I understood why Samantha was hiding behind the menu.

We all picked up menus, except Aunt Ellen and Jessi, who had plates sitting in front of them. They bent their heads down and start shoveling in food. None of us wanted to talk to any of the three women who had just entered, Allyson Wright, leader of the anti-party group, followed by Chris Johnston and Jan Paget.

The three women were having a heated discussion. They sat down at a table in the corner far enough from us that I felt safe from idle chatter. They never looked at us. Their eyes were focused on the men sitting at the counter. I had a feeling Theo was going to regret eating in public.

"You ready to order?" Patti, waitress and close family friend, asked.

"Yes, we are." Katie beamed at her. "I think we all want the burritos. Right?" We all nodded, Jake rolling his eyes up in enthusiastic agreement. Patti took our orders for drinks and left to get our food. For a few minutes, we juggled drinks and plates until everyone was satisfied.

Eating always takes me longer. By the time I get done fussing with mashing and adding gravy, butter, or syrup, anyone eating with me is usually halfway finished. I've almost forgotten what it feels like to eat with two hands free.

Jake has trouble controlling where his right hand goes, so I hang onto it to keep it from poking me or knocking food off the table. I feed him and myself with my right hand. I usually try to keep it even, one bite for him, one bite for me. I've goofed at times and ended up putting his spoon in my mouth. It's not an experience I would care to describe, and it usually results in laughter from those who witness it.

It isn't a neat and tidy process. I seldom run into people rude enough to comment on the messy side effects of eating this way. Jake has a back pack that fits onto the back of his chair. Carrying a roll of paper towels everywhere we go is standard procedure. We go through a lot of them. I try to remember to wipe his mouth often, but it's inevitable for food to spill, and liquids come back out as often as they go down.

At the café, where friends and family gather, it's not a problem. I wouldn't care if it was.

I went through the motions of feeding that I'd been doing for seventeen years. Sight and sounds faded and only bits and pieces of conversation caught my ear.

"Have you lost any more cows?" I recognized Theo's voice.

"Just the one. I check on them twice a day." That was my brother-in-law, Jed's, voice.

"Have you identified what killed the cow?" Theo again. His voice is deep, slow-moving, and restful to listen to.

I heard the clatter of forks hitting plates, drinks being slurped. The air was warm and balmy for October. Jake grunted at me. I must have taken two bites to his one. I grinned at him and held another spoonful of beans up to his mouth. More voices floated to my ears. This time, the voices weren't soft and pleasant, but loud and grating.

"I still can't believe that horrible party is going to happen." I recognized the voice. My eyes slid past Jake to the corner table. Allyson Wright was sitting with her back to the wall. Not a bad idea considering the hot emotions she'd aroused with her verbal outbursts protesting the Halloween party sponsored by the church. She had single-handedly divided the congregation.

Jake grunted at me again. When I glanced at him, I saw his eyes, intent and unblinking, staring at my hand holding a bite just out of his reach.

"I'm sorry." I whispered a quick apology and moved the spoon to his mouth. I leaned closer to him. "I was trying to see Allyson. I have a feeling somebody is in for it."

Before I could stop him, he swiveled his head in her direction. Jake doesn't know the meaning of subtle, and his streak of curiosity has mine beat.

His rapid head turn triggered a primitive reflex and his mouth flew open. I wasn't fast enough to get a paper towel in place. The three women sitting in the corner got an excellent view of Jake's tonsils. Or would have if they could have seen past the beans and cheese that came spilling out of his mouth.

I wiped up the mess as best I could. Mitchell giggled.

"Turn around here where I can reach you." I pulled another sheet of towels off the roll. "And quit being such a snoop." He turned to look at me and gave me that wonderful grin that makes my heart happy. He's such a handsome young man; sweet, loving, and kind.

Out of the corner of my eye, I saw the three women whispering. I was pretty sure what they were saying. At least, if they were talking about Jake and me, they might leave Theo and Samantha alone.

We might have gotten through lunch without further incident if the door hadn't jingled again and in walked Dana Franklin and Ann Richardson, the leaders of the pro-Halloween party group.

Katie leaned toward our table, laughter curving her lips and lighting her eyes. "Look at Mick. He's going to have a stroke."

We all turned to look. Mick stood behind the counter wrapping burritos and shoving them into a sack. Even sitting at the back of the room like we were, we could see his wild eyes and pale face. Logan's distinctive laugh filled the air. Buddy looked like he was having convulsions. Only Uncle Harry seemed unaware of the potential bomb that had just walked into the café.

"How many burritos did you say you wanted?" Mick's words were as rushed as his movements.

Dana laughed. "I thought you'd have it all ready to go. That's why we called ahead. A dozen ought to do it. Make sure there are enough spoons and napkins in the sack." Her eyes slid to the table where Allyson sat. "We have quite a nice group working today. The spook house should be done right on time."

And that's all it took. Allyson heaved herself up and went toe to toe with Dana. My chin dropped. I glanced around to see almost everyone in the café had done the same thing. Most of us remembered to swallow first.

"That party should never happen," Allyson screamed. "Look what it's doing to our town. Animals are being slaughtered. Homes have been vandalized. The grade school is shut down. And you want to expose our children to evil influences. What kind of Christian values do you have?"

"Oh, stop it," Dana drawled. "You're exaggerating. Cows die all the time." She held up one of the bags of burritos that Mick set in front of her. "We wouldn't be having beef burritos if that wasn't true. It was one home vandalized, and I very much doubt that children were responsible. The school has a water pipe leak. That's hardly evil. It's just life."

"There was that dead dog." Uncle Harry started to speak. Logan poked him in the ribs and he shut up. Logan was having too much fun. I frowned at him, still miffed at being left on foot to walk through town with my rear hanging out, regardless of how much duct tape had been plastered to the tear.

"Better stay out of it, Unc," Buddy advised Harry. "It's a hen fight."

That earned Buddy the glare of all his sisters. Being raised in a family of girls, he should have known better than to make a remark like that.

Chris and Jan rose from the table and flanked Allyson. Looking at the two groups, the women from the anti-party group made me shiver. "It's too bad we can't hang pictures of them in the spook house. It would terrify the kids."

"You've got that right." Jessi nodded.

Allyson was so mad I could see her shaking. She leaned in until she stood literally nose to nose with

196

Dana. "This is not over." Each word shot from her mouth with deadly precision. "That spook house is an abomination. Mark my words; something awful is going to happen."

With that she spun on her heel and marched out the door. Jan and Chris followed her like well trained puppies.

Whew." Buddy did an imaginary swipe across his forehead. "I didn't know you offered a one-act play with your lunches, Mick. What drama."

"I don't." Mick placed another sack in front of Dana. He rang up her order and waited until she'd left the café. Then he walked over to stand in front of Buddy. "If I'd planned a show, it wouldn't have been that one. What I really want to know," he said, leaning across the counter toward Buddy and Logan, "is who's going to pay for their lunch."

For the third time during lunch, mouths dropped open and our eyes swiveled toward Allyson's table. We saw they had cleaned their plates of every crumb of food before they swept out the door without paying.

Patti sauntered over to the table and started piling the dirty dishes into a plastic tub. "Would you look at that?" She stood by the table, dishrag in hand. "That Jan is all right." She turned around and held up her hand. "She left me a fifty cent tip."

Chapter Twenty Six,
Bad News

I wanted to ask Jessi about the keys but didn't dare with Logan sitting at the counter. He seemed determined to leave me on foot. I wasn't sure what he'd do if he found out Jessi had obtained the key freeing my van. I didn't really believe he'd swing back by Aunt Ellen's and let the air out of my tires, but I wasn't willing to take the risk.

Jake grunted at me. I automatically filled a spoon with refried beans and held it to his mouth. He clenched his jaws, staring intently toward the front of the café. I followed his gaze, trying to figure out what he wanted. I didn't get past Mick. He's so earnest when he talks. I could hear him explaining, "I can't give food away. It's hard enough to have a profit margin when everybody pays, let alone when three people walk out the door without paying."

I tried to give Jake the bite of food. He shook his head no. The intensity of his gaze told me he wanted something, but what? Once again, I followed his gaze to the lunch counter. Person by person, object by object, I examined each thing. Then I glanced at Jake, trying to figure out exactly what he was looking at. One thing I could count on with Jake, he's usually one-hundred percent accurate with his eye-gaze.

Katie's snort of laughter, quickly swallowed, distracted me. I looked over at her to see her staring toward the front of the café. I put the unwanted bite of food back on Jake's plate and looked to see what everybody was now looking at. My brother, tired of Mick's complaint, scooped up a clean coffee mug. He dug in his pocket for loose change. I heard the coins clink as they hit the bottom of the cup. He passed the cup to Logan, who did the same thing. As coins were dug out of purses and pockets, Jake lost control and laughed until he couldn't breathe. I was pretty sure Mick would end up with a profit, and the small change each person contributed was well worth the silence it would buy.

Jake grunted again. I sighed and asked him, "Are you going to eat your beans?" He shook his head no. "The rice?" He shook his head again. I could tell he was getting impatient with me. It was mutual.

"Are you going to eat anything?" He surprised me with a rapid eye movement upwards, indicating a yes.

I looked down again at the food on the table and then back at Jake. He was staring again. I knew it involved food, so I followed his gaze again and did a mental head slap. "For Pete's sake," I muttered. This time, I looked behind the counter where the desserts were on display. Pie. Of course, it was pie, and I was pretty sure which one he wanted. "Blueberry pie?" Jake whipped his head toward me and his joyful smile made me feel good.

"Patti," I called, "pie for Jake." Katie, Aunt Ellen, and Jessi asked for pie too. At least I wouldn't end up sitting at the table alone while Jake ate.

I never have trouble getting Jake to eat sweets. When it comes to dessert, more goes down than out. A loud scraping noise filled the air as Logan pushed away from the counter.

"Let's go." Logan stood up and waited impatiently for Buddy.

Once again, he'd caught Buddy with food uneaten. A big piece of lemon pie sat in front of him. I didn't see Buddy leaving that untouched.

"No way." Buddy reached in front of Uncle Harry and pulled some napkins from the holder. With care, he lifted the slice of pie. "I'm taking the pie and I'm eating it. I don't want to hear one word about not eating in your truck." He glared at Logan.

"Whatever." Logan waved a hand and stalked toward the door. "We have things to do. Let's get moving."

Buddy, Uncle Harry, and Theo followed him out the door. When Logan hustles, everybody with him does the same. That's what being ex-military does for a person.

"Thank goodness." Relief washed over me. I spooned another piece of pie into Jake's mouth without thinking about it. I turned to Jessi. "I want to know how you got the keys. And how did you get them without Logan finding out?"

"Mom remembered where Dad keeps the spare. If you hadn't been here for lunch, we would have stopped by the house. She figured you'd need the van soon. We both thought the men needed a lesson." She grinned and a fierce gleam entered her eyes. A warm feeling spread through me to know they had come through for me.

"How's the haunted house coming along?" Aunt Ellen was curious. I can't blame her. The whole town seemed to be involved in the party in one way or another, either by supporting it, anticipating it, or being up in arms and screaming about it. It wasn't often the entire town of Weary got so excited over anything.

"Samantha and Katie know more about it than I do. I've spent most of my time avoiding the whole project."

Katie laughed and rolled her eyes my way. "Elliott and Lili are over there right now helping to put the finishing touches on. In fact, I think you'd better plan on having a houseful of kids this afternoon. With the school closed, they'll be at loose ends."

Invasion by children, I sighed. Maybe I could lock myself in the back of the house and ignore the whole mess. Most of the time, I enjoy the children, but with Halloween coming and the anticipation of the party, they were bouncing off the walls.

Katie added, "Elliott stopped by Mr. Whitaker's house and interviewed him. Somehow Elliott found out that Mr. Whitaker lived in the house when it was a mortuary. He thought he could get some information from him about what the house was like."

Mitchell pushed against Samantha. "Let me out, Aunt Sammi. I want to go talk to Uncle Mick."

Samantha stood up to let him out, then sat down in the empty chair at our table. We watched Mitchell scamper to the lunch counter. Patti picked him up and sat him on an empty bar stool where he proceeded to spin in circles.

"Did you really know the house was a mortuary?" Samantha directed this question to our aunt.

She nodded. "I vaguely remember it, but by the time we were living in Weary, it was just a house. It seems to me there was talk of an accident. I can't remember any of the details. It's been a long time. I don't think it was anything I really knew about. Every small town has such stories."

"Who would know?" Phoebe asked.

"The obvious person would be Mr. Whitaker." Jessi spoke. "Maybe someone could take Elliott back to do a second interview."

"I wonder if he knew Elizabeth Jordan." I spoke without thinking.

"What about her?" Jessi's curiosity bump is as big as mine.

"That's the name on the headstone of the grave that was robbed. I'd love to know what happened to her. She died at seventeen on Halloween. What killed her? Was it an illness, an accident, or something worse? Most of all I want to know why somebody took her body. Why now?

Phoebe slid out of the booth, grabbed an empty chair, and pulled it up to our table. "Scoot over." Jessi and Samantha obligingly moved, and Phoebe slid her chair into the opening. "I couldn't hear very well," she explained. "What would be worse than an accident or illness?"

"Murder," Jessi answered. I resisted the urge to kick her.

"Shhh," I hissed at her. "Don't even say that word. That's all I need, a Halloween party in an old mortuary and a murder. Next thing, you'll tell me she died in our house."

Aunt Ellen, in the act of sipping from her glass of water, choked and coughed.

I put the last spoonful of pie back on Jake's plate and stared at her.

"Don't say it," I pleaded.

"Surely not," Phoebe protested.

Samantha simply sat, shaking her head back and forth.

Jake grunted, wanting the last bite of pie. I ignored him.

"Mom?" Jessi prodded, finally giving her mom a firm slap on the back. "Are you okay?"

Aunt Ellen gave a last cough and wiped her tearing eyes on a clean napkin. "Yes, I just swallowed wrong. Don't you think you should feed that boy?" She waved toward Jake. His eyes shot his up in an enthusiastic yes.

I scooped the spoon up and shoved the pie in Jake's willing mouth without taking my eyes off my aunt. "Go on. Do you know what happened to Elizabeth?"

She gave a reluctant nod. "Yes, but you'd be better off talking to Patti."

Katie sat up straight and bellowed, "Patti, we need you over here."

Aunt Ellen fell silent. Jake finished his pie and grunted again. I glanced at him and saw him staring at the glass of root beer. I held the glass up for him, all the while waiting for Patti to finish taking care of customers so she could talk to us.

As she approached our table, Jessi beat me to the question. "What happened?"

Patti looked puzzled, "When?"

We all spoke at once. Patti held her hand up, stopping us in mid-sentence. She pointed at Jessi. "You tell me what you want to know. The rest of you, shut up."

Jessi spoke. "We want to know about the body that was taken from the cemetery. Elizabeth Jordan. Who was she? How did she die? No detail is too small."

Patti nodded and yelled over her shoulder, "Mick, I'm taking my break early." She pulled a chair from the next table and sat down. We all leaned forward to listen.

"I heard all this from my grandmother. She was a little girl when the accident happened. Now remember," Patti warned us, "Granny is ninety-six years old and she's not too sharp anymore, but she seems to remember her childhood okay."

"According to Granny, Elizabeth was a friend of the Whitaker boys. In 1936 Evan and his twin brother were sixteen years old. On Halloween day the Whitaker boys held a big party. According to Granny, both boys had a crush on Elizabeth. Whether that was true or not, she attended the party. She fell through a window and died on impact when she hit the ground. The fall broke her neck."

"A window?" A cold chill settled on my shoulders. I locked eyes with Samantha and Phoebe.

"A Halloween party?" Samantha asked.

"Where was this party held?" I hoped with every ounce of my being she wouldn't say the words.

She gave a big sigh. "I'm sorry. The party was held at the Whitaker mortuary. Elizabeth's death is the reason the funeral parlor closed its doors. She fell from the third story window."

I heard Phoebe murmur, "The window with the bars. I wondered why it was so secure."

"It was an accident, wasn't it?" Jessi tried. I know she wanted an answer that would reassure us.

Patti shook her head. "Sorry, it was never decided if it was an accident or murder. There was some controversy. An eye witness reported the girl was deliberately pushed, but they couldn't use his testimony in court."

"Why not?" I asked.

Patti shrugged. "The eye witness was Ansel. He was only nine years old when it happened. As you can tell, he's mentally challenged. The Whitaker family had money and, for a little town like Weary, some clout. Nobody was charged but there was talk. The funeral parlor closed. Elizabeth was buried and the whole story sort of swept under the rug."

"Great." I leaned back in my chair. "Just great. So sometime back in the 1930's, our house had a Halloween party that resulted in a death. Now we have that same house, we're getting ready for a Halloween party, the young girl who died has been dug up, and her bones are missing"

"I hate to say this." I glared over at Samantha. "I never was for having a party in our house. Not because I'm against Halloween parties, but right now, I'm solidly on the anti-party side. I never thought I'd agree with Allyson about anything, but I wish this party would never happen. I hope we don't blow any more fuses because I'm never going in that basement again if I can help it."

Chapter Twenty Seven
Enter Mr. Whitaker

It's a short walk from the café to Aunt Ellen's house. Getting my van back proved ridiculously easy. Jessi moved her dad's pickup; I unfolded the lift and lowered it. Logan pulled up behind the van. I hated to suspect him of keeping an eye on it, but with him I never know. He looked at me loading Jake onto the lift, let out an audible, "Shit," and took off. It's good to remind him the van is the only way I can transport Jake anywhere. Logan didn't need to find out I was only taking him home.

Phoebe, Samantha, Katie, and Jessi rode home with us. Aunt Ellen and Mary Lee decided to follow in Aunt Ellen's car. Even the van has its limits on how many passengers I can carry.

We usually prefer to gather around the kitchen table, but with the house full, we overflowed into the dining room. With the wide, spacious doorways, it felt like we were in the same room. With the grade school and junior high closed, we had a houseful of children. Right now, I wished my nephew, Elliott, was far, far away.

He stood in front of me, pinning me with smoky blue eyes. He's unbelievably persuasive for his age. I tried to resist the entreaty in his blue eyes.

"Elliott," I protested, "I don't' want to go down to the basement."

He shook his head in disbelief. "Aunt Charly, you don't want to see the cool haunted house?"

I wanted to tell him that I was living in a haunted house, but I was still hoping we could keep the details of that long ago party secret. The last thing I needed was a murder attached to the house. It was bad enough the house had been a funeral parlor. I didn't even want to think about the number of dead bodies that had come through the doors of this house.

"No, Elliott. I don't want to see the haunted house. I'm quite happy never seeing another haunted house as long as I live." I did what I always do when I get stressed. I filled a glass with ice and opened a can of Diet Coke. Thank goodness my husband was wandering the outback of Australia and couldn't see me chugging down the forbidden drink.

He's the one who forbade it. He thinks Diet Coke is the reason I have migraines. I told him if that was the case, why do migraine medications have caffeine as one of the ingredients? He's impervious to logic, but he wasn't here, so I drank my pop with enjoyment and maybe a smidgen of rebellion.

I brooded while I drank. Brooding is something I'm really good at. There I sat, listening to my charming nephew beg me to see the basement. Samantha, Phoebe, Jessi, and Aunt Ellen were in the kitchen with Elliott and me. With the big pocket doors open, I could see Mary Lee sitting at the dining room table surrounded by Lili, Téa, Keira, Mitchell, and Jake. You can't have Mary Lee around without a game of some kind going on. They were playing Yahtzee. Jake was winning. He usually does. Life might have shortchanged him in the physical department, but he was given an extra dose of luck.

"Aunt Charly," Elliott prodded, bringing my attention back to him, "you have to see the basement. It's the best haunted house ever."

The doorbell brought all conversation to a stop. "I'll get it," Samantha sang out.

The surprise in Samantha's voice drew the rest of us to her like a magnet. We circled around her and stared at the man standing in the doorway.

I could see the remnants of a big man in the frail old body standing in front of me. Even hunched over holding onto his walker, he still gave the illusion of the strong man he must have been. Hawk eyes stabbed us. They were so dark they looked black, but they might have been shadowed by the overhanging bushy white eyebrows. Even wrinkled and old, I could tell he must have been strikingly handsome in his youth.

Standing to one side, eyes downcast and looking decidedly uncomfortable, stood a cleaned up Ansel. I gave Samantha an approving glance, but she looked confused and shook her head. By that I knew she hadn't been responsible for Ansel's improved appearance.

"Hi, Mr. Whitaker," Elliott's voice broke into my thoughts. I was grateful because it stopped the burst of laughter that threatened to overwhelm me every time

I thought of Samantha approaching Mr. Whitaker on the topic of Ansel's hygiene.

A smile creaked across the old man's face. "Hello, young man. After that visit from you yesterday, I got the urge to come see this old house opened up and lived in again." Those sharp bright eyes darted to each of us. He wasn't sure who to ask permission from. He settled on Samantha. "Would you indulge an old man? Let me see the old place again?"

Since Josie and Roni were still at work, she glanced at me. I took over. "Mr. Whitaker, please come in. You're welcome to look around; just remember that a lot of people live here, so ignore the clutter."

Clutter was an understatement. The redeeming value of the big house was the clutter was spread over such a large area that it looked lived in rather than messy.

We moved back to give Mr. Whitaker room to come through. Ansel reached down and picked up a bag I hadn't noticed before. He ducked his head when he saw me looking. Mr. Whitaker noticed my interest in the black bag. "Sorry, ma'am. When you get as old as me, you have certain things that need to accompany you. Medical stuff. A nuisance but necessary. I might never need the things in here, but better safe than sorry." He gave me a look that I think was supposed to be cheerful, but on that old, wrinkled face and in my present state of mind, it would have been right at home gracing the walls of the spook house.

Elliott tugged on my shirt. I leaned over so he could hiss in my ear, "Aunt Charly, the basement. How long do we have to wait?"

I sighed. Better to get the kids out from underfoot. They would fidget and wiggle until they drove us crazy. "All right, just give me a minute." I straightened back up.

"Samantha, you've already seen the basement. Would you show Mr. Whitaker around and the rest of us will go tour the basement?"

Now, I should have been the one to stay with Mr. Whitaker. Technically, I owned the house, but, to be honest, Mr. Whitaker freaked me out. I couldn't figure out why, but he made me uneasy. It might have been his age. It might have been his eyes that stabbed a person with the intensity of his gaze or the frown that pulled those bushy eyebrows down, a frown that belied the smile he kept plastered on his face. I don't even know why I felt the smile was false.

There was something wrong there that I couldn't put my finger on. Ansel looked so uncomfortable, I felt sorry for him. He clearly wanted to bolt again, and bolt is what he did when the kitchen door opened. I knew by the scrabbling of dog claws on the floor that Molly and Murphy were racing to greet one of their favorite humans.

We heard Buddy say, "Molly, Murphy," in that cheerful happy way he saves for the four legged critters. Then we heard the front door open and close as Ansel bolted for freedom.

As Buddy came through the kitchen door into the dining room, he drew all eyes but mine. I was caught by the sight of Mr. Whitaker. He was staring at the front door where Ansel had disappeared, and the false cheerfulness had left his face. The fierce, angry light that lit his eyes chilled me to my bones.

The look was so fleeting I might have imagined it except for the feeling it left behind. I knew, without a doubt, there was more behind Mr. Whitaker's visit than just revisiting his home. They had owned the house all these years, and it had stood empty for the last ten. He'd had ample opportunity to come here. I didn't know what Mr. Whitaker wanted, but a walk down memory lane wasn't it.

He spoke first. "Why don't I just sit down and wait for Ansel to come back? I don't know what gets into him at times. He's slow, you know." Those sharp eyes darted at us. "He'll come back for me." And that's what he did. With slow steps, pushing the walker in front of him, he moved toward a comfortable easy chair. We, at least I know I did, held our breath as we watched his slow maneuvering into a position to sit. As he moved, I wondered how he had made it up the stairs of the big front porch. When he left, I'd make sure he went by the kitchen door using the ramp instead of having to manage stairs.

"I'll get you something to drink and snack on." Samantha moved toward the kitchen. "You guys go ahead to the basement. I'll get Mr. Whitaker settled."

With relief, I agreed. We gave our polite leave from Mr. Whitaker and trooped toward the kitchen. One by one, my family disappeared from my sight, stepping into the black hole of the basement entryway. No help for it. It was face the spook house or go back and face the spooky old man.

"Come on," Elliott prodded me.

"Don't push," I was irritable. "You go first."

He grinned at me and vanished through the open doorway. I could already hear the others 'oohing' and 'aahing' and that did it. Curiosity, the driving force of my life, pulled me down the stairs.

I stood at the bottom of the basement stairs and felt...disappointed. To my eyes, it was just our basement with sheets and blankets hanging from ropes stretched along the beams, messy but not scary.

"Isn't it great?" Elliott pulled me toward the center of the basement. I fought off the blankets that whapped me in the face.

"Elliott," I protested," I thought this was supposed to be a spook house. Where are the spooks?"

I wanted to swallow my tongue when I saw the ladies standing around a big box in the middle of the room. Bad mouthing a project is one thing but doing it in front of the people who created it is bad-mannered. Manners are so ingrained in me I could feel Mom's disapproval from beyond, a ghostly presence I would always welcome, but uncomfortable under the present circumstances.

Elliott saved me from further embarrassment. "Look." He pushed in between Ann Richardson and Dana Franklin, the two people most responsible for the haunted house in my basement. "This is the coffin. A body will lay here." I shivered as Elliott's voice sank to a creepy whisper. "At just the right moment, the body will rise from its coffin and, 'Boo!'" He cackled when we all jumped.

I yelped. "Stop that. Elliott, you're a menace." I ignored my sister's giggles. They weren't immune to our young nephew either. If he hadn't scared them this time, he'd get around to it before Halloween was over.

"Who's been chosen for the honored spot?" Aunt Ellen spoke up. I could hear the genuine interest in her voice. I don't know how she does it, but she exudes excitement. I've never heard negative comments from her. Someone would have an idea or a dream, and Aunt Ellen would say, "Go for it." Somehow she encourages people to live their dreams.

Here I stood, resenting this party with every ounce of my being instead of throwing myself into making it the best party ever. I surveyed the box in front me. "Who is the lucky victim that gets to lie in a box for hours?"

"I wanted to," Elliott explained, "but they wanted somebody in high school. They thought an older person would be scarier. Once they found out about the open grave at the cemetery, they thought a girl might be good, a girl the same age as the stolen girl." He looked at us, his blue eyes sparkling with excitement.

Who could resist that face? I couldn't. My reluctance slid away. I couldn't be the one who spoiled this party. It would only be for one night.

"So Karen Wright volunteered." Elliott's smile widened to a grin.

"You're kidding." It's not often we see Aunt Ellen with her mouth hanging open. She's hard to shock. "Does her mother know about this?"

"She does." Dana sounded grim. "We made sure of that. Karen brought us a handwritten note, but we called Allyson and double checked."

Ann nodded her head. "There's been so much controversy over this party we wouldn't take a chance on making it worse. In fact, we wanted to refuse Karen's offer, but we didn't dare."

"Why would you want to do that?" Jessi spoke up.

"It would be simpler." Dana's voice sounded crisp and harsh to my ears. "We thought Allyson was putting her kids here as spies and reporting back to her everything that goes on."

"Fuel for the fire," Ann added. "She was getting information somewhere, and we figured it had to be Karen and Duncan, but what could we do? They're kids. We didn't want to put them in the middle, so we accepted the fact they were here and tried to be careful what we said in front of them."

I appreciated the delicate situation this caused the party committee. It had to be hard having the children of the anti-party leader hold such prominent places in the party itself. What a situation.

Elliott interrupted, "Come on." He tugged, pulled, and pushed to get us moving. "You have to see this." With those words he proceeded to drag us through the spook house, first turning on the sound effects recording and the red lights that cast an eerie glow over the basement. As Elliott explained each section of the basement to us, I could visualize the spook house and did a rapid reassessment of my first impression of the basement. The committee had done a superb job.

"It helps that this was an actual working part of a mortuary," Katie spoke.

The slamming of a door made us all jump. We moved various blankets and sheets aside to see Samantha coming down the steps leading to the kitchen.

"That didn't take long," Jessi said.

"Did Mr. Whitaker enjoy his tour?" Aunt Ellen added.

"Did Ansel come back?" Buddy asked.

"I don't know." Samantha stopped to catch her breath. "I left Mr. Whitaker sitting in the living room while I went to the kitchen to get him something to drink. When I went back to the living room, he was gone."

Chapter Twenty Eight
Screams

We trooped upstairs to the kitchen, leaving the volunteers to put the finishing touches on the haunted house. Halloween was fast approaching.

"They are going to clean up afterwards, aren't they?" I slanted a look toward Samantha.

She halted on her way to the pantry. "They said they would."

"I hope so." I could feel myself sliding back to the dark place, the grouchy, bad-tempered hole I'd been in since I'd first been outvoted on having the party in our basement. Truth be told, I'd been in it ever since I discovered I was living in a house of dead people. I knew, in my mind, those bodies were long gone, but they'd still been here. It doesn't pay to have an overactive imagination. Right now, I wanted to trade mine in.

The basement door slammed, making me jump and interrupting my mental dialogue. Elliott entered the kitchen. "Everybody's leaving. They sent me up here, said nobody is allowed down there until the party." He tried to frown but a flashing, ornery grin lit his face. I swallowed a snort of laughter. They were smart ladies to ban him from the basement lest they acquire a few unexpected touches to the décor.

More doors slamming distracted my attention from my young nephew. Voices, footsteps, and laughter reached my ears. From the noise volume I expected to see a dozen children pour into the kitchen. Keira and Téa breezed in followed by Katie and Lili.

"Aren't you home early?" Samantha still hadn't made it to the pantry.

"School's out." Keira grinned. "They had to shut the water off in that whole section of town to fix the leak at the grade school. It's such a mess they decided to let everybody go home early."

The side door off the kitchen opened again. Josie and Roni tumbled in. I knew they were racing each other to be first. Grown-up doesn't always mean being adult. Big as the kitchen was, it felt crowded; time to overflow into the dining room. Aunt Ellen and Jessi were already sitting at the one piece of furniture purchased specifically for the house, a dining room table expanded to seat twenty people if they sat close together.

Samantha finally made it to the pantry and started fresh coffee brewing. I wrinkled my nose and grabbed a glass of ice and a diet cola. No coffee for me.

From the back part of the house, Phoebe heard the commotion and wheeled Jake in to join the chaos and confusion.

I realized for someone who'd been isolated in the rural countryside of Illinois for twenty plus years, I was happy. Each voice carried a different tone, a different cadence, but together the noise they made created beautiful music to my ears. Not a discordant note among them. I smiled at my own whimsy and snagged a chair before Josie could get it.

The phone rang. Phoebe answered it. I didn't envy her trying to hear over the noise. She disappeared into the living room only to return a few minutes later to holler. "Shall we eat here tonight? Blair wants to know what's cooking."

I shrugged and caught the eyes of Josie and Roni.

"Why not?" Roni matched my shrug. "As long as I don't have to cook, I say the more the merrier."

Phoebe relayed the message to Blair and clicked off the phone. "Who all is staying?"

I wasn't surprised to see all hands in the air, including Aunt Ellen and Jessie. And I wasn't surprised when Phoebe clicked the phone back on and called Mary Lee. If we could get her over here, the food problem would be solved. She's the master organizer in our family and not bashful about giving orders. If we weren't clever at hiding, she'd give each one of us a job. Before you knew it, the table would be groaning under the weight of more food than even our army could eat.

The kitchen door opened again and Josie's eldest daughter, Anna, breezed in. We don't see a lot of her. Her grin reminds me of Elliott's. Not that they look alike, but they both flash and sparkle and make you happy when they smile at you.

"What's going on? Am I missing something?" She turned her smile on everybody, eyes moving from face to face, making each person they landed on feel special.

Josie brought her daughter up to date. Anna headed for the kitchen and disappeared into the pantry. Sometimes I think the pantry is the most used space in the house.

Conversation flowed and ebbed and eventually slowed enough that silence reigned. The silence sounded louder in my ears than the babble had.

Roni spoke. "Elliott, tell me how the party goes. What's the schedule for it?"

"It's so cool, Aunt Roni." Elliott moved closer, dragging a bar stool with him. He sat down by Roni and leaned toward her. "The party starts at five. Everybody will gather in the backyard. There will be Chinese lanterns hung around the backyard with yellow and red lights. It should look really spooky.

"There will be tables set up for food. We wanted a bonfire, but Mrs. Winters said that was too dangerous around so many children." We all hid grins because, without thinking, Elliott mimicked Mrs. Winter's voice to a tee. It was obvious what Elliott thought about danger. Nothing seemed too dangerous to him.

"From what I heard, there will be hot dogs, chips, hot chocolate, cookies, and bowls of candy." Enthusiasm colored his voice.

Keira and Téa moved closer to him. Keira broke in, "The outside entrance to the basement will be opened up. That's the entrance to the haunted house. Volunteers will be in place, and one by one, the kids will be taken down the steps and led through the basement."

"It's going to be so scary." Téa's big brown eyes widened as she thought about the basement. "I'm not sure I want to go through it."

I hunched down. I knew I wasn't going through it. Not if I could help it.

Jake startled me with a loud noise. I'm not sure what to call it. It's not a grunt. It's his voice, but I'm never sure what he's trying to say. Sometimes he kicks his foot, sometimes he vocalizes, but they all accomplish the same thing. He gets my attention. I looked over at him and he raised his eyes upward.

"Yes?" I asked. Most often, eyes going up means yes, but it can also mean big or a lot. Eye's flew toward the ceiling again. Whatever he was telling me was important to him.

"A lot?" I asked. He shook his head no. Then he dropped his gaze to stare intently at his fist.

I knew that sign. "You want? You need?"

Again his eyes flew up. Yes. He needed or wanted something. Now, what would that be?

He turned his gaze on Elliott and Téa and stared with an intensity that I could feel. His cousins are learning how to communicate with him. They pelted him with questions that he ignored, never taking his eyes off Elliott and Téa.

Mitchell watched this with his own intent gaze. His eyes are so blue they burn. Finally, he gave a snort and turned to his mother, Roni. "He wants to go through the haunted house."

Oh, no. The one thing that hadn't occurred to me. Of course Jake would want to see. He doesn't like to miss out on anything. I did a mental count of the steps leading downward, too many for his portable ramp; relief flooded me. If it isn't possible, then I didn't have to take him through it. Samantha shot that idea down.

"Don't worry, Jake. Uncle Theo and Uncle Logan will figure it out. They'll get you down there."

I swallowed a groan and gave up. One way or another, my son would go through the haunted house. It wasn't about me, but about him. Sometimes, I have to back off, keep my personal views private, and let my son make his own decisions. That's life and that's fair.

Mary Lee arrived a few minutes later. I knew from the look on her face she'd already thought up a menu for supper. I also knew it would be something fast, filling, and would probably involve her putting a lot of us to work.

Her arrival started a migration back to the kitchen. Mary Lee doled out jobs, and the kids did their part by whining and complaining. Boredom set in. The children were restless.

Mary Lee can only endure a certain amount of griping, and she reached her limit quickly. "All right, I've had enough. If you don't want to help in the kitchen, what do you want to do?"

"Something fun." Téa lit up.

"Something exciting," Elliott added.

"Something we've never done before," Keira joined in.

Not such a small request. I lowered my head and concentrated on chopping onions. No eye contact. That's the secret. Samantha hasn't learned that yet. She's still a soft touch.

"I have an idea." She clapped her hands and leaned back against the counter. Elliott, Keira, Lili, and Téa gathered around her.

She looked over at Josie and Roni. "Mr. Prescott did get the fruit cellar cleaned out, didn't he?" They nodded. She turned back to the kids.

"When I was a little girl, I used to have a lot of fun playing in the fruit cellar. It had the best sand. I'd open the doors, and the late sunshine would shine right into the cellar, lighting up the inside. I'd have more fun digging in the sand. The humidity in a fruit cellar is usually just damp enough so the sand holds together and you can build huge castles."

I stopped chopping and eyed the faces of the kids. I could tell she'd lost Anna and Keira. Playing in the sand didn't hold much interest for them, but the younger ones looked intrigued.

"What about spiders?" I ignored Josie's yelp. We've long become used to her phobia. "And snakes? There aren't any snakes in there, are there?"

That comment clinched it for Elliott. In his eyes, snakes and spiders would be a plus, but Lili and Téa's decision hinged on Samantha's answer.

I reminded them, "That's why I asked about Mr. Prescott. He was supposed to check the cellar and clean it out, so there shouldn't be any bugs, spiders, or snakes."

"Then I'm in." Téa stood up. Lili joined her. Elliott moved toward the door.

"Wear a jacket, Elliott." Katie didn't look up. She knew her son well.

"I need to get ready to go out tonight." Anna spoke. "Blair's coming over soon and I need to go to the attic. Keira, you have to go with me. I won't go alone."

"Thank goodness," Keira said. "I need some stuff for tomorrow and didn't want to go by myself either." Without another word, Anna and Keira headed up the backstairs.

Samantha, Téa, Keira, and Elliott grabbed jackets and headed for the door only to stop when Mitchell yelled. "Me too. I want to play in the sand."

Roni bundled her young son up and Mitchell trotted out the door with his cousins. He wanted an adventure too.

***

The aroma of spicy chili warmed the kitchen. Several sisters disappeared into the pantry to emerge carrying soft drinks and bags of assorted chips. One perk of merging three families is the diversified food choices gathered by those families. There's a lot to choose from, and feeding a large group of people isn't hard at our house.

Mary Lee popped some kind of casserole into the oven, and it soon added its own scent to air. Life is good when there's hot food and family in the same room.

The kitchen door swung open and Buddy came in. Molly and Murphy met him at the door. They adore him, and he never fails to greet them with great enthusiasm.

."You're by yourself?" Phoebe looked surprised.

"Yes." Buddy gave the dogs a final pat and stood up. "Logan and Uncle Harry have plans to pitch horseshoes. Theo said he's busy at the office and would Samantha please send him over some food. So, I'm it. I'd rather be here than throwing horseshoes around."

"You might win." Josie stopped in front of him, her arms full of paper plates and plastic forks.

I swallowed a snicker. Winning a game against our uncle, one of the top-ranked pitchers in the state, wasn't likely to happen anytime soon.

Buddy shook his head. "Nope, I never win. Anyway, I need a break. Ansel's seen me with Logan all day long. I'm hoping he'll follow Logan's truck, and I can have a peaceful evening without feeling eyes boring into the middle of my back." He gave a visible shudder.

One thing Buddy can count on from his sisters is sympathy. We give him a hard time, but he's our only brother and we're protective toward him. He's always there when we need him, and he knows we're there for him.

"Have you figured out why he's following you?" Mary Lee stopped stirring the chili to turn toward Buddy, her eyes dark with worry.

"No idea." Buddy sniffed the air. "Is that fresh coffee I smell?" He wasted no time pouring a cup and moved into the dining room to sit at the table by Aunt Ellen.

She smiled at him and opened her mouth to speak. Before she could utter a word, the sound of an upstairs toilet flushing reached our ears, followed by a slamming door. A moment of silence, and then we heard screams, piercing screams that can only be produced by teenage girls. Footsteps pounding from the upper regions of the house added urgency to the yells. Anna and Keira wanted downstairs. From the noise pattern, they would fly down the front stairs.

Buddy set his cup down with a slam, sloshing hot coffee onto his hand. We ignored his yelp of pain and rushed into the hallway just in time to see both girls make a spectacular descent. I think Keira slid halfway on her rear. I didn't doubt she'd have some spectacular bruises.

"Mommy," Anna wailed. Gone was any resemblance to adulthood. Keira regained her feet, and both girls flung themselves at their mother, clinging to her in a way that reminded me of their three-year-old cousin, Mitchell.

"What's going on?" Buddy, being the only man in the room, tried to take charge. He's good at sounding the part.

"A ghost." Anna visibly trembled. Keira's head bobbed up and down in agreement.

"A scary ghost." Keira inched closer to her mother. "It was in the upstairs bathroom."

I frowned and voices babbled around me, too many words coming too fast to decipher. The girls tried to describe the ghost, and everybody else asked questions. The screaming had been less noisy.

"Hold it!" Buddy yelled. To my surprise the girls shut up and stared at him with big, round eyes. He cleared his throat, and when he spoke his voice sounded calm and soothing. "You say you saw a ghost?"

The girls nodded. I noticed they had loosened their grip on Josie but still stood plastered by her side.

226

"This ghost, she was in the upstairs bathroom?"

"He," Anna blurted out. "It was a man. I think it was a man." She looked over at Keira.

"It was wearing men's clothing, but it was boney. Maybe it was a skeleton." Keira darted a fast glance up the stairs.

"You saw a skeleton in the upstairs bathroom?" Buddy repeated.

The girls nodded again.

Buddy frowned, deep in thought. "But why?" He shook his head. "That doesn't make sense. Why would a ghost use the toilet? Could it have been one of the volunteers?"

"No," Mary Lee answered. "A volunteer wouldn't go all the way upstairs to use a bathroom, and the last time I looked they were all women."

We pondered in silence. I don't know about the others, but I know the girls. It was possible their nerves got the better of them. One thing my family is long on is imagination. But we had all heard the toilet flush.

I looked over at Roni. "Would your cat flush a toilet?"

"It's possible." Roni nodded. "He's played with the handle before, causing it to flush."

Anna drew herself up and glared at us. "Oh please. Would your cat be six feet tall and wearing men's baggy clothes? We saw it."

"I thought you were in the attic." Josie asked, "How could you see someone in the upstairs bathroom if you were on the third floor?"

"It came upstairs," Keira whispered. "Anna was brushing my hair, putting it up for me. We were

227

looking in the mirror, and behind us we saw a figure plain as day."

The girls moved in closer to their mother, fear radiating from them. I felt the hair on my head stand up.

"What happened next?" Buddy pushed them for details, "when you turned around, I mean?"

"Nothing." Anna's voice dropped to a whisper. "There was nothing there. That's when I knew it had to be a ghost. I wanted downstairs, so I ran."

"Me, too," Keira shivered. "I didn't want to be left up there by myself."

I mulled over possible scenarios in my mind. The one I preferred involved the girls having overactive imaginations, but we'd all heard the toilet flush. Where was the cat anyway?

"What's that sound?" Jessie asked.

"What sound?" Mary Lee cocked her head to listen. And then we heard it, distant and faint at first, but growing louder, moving closer.

Screams. More sound than one person could make.

Chapter Twenty Nine
Something Lurks in Yonder Sand

I recognized full-throated panic when I heard it. Faint and far away, it took me a minute to pinpoint where the screams were coming from. I started running the minute I figured it out, heading for the back part of the house. My rooms where I knew windows faced the back yard. Hopefully, from there I'd be able to see the fruit cellar. A thundering herd followed at my heels.

"What's going on?" Phoebe sounded winded and I risked a glance back. Red-faced, she hadn't forgotten Jake. Pushing a wheel chair and trying to run isn't an easy combination, especially when you aren't used to it.

I didn't stop to help her. I headed for the window that I hoped had the best view. Pressing my nose to the window, I strained to see through the row of lilacs lining the back edge of the yard. The old fruit cellar lay behind them. Even without their leaves, the branches on the ancient shrubs were thick and hard to see through.

I caught sight of movement and I goggled. A quick sidewise look let me know I wasn't the only one gaping. I turned back to watch.

"Who knew Samantha could scream that loud?" Josie spoke. She sounded almost proud of Samantha's full-throated shrieks.

"I think Elliott should consider going out for track," my cousin, Jessi, commented. "He's flying."

Indeed he was. Well in the lead, Elliott led the pack. I noted he was in fine tone too, his voice cracking into a range high enough to embarrass him if I could catch it on tape.

As we watched, Lili closed the gap between her and her brother. Téa easily kept pace with her cousins. In fact, I narrowed my eyes to see clearer. She looked like she might kick it up a gear and overtake Elliott. *What in the world had scared them?*

"Mr. Prescott must have missed a snake," Aunt Ellen commented. Her quiet assurance brought a measure of safety and peace to me. She probably doesn't know she can do that, but I always feel safer when she's near.

I turned my gaze back to the runners. Mitchell's little legs were churning, moving as fast as three-year-old legs could move, but not fast enough for Samantha. She reached down and scooped him into her arms. Then I saw her run like I've never seen her run before. I hoped the effort didn't kill her.

They headed for the nearest door, which happened to be the one opening into my section of the house. Buddy hurried to pull it open. The runners tumbled in. Once safe in the house, the screams faded, but the noise level remained high. Too many voices talking; I'd spent years living in quiet solitude. I did the only thing I could think of. I stuck my fingers in my mouth and blew, proud that I could still manage a whistle loud enough to halt my family in mid-sentence.

I felt bad about scaring Mitchell. He looked at me with wide blue eyes, burst into tears, and reached for his mother. Samantha handed him over to Roni. Mitchell buried his head against her neck and wouldn't look at me, no matter how much I coaxed. As upset as Mitchell was with me, I made points with Elliott. From the look he gave me, I knew at the first opportunity he'd bug me to teach him how to let loose with the loud whistle. The others just stared at me in stunned, blessed silence.

I did what we always do in our family. We start with the eldest. I pointed at Samantha. "What happened?"

She gave a hard swallow. "I took the kids to the cellar. We opened the door and found out there is electricity down there."

"With a light switch and everything," Lili broke in. "It lit up the whole inside."

Samantha continued, "When I saw the light switch, I thought the floor might be cement. If they updated the electrical, they might have poured a floor, but they didn't. There are shelves along the walls, but the floor was nice, thick sand."

"I made the kids stay outside while I checked for snakes." I swallowed a snicker at my mental picture of Samantha hunting for snakes. I almost wished I'd been there to see it.

Elliott opened his mouth to speak, impatient with his aunt for taking her time. Katie shot him a glance only a mother can give. He snapped his lips together.

Samantha folded her arms against her stomach. I could see her shiver. "We had light; the sand was perfect. I showed them how to make blocks of sand to build walls. We were having a lot of fun when Mitchell found something."

She stopped, her eyes widened, and she made a retching sound, a bad sound to make in our family. We're sympathy heavers. One person pukes; we all join in. If Samantha vomited, a chain reaction would likely follow.

"Bathroom," I shouted and pointed toward the door leading to my private bathroom. "Don't you dare throw up on the floor. You'll have to clean it up if you do."

She managed to glare at me as she fled for the bathroom. It was thoughtful of her to close the door after her, but we could still hear her awful retching. Luckily, being out of sight and safely away behind a closed door, we were no longer in danger of joining in. Keira, Téa, and Lili looked decidedly green. Mitchell stopped crying and peeked at me from his mom's shoulder. He'd stopped being afraid. I knew later on he'd ask me how I'd made the loud noise. Sometimes, curiosity can be a good thing.

I heard the water run. A few minutes later Samantha returned.

"I'm so sorry," she said. "Nerves." She moved over by the girls. They scooted closer to her.

Samantha resumed her story. "The sand was perfect for building, holding its shape. Then Mitchell found something." Her voice quivered. For a minute I thought she'd be heading for the bathroom again. "He brought it to me, and I took it from him, trying to figure out what it was. Then Lili uncovered something. She started yelling at Elliott."

Lili broke in. "I thought Elliott hid the skull in the sand to scare us. He's been pranking everybody all week. When I uncovered a human skull, I thought it was the one he borrowed from the science class for the party."

"But it wasn't the same one," Keira added. "This one was old and dirty."

"Wait a minute." Concern brought a frown to Buddy's face. "You found a skull in the sand?"

"Not just a skull." Samantha's voice shook. "Bones. Lots of bones."

Roni squeaked. That's the only way I can describe the sound that came out of her mouth. "Bones? Mitchell was holding a bone? A human bone?"

"Yes," Excitement bubbled in Elliott. I could see him going from fear to excitement now that he was safe in the midst of family. "He found a finger bone."

"Oh, eeyew." In a family of weak stomachs, Roni holds the record. She peeled Mitchell off of her and holding him at arm's length, rushed him into the bathroom. I figured she'd scrub her young son within an inch of his life. I wasn't the only one grinning when we heard her run water into the tub. A full bath. Well, I probably would have done the same. If I wasn't mistaken there were four people standing in front of me who would head for showers as soon as possible.

I didn't count Elliott. Finding bones, for him, would turn into a badge of courage.

"Why would there be bones in the fruit cellar?" Puzzles. I can't resist them.

"Think about it, Sis." Buddy elbowed me just like he'd done when I was ten. "What bones are missing?"

"You think we've got Elizabeth Jordan in our fruit cellar?" I did another mental eeyew. For some reason having a name for the bones made it all too real. I wanted the bones, the party, the whole mess to vanish. Tomorrow, I promised myself. It would all be done tomorrow. Halloween never looked so good.

***

Three hours later we sat around the dining room table.

"I hope I don't look like you do." I eyed my unhappy nephew.

Elliott raised his head and glared at me. His smoky blue eyes, usually so full of laughter and mischief, carried storm warnings. If the corners of his mouth went any further south, they'd meet up with his chin.

I eyed the people sitting around the table, stopping to examine each face. They all mirrored Elliott's unhappy countenance with the exception of Mitchell and Jake. Roni, with superb forethought, put Mitchell to work coloring pictures. I smiled to hear her tell him the church ladies needed help decorating for the Halloween party. Jake sat in his customary place at the corner of the table closest to the kitchen and laughed at us.

"I can't remember the last time I've been scolded," Buddy muttered and reached for his coffee cup.

Finding it empty, he stood up and headed for the kitchen to refill it.

"Me, either." Samantha looked glum. Then she burst out, "But I know what we saw. I know there were bones in that cellar."

Téa and Lili bobbed their heads in agreement. "We all saw them, Aunt Share-Bear." Téa reached out and patted Samantha on her shoulder. Her older sister, Anna, gave Samantha the nickname, but all the girls use it.

Buddy came back to the table and sat down. "You know the worst part?" he asked. He fell silent and we waited. He raised his cup and took a careful sip of the hot coffee.

"What?" Elliott finally burst out. "What was the worst part?"

Buddy smiled at his young nephew over the rim of the cup. I knew from that smile my brother was doing what he does best, making us feel better, putting a spin on things that would help cheer up the kids.

Buddy set his cup down, careful not to spill a drop. His slow, deliberate movements exasperated me, but I saw the children lean forward, drawn toward their uncle, hanging onto every word that would come from his mouth. A grin twitched my lips when I noticed that all of us, even me, waited for Buddy's words of wisdom.

"The worst part wasn't the police coming here to search the cellar; it wasn't even Logan showing up. We're used to him yelling. It wasn't learning the bones were gone. The worst part...." Buddy leaned back in his chair. His voice turned gloomy and his face took on a sad hound dog look. "The absolute worst part is the fact the county sheriff is our uncle."

I cringed. Oh, yeah, that had been bad.

Buddy spoke again. "A sheriff should have stayed professional. He crossed the line when he treated us like family."

The kids nodded their heads in agreement. I caught Samantha doing the same.

"You would think he'd realize I wouldn't be part of such a trick." She sounded so indignant; I had to swallow another giggle. Jake didn't. His shoulders started to shake. I stared at him, willing him to be polite, but stopping him is like stopping the wind. He laughed so hard I wanted to join in.

Elliott's frown deepened. "I'm not a prankster. He made it sound like all I do is play jokes."

I had some sympathy there with my uncle. Elliott did like to play jokes, but not even his inventive mind could conjure up a full skeleton. The skull he'd borrowed for the Halloween party was present and accounted for and definitely not real. Uncle Claude checked that out.

I believed Samantha. She wouldn't have mistaken human bones. Even if they had been misidentified, they would still be out there buried in the sand. And they weren't.

"Where could they have gone to?" Josie puzzled. "There wasn't a lot of time between Samantha and the kids being out there and the arrival of Logan and the police. Maybe thirty minutes, tops."

That puzzled me too. If the bones were there, and I believed they had been, what happened to them in that short time frame? None of us had gone back to look. We'd wanted to, but a stern warning from the police relayed to us by phone through Buddy kept us waiting in the house.

I sighed. Would we ever be done with questions and puzzles? My life seemed full of them, and I blamed it all on the party. "Tomorrow," I frowned at Elliott, matching him scowl for scowl. "Tomorrow is the Halloween party and all these stupid problems will go away."

Chapter Thirty
A Few More Shocks

The morning of Halloween dawned in disgusting glory, with air so crisp and clear it hurt my eyes.

"What in the world is that?" I blinked my eyes and leaned forward over the kitchen sink to peer through the window into the back yard, illuminated this early in the morning by the corner street light. "I should have realized," I muttered as I sank back on my heels and let go of the sink. "I guess it's better than having everybody troop through the house." I rubbed my eyes and looked again. A big, gaudy tent sat like a fat mushroom in my backyard. When did it get put up? And why did Uncle Claude let them?

"Oh, yeah," I grumbled, "because he didn't believe us. He thought the whole skeleton thing was a hoax. He thought it was a ploy to get more hoopla for the Halloween spook house as if we needed any more excitement around here."

I sighed and headed for the pantry. I needed a Diet Coke and needed it bad. So what if it was breakfast? Drinking a soda wasn't any different than a cup of coffee.

My brother's voice, coming from the dining room doorway, halted me in my tracks. "Coffee."

Seeing my brother up at six in the morning without somebody having to throw something at him was almost as big a shock as seeing a tent perched in my back yard.

"You'd risk drinking coffee I make?"

"Oh, yeah," Buddy groped his way to a kitchen chair and struggled to get his eyes open enough to focus. "I forgot you make the worst coffee in world. Do you have any instant?"

I pulled a glass out of the dishwasher, filled it with ice, and poured in the Diet Coke. "Actually, I do. It's sitting on top the microwave cart."

Before Buddy could gripe about the instant coffee being decaf, the kitchen started filling up with people. Josie and Roni came tromping down the back stairs. Samantha and Phoebe arrived through the side door. Before I knew it, the kitchen was full of people. So much for my quiet time; I'd be darned if I made breakfast for everybody. But I did. Before long the aroma of frying bacon and sausage filled the air. Biscuits baked in the oven, and the griddle was hot for pancakes.

"Why are you all here so early?" Curiosity prompted my question.

"I felt guilty." Samantha picked up the tongs and started turning bacon. "This whole haunted house thing ending up here is my fault. I didn't want you to have to do a single thing today."

"That was nice. Not doing anything appeals to me, but why six in the morning?" I gulped the last of my

Diet Coke and wondered if I dared get a second one. Phoebe watched me like a hawk, and I knew her opinion of artificial anything.

Samantha shot me a guilty look and turned back to the skillet of frying meat. Uh oh. I knew that look. Something was going on and I hadn't been told. Or I had been and hadn't paid attention, which was a more likely scenario.

Before I could question her, I heard voices accompanied by even louder laughter. "Doesn't anybody ever sleep in around here?" I jumped up and headed for the sink so I could see into the back yard. I groaned when I saw a group of women bustling about under the tent.

A loud beeping assaulted my ears, the kind of noise a big truck makes when it's backing up. The sound came from the direction of our driveway. I moved from the window above the sink to the window facing the driveway, peeked through the curtains, and stood there in stunned silence.

I turned my head to look at Samantha. "Port-a-potties. Three of them. In our driveway?"

"Think about it." She spoke fast. "Little kids. Koolaid. You certainly don't want them trooping through your house, do you?"

No, I didn't. In fact, I intended to lock all the doors and windows as soon as I could get everybody out, although that probably wouldn't work. Josie and Roni had their own keys, and I was pretty sure they would object to being locked out of their own house. And I wasn't aware of any key that would lock the basement door to the kitchen.

Buddy woke up enough to snicker, "Port-a-potties? What will they think of next?"

What would they think up? I was horrified at the parade of ideas that marched through my imagination. Those church women were capable of anything. Panic sent me to the pantry for another soda. I ignored Phoebe's frown. She didn't live here. She could go home. Heck, I might even move in with her until this was all over. That would serve her right.

"If they wake Jake up before he's ready, I'm not going to be happy." I glared at Samantha. She hunched her shoulders and started cracking eggs. I was betting there wouldn't be any soft yolks today.

"This is the most bizarre Halloween I've ever been through." I sank onto a chair. "First of all, we find out we're living in a mortuary. What kind of person lives in a mortuary? I hate knowing there were dead bodies here. If anybody tells me my bedroom was where they held visitation, I'll never get over it."

Buddy gave Samantha a happy grin when she handed him a cup of freshly brewed coffee, the real stuff. Guilt must be weighing heavy on her because she never, ever drinks real coffee. He took a careful sip of the hot brew. "My cars were vandalized and my house flooded. Somebody put fresh sod on a grave at the cemetery and then stole bones out of another grave."

He took another long sip of coffee, carefully set the cup down and frowned. "Add Ol' Ansel to the mix. I still can't figure out why he's shadowing me."

Samantha went back to the stove, carefully split a biscuit open, and covered it with gravy. She added two slices of bacon and one sausage link before joining us at the table. "The church secretary disappeared. The last I heard, the minister hasn't been heard from since he unexpectedly left his post."

Roni emerged from the pantry carrying a can of Pepsi. She too ignored the frown Phoebe sent her way. "Add the blackout, the suspected intruder, and the haunted house in the basement."

"Not to mention the graveyard out front and the circus tent in back." I slumped deeper on my chair. Gloom settled over me like a warm blanket. "I don't even want to think about the port-a-potties sitting in the driveway."

"The worst thing," Josie added, dropping her fork onto her plate and pushing it away, "are the bones. I believe what Samantha and the kids told us."

"Thank you." Samantha gave Josie a grateful look. "I'm glad somebody believes us."

"I believe you," I protested. "The way our luck runs, it had to be the bones from the missing skeleton."

Roni spoke up again, "All that is weird, but for absolute bizarre, I can't get over the fact that Karen Wright will be participating in the haunted house. She'll be rising up out of the casket as the kids are led, one by one, through the haunted house. With her mother so against Halloween, how did that happen?"

Silence descended as each of us pondered the events that had led up to this day. Phoebe broke the quiet. "Well, look on the bright side. By tomorrow morning this will all be over and life will get back to normal."

Normal. I could feel my lips turning upwards in a smile. Normal sounded good.

"Mo-om." We heard Mitchell's voice float down the stair.

A loud yell came from the back part of the house. Jake may not talk, but he can yell with the best of them. Drat the noise. He should have slept for two more hours. I sighed and went to get him up. In the nether regions of the house, I heard a toilet flush.

Chapter Thirty One
Hiding out

"You aren't serious about hiding in your bedroom, are you?" Phoebe sounded shocked, although I don't know why she would be. She knows me well.

I counted the cans of Diet Coke residing in the plastic grocery bag and felt a twinge of guilt when the number hit six. I debated on putting three of them back, then decided it was better to have too many than not enough. I looked up from the sack and eyed Phoebe. She looked worried.

I spoke firmly, wanting to get across to her my serious intention to hibernate the day away. "I meant what I said. I've got drinks, food, and a stack of books waiting for me. I remember somebody telling me I wouldn't have to do a thing today. I intend to keep it that way."

Phoebe tried again. "You do realize that's a whole bag of chips you just added to that sack, don't you?"

"I'm not going to eat it all." *At once*, I added silently to myself, glad that she couldn't see the bowl holding an entire package of cream cheese that I'd turned into my favorite chip dip hiding in sack number two.

"I'll come out to take care of Jake," I assured her. "You won't have to feed him. There are enough people around he won't be alone."

Jake's loud grunt startled me, and I glanced over at him. He sat gazing at the back staircase. From his unmoving intentness, I knew he was trying to say something. He grunted again, adding a foot kick to tell me that whatever he wanted was important to him.

"Do you need to go upstairs?" I couldn't imagine why. Curiosity might motivate him, but that would have happened the first few days we lived here, not now for no reason that I could discern.

He shot me a look of utter disgust and turned his eyes back to the staircase, adding another loud grunt for good measure.

"Is somebody up there that you need to talk to?" To my surprise his eyes shot upwards, following his yes response with a headshake in the negative. I hate it when he does that. It means I'm close, but I have no way of knowing what part of my question got the 'yes' and what part got the 'no'. I started listing everybody who might conceivably be upstairs. He answered each name with a no, getting angrier with each name I spoke.

Usually we communicate without trouble, but once in awhile, I admit defeat. I ran out of names and the conversation stopped, leaving both of us dissatisfied. I sighed and gathered up the sacks of drinks and food, eager to get to the stack of unread books waiting for me in my bedroom.

Phoebe tried one last time. "Don't you think you should stay out here? It looks bad for you to be off hiding."

I shook my head, dropped a kiss on top of Jake's head, and swept out of the room, stopping at the dining room door to look back. Phoebe looked frustrated, Jake looked angry, and I didn't feel any too pleased with myself. I knew I was being cowardly, but what else could I do? I wasn't in the mood to deal with screaming children, dueling churchgoers, or ornery nephews.

I sighed, "I'm really sorry. I don't intend to poke my nose outside my bedroom door except to feed Jake." I paused for dramatic effect, a pose I'd learned from my sister, Roni. "And woe to anyone who disturbs me." With that dire threat, I swept out of the kitchen heading for my part of the house. Once inside my bedroom, I turned the lock in the door and prepared to ignore the noises that were already starting to permeate through the walls.

***

It's not often I can block out an entire day to read, and I eyed the stack of paperbacks with the same feeling a pirate would dig up buried treasure. I'm an eclectic reader, so the stack contained a mix of mystery, romance, science fiction, and biography, heavy on the mystery.

Not ready to commit yet to a topic, I unloaded the sack of food. I set each item carefully on the small bedside table. As the pile grew, guilt gnawed at me. Not guilt for hiding out; it was the amount food staring at me from the table that caused my uncomfortable twinges. Was I really going to eat all that?

"It is supposed to last for an entire day." I spoke out loud, hoping the words would convince me they were true. It didn't work. Even for a whole day, I was looking at a disgusting amount of calories: an entire bag of ripple potato chips, six cans of Diet Coke, a pitcher of crushed ice, three ground-up lunch meat sandwiches, and what I'd told myself was two brownies now looked like I'd taken half the pan.

I plopped down on a chair and stared in dismay. "I'm feeling sick and I haven't even eaten one bite yet."

A timid knock on my door interrupted my dark thoughts. "Already?" I hollered. "I haven't even opened a book yet."

"Aunt Charly?" I recognized Téa's voice. "Could I ask you something?"

I sighed, stood up, walked to the door, and inched it open, making sure Téa wouldn't see the food-laden table. "Ask away," I told her.

She lowered her voice to a whisper. "Uncle Buddy wants to know if you need anything."

My jaw dropped. "That's it? That's the only thing he could think of to bother me with?"

She looked like a shy bird standing there in my doorway, pretty brown eyes, curly brown-blond hair, her lips tilted in an impish smile. I sighed, unable to work up any anger toward her. At her age I'd been no more able to resist my brother's persuasions than she could.

"Tell your Uncle Buddy that I'm fine and to quit bothering me. I meant what I said. I'm going to curl up with a snack, a cold drink, and a good book. I don't want to be interrupted for any reason."

She bobbed her head in agreement and ran off. I closed the door and relocked it. Ten minutes later, my book chosen, I sat down on the bed. I settled back, wiggled around to get comfortable, and opened the book. I barely finished page one when another knock rattled my door.

"Aunt Charly?" Not Téa this time. I recognized her big sister, Keira's, voice. Drat my brother. He knew I wouldn't ignore the children. I sighed, put my book down, slid off the bed, and went to the door, not bothering to worry if Keira saw the food on the table.

"What now?" I tried to glare at her. She's seventeen. I'm not so worried about hurting her feelings as I had been with Téa.

She hesitated, then held out a magazine. "Uncle Buddy said you needed this and asked me to bring it to you."

I reached out and took the magazine, glancing down to see an old copy of <u>Golf</u>. Each face on the cover sported artistically inked facial hair. My brother had added a big smiley face to the golf ball.

I sighed. "He couldn't even send a magazine I might actually read?" I did appreciate his artistic effort though. A smile tugged at the corners of my mouth. I glanced up at Keira and asked, "How many more kids does he have lined up?"

She shrugged and grinned. "He's sitting at the kitchen table drinking coffee. Jake and Mitchell are laughing so hard."

"I can just imagine." I felt, more than glimpsed, movement down the hall. I raised my voice, "If I were you, Keira, I'd tell everybody else to start charging your uncle a hefty fee to knock on my door. Tell him it's gotten dangerous, and you all need hazard pay."

Her dark eyes lit up with laughter." I'll do that. Bye." She went running back toward the kitchen, and I once again shut the door and locked it. I suspected the movement I'd seen had been Elliott, and if I knew my nephew, it would cost Buddy some money to continue this little game.

Elliott showed up thirty minutes later, a big grin on his face. From the way he patted his pocket, I hoped he'd clipped Buddy for at least five dollars.

My brother possesses an uncanny knack of knowing just how hard to push me. He also knows that if he can make me laugh, my temper can usually be controlled.

After Elliott's visit, I merged to feed Jake lunch, then retreated to my bedroom and my book. With diabolical timing my brother gave me another thirty minutes of peace before the disturbances started in again. Interruption number four set me off. "That's it." I stepped outside my bedroom door and screeched in a way that would have gotten me in big trouble if Mom had been around to hear it. "I'm not opening this door again today except for life and death emergencies. I'm shutting off the phone. I really mean it this time."

My brother knows me well, and he knew I'd been pushed far enough. I got in two hours of peaceful reading before all hell broke loose.

I truly meant to ignore any sounds I heard, but when every girl in the house started screaming, the dogs started barking, and I could hear Jake yelling over the din, I knew something truly cataclysmic had happened. Curiosity overpowered stubbornness. I left my bedroom at a run.

Entering the living room, I did a head count, making sure that Jake and Mitchell were safe. My son was in full wind-up mode, one hand cranked back by his ear, and his head turned the opposite direction. It's a primitive reflex pattern that all infants have and lose as their nervous system develops. Jake didn't lose his. When he gets emotional, the reflex triggers, and he ends up with his body going several directions at once. Seeing this pattern told me clearer than words how upset he was.

Keira and Téa clung to their mother. Keira stood as tall as her mother. Her eyes were wide with fear. The screams she emitted took me back to childhood. She is her mother's daughter.

Buddy, Phoebe, and Samantha came from the kitchen area and stood grouped in the doorway. They looked as helpless as I felt.

I did what I always do when the noise level makes it impossible to be heard. I stuck my fingers in my mouth and whistled. Blessed quiet followed. "What in the world is going on? I thought the screaming would come from the haunted house."

"We're living in a haunted house," Keira snapped.

Téa's eyes were lemur big as she nodded agreement. Lili, unable to get close to Josie, scampered over to stand between Buddy and Phoebe. I turned a wrathful gaze onto Elliott. "Have you been pranking again? Today of all days?"

He gave me a wounded look. "It's not my fault this time. I was watching TV. I didn't do anything."

"He didn't." Lili spoke up. "It really isn't Elliott's fault." She shuddered and drew in a big breath. "It's the ghost. We all saw the ghost."

"We? We who?" I frowned.

Lili, Téa, and Keira all pointed at each other. "All of us," Keira added. "We were upstairs. Why, I'll never know. I thought it was just the third floor that had the ghost, but it isn't." She started to sound panicked. "He's everywhere."

She tugged on Josie's arm. "I want to move. Can we move in with Aunt Katie and Uncle Mick?"

"No." Josie rolled her eyes. "We're not going anywhere. There's no such thing as ghosts."

Thank goodness I kept my mouth shut because I'm not convinced there aren't, but the girls didn't need to be burdened with my fears. "What did this ghost look like?"

"Old." Keira shuddered again. "Really, really old."

"White hair, eyes of blue fire," Téa whispered.

"He shuffled when he walked," Lili added.

"And where did you see this ghost?" Phoebe asked.

The girls looked uncomfortable and hesitated before they answered. Finally, Keira spoke. "In the upstairs bathroom. We went in."

Téa blushed red. "He was using the toilet. He looked at us, zipped up his pants, flushed the toilet, and vanished."

Buddy frowned. "Wait a minute. You saw him in the bathroom? Why would a ghost use the bathroom?"

The girls shrugged and looked away. Keira muttered, "I don't know. Maybe he died in the bathroom?"

I could see that thought clearly disturbed the girls.

"He vanished? Just disappeared?" Josie met Buddy's eyes.

"Sort of," Lili said. "He went through the door."

"Did any of you touch him?" Phoebe wanted to know.

The resulting eeuuws rivaled the screams for noise level. "No way." Keira shook her head. "We fell over ourselves not to touch him."

Jake grunted at me again, loud, insistent. I looked over at him and knew from the twisted body position he was still agitated. He caught my gaze and flicked his eyes to the empty couch. I frowned, unable to decipher his message. I puzzled a moment, then gave up, and turned back to the girls. Jake barked another grunt at me and kicked his foot.

"What?" Frustration caused me to speak with more impatience than I meant. He moved his eyes slowly, with deliberate intent, making me feel like a fool knowing that he wanted to tell me something but I was too dense to understand. "I don't know what you want."

Mitchell looked from his cousin to me and back to Jake and gave an exasperated sigh. You haven't lived until you've been chastised by a three year old. "That's easy, Aunt Charly. Jake wants to show you the thing."

"What thing?" Phoebe, Buddy, Josie, and I all spoke in varying degrees of curiosity.

"This thing." Mitchell ran over to the couch, crawled up on the cushions, stood up, leaned over the back, and reached down. "I can't get it up. It's stuck tight."

Elliott and Buddy went to help. Elliott got there first and crawled up by Mitchell. He knelt there beside Mitchell and looked over the back. "Oh, cool. Look at this, Uncle Buddy."

With Buddy's help, Elliott pulled something metallic from behind the couch. Buddy lifted it free and set it on the floor.

"What is it?" Phoebe spoke.

We all moved closer. He unfolded the metal pieces, and we realized we were looking at a walker. "Uh oh," Buddy murmured and I think that's when we realized who our ghost really was.

Chapter Thirty Two
Hunt for Mr. Whitaker

"Has that old man been wandering in the house ever since he came here?" Buddy shook his head.

"It also explains all the toilet flushing we've hearing," Josie muttered.

"We need to find him," Phoebe added. "How could somebody stay hidden with everybody living here?"

Buddy slanted a look at me. "Don't you have dogs in the house? Wouldn't they bark at an intruder?"

"Yes, they would," I shot back at him," but how would they know he wasn't welcome? We sat and talked to him. We gave him snacks. How would they know, out of all the people that come tramping through this house, that one old man wasn't supposed to be here?"

"Anyway," I added, "I'll go get the dogs. I've been keeping them confined to the back of the house because of all the Halloween traffic going in and out. They might notice if somebody is hiding." I didn't hold much hope for it, but I left to retrieve Molly and Murphy, leaving the others to divide into groups. With all of us hunting, I didn't think it would take long to find Mr. Whitaker.

Thirty minutes later we gathered in the kitchen. The dogs, tongues hanging out, headed for their water dish. The rest of us grabbed our drink of choice, then settled around the table and stared at each other in gloomy silence.

Josie broke the quiet first. "How could one old man elude all of us? He's ninety years old, isn't he?"

"Ninety-one," Elliott spoke, a mistake on his part because it drew all eyes to him and we noticed him sitting on the kitchen counter. Before his mother could yell at him, he slid downwards to stand. "I interviewed him, remember? He said he was born in 1920. His father was a mortician. When he grew up, he became one too."

"What else do you know about the family?" Buddy leaned back and eyed his young nephew.

Elliott grinned and continued. "He had a twin brother and a sister. The sister was ten years younger. Old Ansel lived here too. He's a cousin. I don't know what happened to his family, but he lived here and grew up with Mr. Whitaker's family. Mr. Whitaker told me that there wasn't anywhere else for Ansel to go."

"Where does Steven Whitaker fit in?" Josie spoke. "You know, the guy who showed us the house?"

"He's Mr. Whitaker's grandson. I saw him when I did the interview. In fact," Elliott said, stopping to frown, "he stayed in the room for the whole interview. He never spoke, just sat in a chair and stared at us. It made me uncomfortable."

That statement stopped us in mid-motion, and we stared at Elliott. Nothing made him uncomfortable. His people skills didn't come from the Russell side of the family.

"Hmm." Phoebe narrowed her eyes. She's a mystery buff, the old who-dun-it kind. I'd bet money she was fitting information together the way I'd work a jigsaw puzzle. Her brain is wired that way. Mine? It hurt.

"Well, I don't like it," Keira burst out." We spent thirty minutes looking for that old man. Every time I opened a closet door, I thought he'd jump out at me."

Téa's head bobbed up and down. "Every time I looked under a bed, I was afraid I'd find a dead body. I'm not looking anymore. I'd rather go stay with Lili until this all blows over."

Oh, good. I fought to keep the grin off my face at the idea of children leaving the house on Halloween. That could only be a good thing. "That's actually a really good idea." I looked over at Josie waiting for her decision.

She shrugged and I looked at Katie. She threw her hands in the air and said, "Why not? The more the merrier."

Keira whooped and Téa sagged. They started for the back stairs only to freeze in their tracks. Even though we'd combed the upstairs, they weren't convinced Mr. Whitaker wasn't hiding up there.

"If he's spent the last twenty four hours hiding, he's not going to choose now to appear." Buddy sounded exasperated. You'd think growing up with seven sisters would have taught him better. Girls do not function by using logic. It's pure emotion with them, and Keira and Téa were spooked. Lili didn't budge. In fact, she scooted her chair closer to her mother.

Keira's eyes traveled the circle: Phoebe, Katie, Buddy, Jake, Elliott, Roni with Mitchell sitting on her lap, Josie, and me. She gave up. "Never mind; Mom can bring our clothes by later. I'm out of here." She moved to the kitchen door, Lili and Téa close on her heels. Elliott hesitated, then leaned back against the counter. Girls vs. mystery? He chose the mystery. I couldn't blame him. I would have made the same decision at his age. Today? I wanted to follow Keira.

"What do we do next?" Phoebe emptied the Pepsi can sitting in front of her over a glass of ice. "We searched every nook and cranny of this house. He has to be here somewhere."

Buddy snickered. "I thought sure the dogs would find him, but they never left Charly's side."

"It's not my fault." I glared at him. "I took both dogs through obedience training. They think they're supposed to stay by my heels. They don't understand the word search. We never got past the basics." I tried not to think about Murphy crawling on her belly after I gave her the down-stay command. She'd stayed down all right. It was the left behind bit she'd had trouble with. "They would have searched if they'd understood what we wanted."

"Yeah, yeah," Buddy muttered. "It still leaves us with one old man hiding in the house."

"There's one place we haven't looked." Phoebe spoke.

"Where's that?" Katie asked.

Josie answered for her. "We haven't been in the basement yet."

"For Pete's sake," I burst out, "he's ninety one years old. Could he even get to the basement?"

"He managed to get upstairs just fine if he's the ghost that's been scaring the girls," Phoebe retorted.

I had to give her that. That old man had run circles around us. "The walker certainly misled us," I admitted.

"We better hurry," Josie prodded. "The haunted house is set to start in one hour. If we want to search the basement, we better do it now."

"I can't leave Jake and Mitchell up here by themselves," I protested. "I'll stay with them."

"No you won't." Buddy nudged me toward the basement door. "Elliott can stay with the boys. He'll holler if he needs us."

Elliott's frown matched mine. "Uncle Buddy," he started to argue, but Buddy headed him off.

"No. You stay up here. Knowing you, you'll want to go through the haunted house later. You won't want the experience spoiled by knowing too much."

"I already know everything," he protested. "I helped design it."

He had too. More than once I'd heard one of the decorating committee call out to get Elliott on the phone for his input. The kid possessed a diabolical mind, and they'd taken full advantage of it.

"Never mind," Buddy told him again. "We need you up here. Keep Jake and Mitchell in the kitchen, and the basement door stays open. Make sure Mitchell doesn't go down the steps. I mean it." Buddy frowned at his young nephew. "I'm counting on you to take care of those boys."

It's a guy thing. I swear I saw Elliott's chest puff up, and that quick he became the protector. Just what Buddy intended. Rats. That meant I would be going to the basement.

One by one, we filed through the basement door heading downwards. In my mind I heard the music of a death march. Dum dum de dum.

"Lot's different from the house on South Douglas, isn't it?" Josie called over her shoulder.

We'd held our own Halloween parties in the basement of that house, and to enter the basement we had to go through a trap door in the dining room closet. At the time we considered it a very cool feature. I was grateful this house didn't possess one.

I intended to be last in line, but Buddy spoiled my plan. He waited for me to go ahead of him. He knows me too well. I probably would have joined Elliott at the kitchen table if I could have gotten away with it. With Buddy behind me, my escape plan faded.

The decorating committee had used sheets and blankets to partition the basement into a maze of little tunnels and rooms. "We could search for an hour, and he could elude us by stepping behind sheets. This is impossible." I cringed at the sound of my own whining.

We spread out, working our way from the outside in. I ignored the shrieks, grunts, and moans, hoping the others would ignore the similar sounds I made. The ladies had outdone themselves on special effects. The prize for screaming came from Josie. She is phobic about spiders, and there were a lot of them hanging on strings from the rafters. Her periodic shrieks kept us well informed as to her progress. I'm glad Mom couldn't hear the swearing. I didn't know my sister ever used that kind of language.

We met back in the center of the basement, a big area dominated by a cardboard casket. I'm ashamed to say we all screamed when a body sat up.

"Sorry." The girl spoke. Her stark white face enhanced by black mascara ringing her eyes gave her a ghoulish look. Yards of white satiny material shrouded her body. Her hair hung limp and stringy around her face. I recognized Karen Wright.

"Did your mother really give you permission to do this?" Skepticism tinged my voice.

"Yes, she did." Karen spoke, her voice just short of snippy. "Mrs. Franklin called and made sure. Mom said she might not agree with the concept, but if I wanted to do it, she would give her permission. Mom is good that way. I'm allowed to have my own opinions."

Ouch. "Sorry, just checking." I knew I didn't want to lock horns with Allyson over anything, especially if it involved one of her children.

"What exactly do you do?" Phoebe is a peacekeeper. She changed the subject.

"It's really cool." Karen perked up, a nice change from her earlier prickly defensiveness. "Every time they bring somebody through the haunted house, they walk through here. I moan and groan and rise up slowly from the casket. It will scare the little kids silly." A grin lit her face and I shuddered. It must be true the young are truly bloodthirsty. They haven't lived long

260

enough to know grief and despair. They don't yet fear death.

I sighed. More screams in my future. Maybe I would take Jake and go over to Katie's. Ann Richardson, coming through the sheets, distracted me. She stopped, startled at seeing all of us.

"Is anything wrong?" I could hear panic underlying her words. In less than an hour, a long line of children would be led through the basement. She certainly wouldn't want complications at this late date.

We told her about the possibility that Mr. Whitaker might wander through at an inopportune time. She took the news well and promised to inform everyone working the party to be on the lookout for him. We retreated to the kitchen and gathered back around the kitchen table. I can't remember the last time I'd endured such a useless day.

Some of us, not me, thought about supper and busied themselves finding food for everybody. I slumped at the table, lost in my gloomy thoughts. Someone else filled plates for Mitchell and Jake. I did stir myself to feed Jake. I've done it so many years I could do it in my sleep. Sunk in my own thoughts, I didn't notice his worried eyes or his grunts to get my attention. Did we still have a ninety-one-year-old man hiding out in our house? Had we missed him? Or had he sneaked out before we got organized to hunt for him?

I found the idea of the old man eluding us ludicrous, but he must have because none of us had caught so much as a glimpse of him. The only evidence of his presence came from finding a rumpled bed on the third floor that indicated someone might have slept there and a toilet seat lid in the up position. Buddy and Elliott denied using it, and I, unfortunately, believed them.

Outside we heard excited voices as happy, exuberant children started arriving. I shuddered and sank even deeper into dark thoughts. I heard voices moving into the basement. Shrill shrieks and laughter drifted up through the floor boards. The haunted house seemed to be a success.

"How late does the haunted house run?" Josie asked. "When will it be over?"

That question caught my ear. Sometime this evening it really would be over.

Phoebe responded, "It shuts down at eight. Tomorrow the cleanup crew will show up and we can forget this ever happened."

Three hours. I only had to get through three more hours, and life would return to normal. A smile tugged at my lips and hope surged through my body. No more interruptions. No more ladies tramping through the house asking for tools. Elliott would stop putting on masks and popping up and scaring the daylight out of us.

Another shrill scream lifted the floor boards, not a child this time. This was a full-blown, wicked-loud, adult scream that put Josie's best efforts to shame. Hope fled and dread came rushing back. I watched Buddy, Phoebe, Josie, and Roni bolt for the basement door. Me? I was getting really tired of hearing screams.

Chapter Thirty One
Bones in the Casket

Everybody headed for the basement door. I grabbed
Mitchell and swung him off his feet. "No way, little guy,
you stay here with Jake."

He started to argue with me, but he's a smart child,
and he recognized this wasn't the time to argue with
his Aunt Charly.

I sat him back down at the kitchen table and put
some cookies and milk in front of him. I didn't trust
him not to bolt for the basement door, so I kept a close
eye on him.

Jake grunted, catching my attention. He flicked
his eyes to a glass sitting on the table, then back to
me. I didn't respond fast enough, so he repeated the
movement with rapid insistence.

"I know, I know. You need a drink." Jake's eyes
flew upwards and I felt guilty. The speed of his yes
signal told me how thirsty he was, and I tried to
remember the last drink I'd given him. "I'm sorry," I
apologized and held the glass for him. While he drank,
I strained my ears to hear sounds from the basement.

I could hear voices, the words so rapid and unintelligible they might have been speaking Chinese. Footsteps pounded up the stairs, too light and rapid to be my brother.

"Aunt Charly?" Elliott bounded into the kitchen. "Uncle Buddy needs you in the basement."

"No way, Elliott."

Jake grunted. I turned to him, and he raised his eyes rapidly letting me know he wanted more. I gave him another drink. "I'm not leaving Mitchell and Jake by themselves."

"I'll stay with them." Elliott pulled out a chair next to Mitchell and threw himself onto it.

I cocked an eyebrow at him. "You're willingly offering to stay up here? Why?"

"Mom said I could come up here and sit with Jake and Mitchell or I could spend the evening helping Dad at the café."

Elliott's face left me no doubts on his opinion of cleaning tables on Halloween. I hastily swallowed a giggle. "I feel for you, I do, but I don't want to go down to the basement. I'll take care of the boys."

Elliott shook his head. "Won't work. I'm stuck up here and you need to go downstairs." His blue eyes turned so serious I felt fear skitter across my neck. "You really do," he urged.

I offered Jake another drink. He gave a small negative head shake. I put the glass on the table. "Okay, I believe you. Tell you what." I handed him my cell phone. "You call in everybody you can think of. I have a feeling we're going to need the whole family here tonight."

Elliott took the phone from me, pulling the stored numbers up with ease. He should know how; he programmed it for me. "I'll do it but I don't think Uncle Claude will appreciate it."

I froze at the top of the basement stairs and turned toward him. "What did you say?"

Elliot held the phone to his ear, looking at me with a clear, steady gaze. "Nothing. Just go downstairs and see."

Before I could ask further questions, he spoke into the phone. "Aunt Mary Lee?" I sighed and headed down stairs.

Phoebe, Buddy, Josie, Roni, and Katie stood as far from the cardboard casket as they could manage and still be inside the blanketed area. I'm good at non-verbal communication. I have to be, living with a child who can't speak. Faster than words, I registered their body language and followed their gaze to the casket. What I saw stopped me in my tracks. "Where's Karen?"

One by one, they dragged their eyes from the box and looked at me. Disbelief and the dawning of worry and anger showed in varying degrees on their faces. Where Karen had lain reposed a pile of bones, the skull placed with care on top, staring at us with empty sockets.

I shuddered. "I take it that's our missing body? No hope that skull is the one Elliott brought over?"

"We couldn't be that lucky," Buddy muttered. "From what I can see, this is the real deal. Looks like the spook house will be closed until further notice."

"We can expect Uncle Claude back?" After our last experience, talking to Uncle Claude was the last thing I wanted to do.

Everybody nodded. Nobody looked happy. Josie spoke. "At least this time we have proof. The bones are here, and we're not letting them out of our sight until someone in authority shows up."

"What happened to Karen?" I asked again.

"We don't know." Buddy shook his head. "She was here; now she isn't. The ladies were lining up the children, getting them ready to come through the spook house. Ann is the one who screamed. She brought the first group of kids through, found the bones, and let out a blood-curdling screech. She herded everybody out and hasn't been back."

"Has anybody called Uncle Claude yet?" From the way the others cringed and avoided eye contact, I figured they weren't any happier about calling him than I was.

Phoebe sighed. "I'll go check with Ann to see if anybody has called yet. If not, I'll get hold of him." She gave the bones one last glance, pushed aside the blanket hiding the outside stairs, and moved out of sight.

Katie may be the youngest in the family, but she's also one of the most analytical. She waved a hand at the bones. "Why would anybody dig up a grave? Why would they take the bones? Why would they put them in your basement?"

A voice coming from behind a blanket answered her. My shriek would have embarrassed me if it hadn't been drowned out by the others, my brother included.

A blanket hiding the interior of the basement moved, and Old Ansel stepped through. With slow steps he moved to the table holding the cardboard casket and the pile of bones. He swept his hat off and held it in one hand. With his other hand he gave the skull a gentle pat. "I knew her, you know." His blue eyes grew shiny and wet. "She was pretty and nice to me, never said a mean word to me. I liked her." He wiped his eyes with the back of his hand.

"Where did you come from?" Josie's eyes narrowed. "How long have you been here?"

Ansel shot a quick glance at her then looked back at the pile of bones. "I've been here awhile looking for Mr. Whitaker. I can't find him." He raised his eyes again, bouncing to each of us. "I think he's hiding but I don't know where. He's looking for the book."

"What book?" Rhonda frowned. "What would he need a book for?"

"He called it a journal," Ansel explained. "He hid it a long time ago."

Buddy regarded Ansel. "Why have you been following me around?"

Ansel gave a start, and for a minute I thought he'd make a break for freedom rather than answer Buddy's question. Without thought we moved, effectively shutting off all possible escape routes.

I watched the expressions flit across Ansel's face. I could tell the minute he decided to talk. With a sigh he relaxed and spoke. "I knew someone was looking for Mr. Whitaker's book. When someone bothered Aunt Clarissa's grave, I thought it was you hunting for the book. If you found it, I wanted to know."

Buddy frowned. "Why would you think that? I never even met Mr. Whitaker before. Why would I mess up the cemetery? I have to take care of it."

With careful hands Ansel laid his hat next to the bones and reached deep into his pocket. He pulled out a handful of papers and handed them to Buddy. We crowded closer to look. Each note bore a crudely lettered message, four in all. As he read them, Buddy passed them on to Josie, who handed them to Katie, and finally they came to me.

The first message read: *I know what you did. I know where you did it. I know where you hid it.*

Message two read: *Justice will prevail. The truth will be revealed.*

Message three: *She doesn't lie forgotten. Her death will be avenged.*

Message 4: *I know it wasn't an accident. Your only escape is death.*

"Oooh," Josie groaned. "I don't like the sound of this."

I didn't either. "Why would you connect these notes with Buddy?"

Ansel shuffled his feet and wouldn't look at any of us. "Every time I found a note, I saw Mr. Russell.

Katie spoke. "You thought Buddy wrote these?"

Ansel nodded. "He takes care of the graves. I thought he found out where Mr. Whitaker buried the journal." Ansel's eyes darted around, seeming to check the dark corners. He lowered his voice, and we leaned closer to hear him better. "I saw where he hid it, you know."

"How old were you?" Roni cocked her head, gazing at him with eyes full of curiosity.

Ansel frowned, thinking hard. "I'm not good at numbers. It happened on Halloween. I remember that." He looked down at the pile of bones. I don't know about the others, but I cringed when I saw him reach out to stroke the skull. I could almost see hair, so gently his hand moved, almost loving in his touch.

"She was a pretty girl. Always nice to me, you know?" He looked at us and his eyes glistened wetly in the dim light. "She never treated me like a dummy. The boys did." He gave a nervous look at the dark shadows and whispered, "Even Mr. Whitaker. But after the accident, he had to be nice to me. He knew I could tell his secrets." He opened his mouth, and it's a wonder we all didn't fall over, so closely we leaned toward him to hear what those secrets were.

"What's going on?" Logan's voice boomed from the darkness.

The chorus of shrieks and yells that answered him did full justice to the haunted house setting. Ansel bolted. I barely stopped myself from following him.

I listened to the babble of voices as everyone filled Logan in on the bones. He may be retired from the Air Force, but every once in awhile he does something that reminds me of his military training. Tonight was such a time.

He took in the scene and listened to the explanations. At the end he gave a silent nod of understanding and spoke. "I'll stay here and keep watch. You all head upstairs and tell everybody what's going on." His eyes stabbed each of us. "Find that old

269

man. I have a lot of questions for him. I'm sure Claude will too. I'll fill him in on what's going on as soon as he gets here."

For one short moment we froze, our eyes darting around the circle, and then we ran. I'm not proud of it but it's a fact. In the wake of Uncle Claude's imminent arrival, we scattered like cockroaches in the light

Chapter Thirty Two
Enter the Clan

We hit the basement stairs at an undignified run with Buddy elbowing us out of the way so he could go up first. Some things never change. I tumbled into the kitchen close on his heels and stopped at the top to catch my breath.

One glance around the room calmed me. I'd left the kitchen with Elliott, Mitchell, and Jake sitting at the kitchen table. I reentered to find the upstairs crowded with people. Somehow, and I shouldn't be surprised by this, one phone call leads to another, and before you know it, every relative in a thirty mile radius has gravitated to your house. Even I, as used to the family as I am, can be awestruck by this gathering of the clan.

Voices and laughter assaulted my ears. The doorbell ringing and doors opening and shutting added to the din. I didn't even bother to count the sisters, in-laws, nieces, nephews, aunts, uncles, and cousins. I long ago gave up trying to figure out the number. It's enough to know that when the call goes out, family responds. At least my family does.

The noise grew deafening until someone let out an ear-splitting whistle. I hoped the crowd sufficiently hid the person responsible. The downside of my family is it's hard to escape the teasing.

Those capable of organizing took charge. That didn't include me. Organizing is at the bottom of my skill list. Thankfully, I have several family members who excel.

Mary Lee raised her voice. "We need to break into groups. I think the kids should look for Karen."

"Only junior high or older," Samantha added. "The younger kids can go trick or treating if accompanied by an adult, so we'll need some volunteers for the little ones."

"Won't they be at the party?" Katie's face is as expressive as her voice.

"We don't even know if the party will continue," Samantha answered. "It's possible Uncle Claude will send everybody out of the yard."

"Just as possible he'll keep everybody here so he can question them," Buddy muttered. I shuddered at the thought; snagged a sandwich off the tray Patti carried by, and hid behind Jake's chair.

He grunted at me to get my attention. I leaned forward to see what he wanted. "Are you hungry? Thirsty?" He shook his head, but the intensity of his gaze told me he wanted to tell me something. I followed his gaze, straight as a beeline, to the dining room. I didn't think he wanted to talk to a person. His eyes didn't follow anybody moving. As far as I could tell, he was focused on the dining room table.

I started listing everything I could see. With each item I listed, he wound up tighter. His grunt and headshake got progressively angrier. "I'm sorry, Jake." I stuffed the last bite of the sandwich into my mouth. "I give up. I've listed everything on the table."

He shot me a look of true anger, a rare sight on his face, and turned back to stare toward the dining room. Watching my family split up into organized groups distracted me. The junior high and high school faction, accompanied by older cousins, headed out the door on their way to locate Karen. I noticed they all had sacks in hand, even the older ones, which told me they all intended to collect treats while they hunted.

Ten adults congregated at the foot of the stairs, and with half an ear I listened to them plan a strategy to search the house from the attic down to locate Mr. Whitaker. With what my mom would have called the noise of a thundering herd of elephants, they headed for the attic.

Roni stayed behind. It looked like she, Phoebe, Samantha, and Katie were in charge of the little ones. "Is anybody left out back?" I asked Phoebe. "I see you brought in a group with you from the backyard."

Phoebe shrugged. "Uncle Claude isn't there yet, but Logan took charge and said the children could go trick or treating as long as there was a list of names so he can locate them if he needs to question them. He wanted the adults in charge to stay until released. The volunteers could leave if they came back by to be questioned. Logan isn't worried about Karen. He thinks it's a Halloween prank. So the children who came have left. I brought our kids in so we could take them trick or treating."

I smiled at Phoebe's use of the word 'our'. It doesn't matter if the children are sons, daughters, nieces, nephews, or cousins. They're family and we all feel the connection equally.

Above our heads we heard pounding footsteps and doors slamming and, once in awhile, a shrill, quick shriek. My family does what needs to be done. That doesn't mean we're brave about it.

"No." Mitchell's loud voice snagged my attention. He pulled away from Roni and ran toward Jake and me. "I'm staying with Jake."

Roni's expressive face revealed confusion. "You don't want to go trick or treating? No candy?"

Mitchell pushed between me and Jake's chair. He grabbed hold of the handles and using the wheels for steps, climbed up the side of the chair. I caught him before he could sit on the tray. The chair was strong, but I didn't think the tray would hold Mitchell's sturdy three-year-old body. Not safely, anyway.

"Whoa, little guy." He wiggled in my arms, and I stood him back on the wheel. He hung on like a little monkey. "What's going on here?"

He is his mother's son. As theatrical as she was at three, he has her beat. He gazed at me with tragic, big blue eyes. "We can't go out. The man might get us."

"What man?" Roni's smiling face turned grim.

Jake grunted at me again and, catching my eyes, turned a deliberate stare back to the dining room table. "What?" I felt bad at the impatience that tinged my voice. The only time I get frustrated with him is when

274

I can't figure out what he wants, and he definitely wanted something.

I moved out from behind the chair and crouched by him, bringing my eyes down to his level. Maybe seeing the room from where he sat would help. I saw my sisters hovering close by, but none of them stood in his line of sight. The only thing he could possibly be looking at was the dining room table.

Mitchell watched me with unblinking eyes. I still heard the distant roar of footsteps, now moving across the second level of the house. My little nephew reached across the tray and poked me. "Aunt Charly."

I ignored him, still crouched and trying to figure out what Jake wanted to tell me.

"Aunt Charly!" Mitchell poked me so hard I nearly fell over.

"What?" I clutched at Jake's tray and regained my balance. "I'm busy here, Mitchell. Jake needs something and I can't figure out what it is."

"I want to know why Mitchell is afraid of a man." Roni pulled the rocking chair around and sat down next to us. She reached for her son. He tightened his grip on Jake's chair and resisted Roni picking him up.

Jake turned his gaze back on me. It disturbed me to see the anguish on his. He stared into my eyes then turned to stare intently at his small cousin. I don't know how to explain, but I could see it happen. Without words, without even body language that I could see, my seventeen year old non-verbal son communicated with my three-year-old nephew.

Mitchell's big blue eyes stared into my son's golden-brown gaze. Then he nodded. "I'm trying," he told Jake. "She's not listening very good." Jake rolled his eyes toward the ceiling in silent agreement.

"I am too," I protested. "I can't figure out what he wants off the dining room table. I've listed everything I can see."

Mitchell gave as disgusted a sound as a three-year-old is capable of. "Not the table. He's looking at the window."

As one, all eyes turned back to the dining room. I saw it now, across the table to the row of windows lining the wall facing the driveway, the windows with the extra-wide sills that held potted plants. And leaning against a terra cotta pot was a sheet of paper.

Katie stood closest to the dining room and reached the paper first. Mitchell hopped off Jake's wheel and helped me push the chair into the dining room. We crowded around her as she read: *The old man is gone. Look for him in the cemetery.*

The thundering herd poured down the stairs, both the front stairs and the back. "Perfect timing." Katie spoke. "You all can quit hunting now. Our missing visitor isn't here any longer."

"How do we really know that's true?" Phoebe reached for the paper, and Katie handed it to her. "Just because this note says he's gone, is he really?"

Everyone fell silent, and with a crowd as large as we had, that was a miracle in itself. I looked down at Jake and Mitchell. It occurred to me that these two boys were perhaps the only two that might have seen who left the note. I moved from behind the chair to face Jake. This time Mitchell reached for Roni, and she picked him up.

"Did Mr. Whitaker really leave?" I asked Jake. His eyes flew up and Mitchell nodded in agreement.

"He was scary." Mitchell's arms went around Roni's neck. "He told us to be quiet. We were, weren't we, Jake?" Again Jake's eyes flew upwards.

"Did Mr. Whitaker leave this note?" Jake did what I call a wind-up. His left arm bent at the elbow, his head turned to the right, and it took him a minute to shake his head 'no'.

Questions erupted as everybody talked at once. Jake ignored them all and stared at me with a steady, intense gaze. I could feel his frustration at needing to talk and being unable to. It had to be agony for him. I know it was for me.

"Did you see who left the note?" Buddy's voice broke through the babble of voices. Jake's eyes flew up and that silenced us all.

"Was it someone in the family?" Jake shook his head 'no'. "But someone you know?" Jake's eyes went up.

"Great," Phoebe muttered. "Everybody and his neighbor have been through this house in the last twenty-four hours. How do we figure out who it was?"

You'd think with fifteen people standing there naming off every name they could think of that someone would hit on the right one, but Jake said 'no' to them all.

Mitchell tuned us all out by turning his face to Roni's shoulder and snuggling in. "No," he mumbled when asked if he knew who left the note. "I won't tell. The man said not to."

Mitchell pulled back far enough to stare into his mother's eyes. "He scared me." Then he buried his face against her shoulder and wouldn't look at any of us.

Chapter Thirty Four
The Hunt

I tuned out the chaos, unable right then to deal with the overload of information, from finding out our house had been a funeral parlor, to the Halloween Haunted House inhabiting our basement, to the open grave at the cemetery and the discovery of the missing bones only to have them appear in our fruit cellar then to disappear again. Add to the mix the vandalism to Buddy's home and vehicles and Phoebe's mutilated cow. I couldn't forget the mysterious vanishing of the church secretary and now a missing child as well as the unknown whereabouts of the elusive Mr. Whitaker.

How could so many things happen in such a short amount of time? More importantly, why? Without giving it any thought, I pulled Jake's chair backward and spun it around to take him back to the living room. We returned to the rocking chair in the corner. I plopped myself down. Leaning back, I placed a hand over his and sat there, the gentle movement of the chair soothing me. I tried to put the recent happenings into some sort of order.

Peripherally, I noticed the children being herded out the door by Phoebe, Samantha, Katie, and Roni. Mitchell must have agreed to go along if his mother went with him. Mary Lee, Aunt Ellen, Josie, Buddy, Jessi, and Patti stood huddled in the hallway.

Mary Lee's voice rang out. "All right, here's what we'll do. Some of us will stay here and answer the door. The rest of you go drive through the cemetery and see if you can find Mr. Whitaker."

I watched Mary Lee and Patti head for the kitchen. If I knew my sister, Mary Lee wouldn't be able to relax until the food was put away and the kitchen back in order. Patti, good friend that she is, would help her. Aunt Ellen started emptying bags of candy into a big empty bowl sitting on small table in the entry way, a job that should have been done hours earlier.

While she did that, Buddy, Jessi, and Josie donned jackets. "Let's go," Buddy called out.

I leaned back in the chair. "Have fun. Watch out for the bogeyman."

Buddy frowned at me, impatience putting a barb in his voice. "Grab a coat, Sis. You're going too."

"Uh-uh." My feet hit the floor, bringing the rocking chair to a halt. "I'm not going near the cemetery, especially at night."

I could see the wheels turning in my brother's head. I determined that this time he wouldn't convince me to do something I didn't want to do. I was an adult now, darn it, surely old enough to withstand whatever manipulation my brother would come up with.

It proved disgustingly easy for him. It wasn't my brother that caused me to hit the floor running. What motivated me was the flashing red lights coming through the dining room windows. Uncle Claude had arrived, and if the red lights were any indication, he'd arrived accompanied by one or more squad cars.

I barely took time to drop a kiss on top of Jake's head before I followed Buddy, Josie, and Jessi out the front door. I'm not proud of the furtive crawling we did to keep to the shadows. I am proud that we managed to do it without groans. I wish I could say the same about the giggles. Never in our whole lives have my brother and I been able to do anything together without laughter. Adding Josie to the mix made it worse. It pleased me to see that Jessi possessed the same genetic makeup for laughter. Blood does tell.

We crouched low beneath the porch railing, not wanting the strobes of red lights of the squad cars to illuminate us. I whispered, "How are we going to get to the cemetery? Whose car are we driving? It's a cinch I can't get to the van. There are three cars parked behind me, and two of them are squad cars."

"Shhh," Josie shoved me. I wobbled and caught the porch rail to steady my crouch.

Further words died in my throat as the porch light lit us up. With started yelps we bailed over the side of the porch and landed in the shrubs. With the grace of hippos, we scrambled free and ran for the dark shadows of the trees. Buddy kept running, and we followed him like lemmings to the cliff. We didn't slow down until we had a block of houses behind us. You'd think grown adults would behave with more sense, but for those few minutes of blind flight, we were kids again, playing games on Halloween night. The laughter that spilled from our throats felt good.

"Do you want to stop at the café?" Buddy asked Josie.

"What for?" She should have known better.

"To make sure you didn't pick up any spiders when we fell in the bushes."

Jessi and I moved back a few steps. We knew Josie would explode, and she did.

"I wish I could see better," I whispered to Jessi.

"Me too," Jessi replied. "It's not so much the dancing around and pulling at her hair. It's the wallops she's getting in on Buddy that I'd like to see."

Josie's spider phobia is legendary in our family. We all know how to set her off. By the time she settled down and Buddy could breathe again from laughing at her, I realized we were within sight of the Weary cemetery. At least, as well as it could be seen in the dark of night.

"Did anybody think to bring a flashlight?" Jessi spoke up. "Because I don't think I want to trip over any headstones in the dark. With our luck, one of us would break something."

Her words stopped us in our tracks. I knew I didn't have a light on me, and from Josie's silence and Buddy's cussing, I figured they didn't either.

"Let's go home and tell them we looked and call it done," I suggested.

"And maybe leave an old man alone in the cemetery? That would be a real nice thing to do." Disapproval of my cowardice dripped from Josie's voice.

"Can we get lights at your folk's house?" Buddy asked Jessi.

"Sure," she answered. "I think Pop has a lantern in the workshop." In the dim light thrown off by the corner streetlight, I saw her teeth flash in a grin. "I get to carry it," and she was off moving so fast that we decided to wait for her rather than try to catch her.

She returned faster than I'd hoped for. The longer I could put off going into a cemetery at night, the better.

"I found the lantern." She held it up and switched it on. The light spilling from it seemed far brighter than the streetlight. She switched it off and reached into her pocket. "I found two regular flashlights too.

I don't know how it happened, but Buddy and Josie beat me to the grab, which meant we entered the cemetery gates with three of us armed with light and me walking in the dark. A feeling that felt all too familiar.

Walking on the road was easy. The others kept telling me to move away after I stepped on their heels a few times.

"It wouldn't happen if I had a light of my own," I protested, but none of them took the hint, so I continued to crowd whomever I stood closest to. Tough, I thought, if they didn't like it. I didn't like being here.

"Where should we look?" Jessi asked Buddy. "You know the cemetery better than we do. Do you know where the Whitaker section is?"

"Yes, but I think a better place to look might be where the light is."

"What light?" Josie asked the question. We stopped walking and looked first at Buddy and then toward where he was looking.

One by one, they clicked their lights off until we stood huddled in the dark of the cemetery looking across the headstones to where a dim flickering light beckoned to us. Clouds skittered across the sky. The big round disc of moon peeked out. The wind picked up and sent shivers across the goose bumps that popped up on my skin. The faint scent of a skunk tickled my nose.

Buddy snapped his flashlight back on. Josie and Jessi's came on almost simultaneously.

"Is there any way to get there by the road?" Jessi asked Buddy. He shook his head just barely visible to me in the dim light.

"No. We'll have to head straight for it."

"Oh, crap," Josie muttered. "First one to fall in a grave is a rotten egg."

Nobody laughed.

"I'm not walking last." The idea of having dark at my back made me want to turn tail and run home. I'd rather face Uncle Claude and a thousand questions than have darkness behind me. "I get in the middle or I'm not going." A false statement if I'd ever uttered one before. Close to light was better than total darkness.

"Fine," Jessi agreed," Buddy first, then you, then Josie. I'll walk last."

"That works for me." And I fell into step behind Buddy.

Nobody spoke as we wove our way through the headstones. Jessi's lantern threw a halo of white light around us. The walking proved easier than I expected.

"I know where we are." Buddy spoke up, his voice sounding loud in the dark night. "That light has to be at the grave where the bones were taken."

As we moved closer, I saw he was right. Even in the dark I recognized the big open hole. The small lantern flickering at the head of the grave could have been a twin to the one Jessi carried.

Step by reluctant step, we drew closer until we stood at the edge looking down. Poor Mr. Whitaker, looking even frailer than the last time I saw him, lay peacefully in the grave.

We stood at the edge looking in. I struggled to think what to do next. We'd found him. Now what did we do with him?

Before I could ask, my brother reached out and goosed my ribs, at the same time giving an unholy squawk in my ear. I shrieked and spun around to run, lost my footing as well as my balance, and toppled backward into the grave. As I fell, I reached out and grabbed hold of the first solid thing I came into contact with.

Buddy gave another unholy shriek as I pulled him into the open hole with me.

The fall stunned me. As I lay there trying to breathe, I saw my brother glaring at me from the other side of Mr. Whitaker. Just bad luck we'd fallen in such a way that we flanked the old man's frail body. *Body?* I gave one horrified look then attempted to fly. I failed. Buddy got in my way and we both slid back. I'm the shortest member of my family. My brother doesn't top me by much. I'd have died if he'd gotten out of the grave and left me there with Mr. Whitaker.

"Get us out of here," I yelled, mostly toward Josie and Jessi, but for anybody who might be within ear-range.

I had to wait for them to stop laughing. If I'd been near enough, I'd have pulled them both in just to show them what it felt like.

Jessi regained her composure first. She held the lantern out so the light filled the hole. "Is he dead?"

Buddy and I locked eyes. Was Mr. Whitaker dead?

"You check," I told my brother. "It's your fault we're in here."

"No way," he protested. "You're the one who trained as an emergency medical technician."

"My card expired. I'm not legally obligated to check anymore. You do it."

"Somebody do it." Josie moved closer to the edge, being careful not to risk falling. "You have to make sure."

I glared at my brother. "If I get down there and you scare me again, I'll hurt you. I also took karate classes."

My brother likes to tease, but he can be serious when he has to. "Don't worry. I wouldn't do that to you. Not now. We'll both check."

We looked down at Mr. Whitaker, stretched out and looking oddly boneless in the dark shadows cast by the lantern glow and the weak light from Buddy's flashlight. Inch by inch, Buddy to the right of Mr. Whitaker and me to the left, we moved closer. More than anything in the world, I didn't want to kneel next to that body, but Buddy dropped to his knees. I followed suit. Fair is fair. I waited. Buddy waited.

"Do it," he hissed at me.

"You do it," I hissed back. I tried to see if Mr. Whitaker was breathing. I leaned forward. Closer and closer, my brother and I moved until our heads almost bumped together, throwing a dark shadow across Mr. Whitaker's face.

I held my breath, hoping if I held still I'd be able to see if the old man still breathed. Without warning, his eyelids snapped open. I heard Buddy gasp. The next thing I knew we were scrambling and jumping at the side of the grave.

Buddy almost made it out, but I snagged his pant leg and hauled him back down. No way would I be in this hole with a ninety-one year old man by myself. Mr. Whitaker might not be a dead body, but at his age he was close enough.

"I'll be more help on top, Sis. Honest," Buddy protested in vain.

I wasn't buying that line. "No way, if I'm down here, so are you."

"Help me up." For an old man, Mr. Whitaker had a loud voice. I didn't know how many more shocks my heart could take.

With reluctance, Buddy and I turned toward Mr. Whitaker. He held his hands out to us. "Don't just stand there. Get me up."

I sighed and heard my brother do the same. We had no choice. Buddy took his left arm, I grabbed his right, and we hauled the old man to his feet. He wobbled and shook for a minute then pulled himself upright. Grudging respect moved in me.

"Now get me out of here," he demanded. My respect fled, leaving me irritated.

"How?" I looked over at Buddy.

"He doesn't weigh much." Buddy shrugged. "Maybe we can boost him up, and Josie and Jessi can pull him out."

"That's one plan." I shot Buddy a look that would have shriveled him if could have seen it in the dim light.

With a lot of grunts, groans, and swearing from Buddy, we managed to lift Mr. Whitaker high enough for Jessi and Josie to grab his arms. With them pulling, Buddy and I were able to grab him around the knees, and with one hand under his feet, we raised him out of the hole.

"Can you boost me out?" I asked my brother.

A disgusted grunt answered me. "You're asking me that after you hauled me back in?"

"We know you can get out," I protested. "You almost did it before, but I'm too short. I need help."

"Hey," Josie shouted, interrupting our bickering, "where are you going?"

Buddy and I backed up a few steps so we could see more than dirt. Mr. Whitaker, step by slow shuffling step, was walking away. Josie grabbed at his arm. He brushed impatiently at her.

Jessi tried to reason with him. "It's dark." She spoke, her voice calm and soothing. "You can't walk in the dark. You'll fall and break a hip."

Mr. Whitaker hit at her, his aim bad and his strength weak. "Leave me alone. I know what I'm doing."

"Grab him," Jessi shouted. "He's making a break for it. They reached for Mr. Whitaker, and the old man surprised them with a burst of energy. He yelled, thrust out both arms, and sent Josie and Jessi tumbling into the grave.

Chapter Thirty Five
Putting the Pieces Together

Buddy and I broke their fall. Can life get any more unfair? One by one, we untangled ourselves and rose to our feet. Thank goodness, the flashlights had fallen with them. Hysteria tickled my voice. "Let there be light."

Josie brushed at herself in much the same way she'd slapped at imaginary spiders earlier. "Great," she muttered, "grave dirt. Is there anything worse?" She raised her head, and even in the dim light, I shriveled under her glare as she said in her best Oliver Hardy voice said, "This is another fine mess you've gotten me into."

"This isn't my fault." I glared back at her with little hope of matching her ferocity. Josie's expressions have always been more potent than mine. "I didn't want to come here in the first place. Blame it on Buddy." I turned around, examining the grave once more to see if any footholds had magically appeared. "How could you let a frail, old man push you both in at the same time?"

"He's a crafty old man." Jessie held her lantern higher, lighting up the entire hole. "And fast. It was just bad luck we were standing too close to the edge. I'll remember that in the future." I saw her frown as she leaned forward. She muttered, almost in an afterthought, " Note to self, stay away from open graves."

Her voice died away and she pushed past Buddy. "Look. There's something over here."

"If it's a spider, I'm out of here if I have to climb on your head to do it." Josie pushed closer to me. I moved to put Buddy between us. He's taller anyway.

"No." Jessie set the lantern down. "I see something sticking up. Did that old man try to bury something?"

Jessie dropped to her knees; the rest of us leaned over to watch. "The dirt is soft. Somebody had to put this here recently. Is this what Old Man Whitaker came here for?"

I heard, low as the night breeze, my sister mutter, "She's digging in grave dirt."

"Got it." Jessie raised her hand in triumph. A gallon-sized plastic bag dangled from her fingers.

"What's in it?" Before Buddy could take the bag, lights lit up the sky. Red flashing lights.

"Maybe we can hide until they leave," I hissed.

Heads swiveled toward me. "Where do you suggest we do that?" Jessie's voice held exquisite sweetness. A sound she reserves for the terminally stupid.

"We're already in a hole," Josie added. "Should we pull it in after ourselves?"

"I want out." Buddy reached down and grabbed Jessie's lantern. "I don't care who does the pulling, but

I want on the topside of this grave." He held the lantern high and waved it. "Help. Over here."

Josie and Jessie added their voices to his. I figured since they yelled loud enough to wake the dead, I didn't need to help.

Uncle Claude loomed over the hole. He stood there, looking down at us and grinning. It's not just Mom's side of the family that inherited laughter. My dad's side got a good dose of their own.

"I'm really getting tired of being laughed at." I might as well have talked to air. Nobody responded.

"We'll have you out in a minute." Uncle Claude leaned over and for a small nano-second I wished he'd join us. That would wipe the grin off his face.

He turned his head and spoke to someone out of sight. "Use the ladder. It's on the ground next to your feet."

A moment later, Uncle Claude and a deputy slid a ladder over the side. Buddy grabbed it first. As he moved up the rungs, he looked down. "There was a ladder?"

"It wouldn't have made any difference." Jessie moved upwards. "We landed in the grave with you so fast we didn't have time to look around."

"That's right." Josie climbed next. "If we'd had time, we could have rescued you."

Her voice faded away. Darkness closed in around me. They had taken the flashlights. I was in a dark grave, by myself. I gave a soft whimper, leaped for the ladder, and moved up it with impressive speed, dark nipping at my back the whole way.

***

"Why do we have to sit in back?" I asked my uncle. "Why can't we just walk home? We'd get there almost as fast."

Uncle Claude held the back door of the squad car open and waved us forward. "Do I have to remind you I'm the law? What I say goes."

"Just do it, Sis." Buddy moved forward and slid in. Josie followed, then Jessie.

I tried again. "There isn't room for four of us. It will be too crowded. I could just go on home on my own. I know the way."

"Get in." Uncle Claude's voice hardened. "We'd be there already if you'd just cooperate."

I gave up and pushed myself in next to Jessie. "I've never been in the back of a squad car in my life. This is embarrassing."

"Think of it as an adventure," Jessie advised and wiggled around to make more room. "What a story you'll have to tell Hal and Russ when they get back from Australia."

That thought shut me up. I had no intention of ever letting my husband know about this fiasco. I wished I could think of some way to keep the family silent about it too, but I didn't hold much hope of that happening.

Five minutes later, we pulled into the drive-way.

"I thought the party was cancelled," Buddy commented as we piled out of the car and stood looking at a house that appeared to have every light turned on from the third floor to basement, as well as every exterior light including the garage.

We entered the house through the kitchen; the distant sound of raised, excited voices assaulted my ears. So many people talking at once words were indistinguishable.

In the hallway between the dining room and living room, Uncle Claude halted and pointed down the hallway toward the back of the house, the area that Jake and I had claimed as our own. "The only room big enough to hold everybody is the room at the back where the wakes were held."

His words stopped me in my tracks. "What did you say?"

I couldn't hear his answer over the laughter of Josie, Buddy, and Jessi.

Uncle Claude frowned at me, impatient with me delaying him. "The big room at the back of the house is the only room big enough to hold a crowd. That addition was added on when the house was used as a funeral home. Wakes and funerals were held back here."

"That does it." I spoke through clenched teeth. "I am going to buy a sage bundle and smudge every inch of this house."

Only Jessie understood me. Sage is traditionally used to clear the air of psychic energy. To smudge a house is the equivalent of cleaning out psychic dust.

Whether this is true or not is irrelevant. I would feel better once it was done, and the result is all that matters.

"Go for it." Jessi, with obvious effort, stopped laughing. "You do realize you have to clean the house too? Before you smudge? It's a whole process."

"The whole house?" Thinking of three stories and uncounted rooms kept me silent as I followed them down the short hallway, past the staircase, and into the big great room, a room I'd been happy with until this moment.

Until you live with a person in a wheelchair, you don't appreciate space and hardwood floors. Even with furniture strewn about, chairs, a table, lamps, and a loveseat, this room still allowed ample room for the wheelchair to be pushed with ease.

Large tall windows lined the back side, giving Jake a view of trees, shrubs, and flowers. Until this moment I had perceived it as a perfect room. Now, everywhere I looked, I saw caskets. Thankfully, they were closed; even my imagination has limits.

Reality was so much worse. People blocked my view, family members, police officials, and townsfolk. I couldn't begin to count them. I looked for and found Jake. Roni and Mitchell stood by him. I appreciated them watching over him. I saw the pro-party group in one area, the anti-party group on the opposite side of the room.

I recognized Gary Prescott standing next to his very pregnant wife. A cute little boy, looking like a miniature of his father, clung to his pant leg.

I saw Ansel, shabby and worried, bouncing from foot to foot, shredding his hat in his hands. And there, in the center of the room, seated in the only new piece of furniture I owned, sat Evan Whitaker.

Chapter Thirty Five
The Final Pieces

I elbowed my way toward Jake, hugging the wall as best I could in the crowded room. After the grave fiasco, I wanted a long, hot shower, but it didn't look like I'd be getting one soon.

"What did I miss?" I slid into my customary place behind Jake's chair. He turned his head and gave me a 'happy to see you' grin. I wanted to ruffle his hair, but looking at my grave-grimed hands, I refrained. But I grinned back at him, happy to see him too.

Roni rolled her eyes and spoke, raising her voice so I could hear over the dull roar of the crowd. "Uncle Claude called in help from the state police. They're down in the basement taking charge of the bones.

"He rounded up the committee heads." She nodded toward the groups of women. "I have to give him credit. He got both sides in here." She frowned and fell silent. "Sometimes, I think I seriously underestimate Dad's family."

I pondered her words, and, to a certain extent, understood what she meant. I love my dad's family, but when I think relatives, the ones that pop into my head first would all line up on Mom's side.

"Makes sense, I guess." I spoke absently while scanning the roomful of people. "Mom's family had it hard. A lot of siblings, a grandfather that took off for parts unknown for reasons equally unknown. Grandma worked hard to keep it all together. Mom's family took care of themselves. Not a normal kind of upbringing, but it established a close bond that nothing can break. It carried over into our generation."

I gazed through the crowd, picking out various cousins that held a place in my heart more near to brother and sister than cousin. I gave a quiet little thank you to my mother for passing that gift down to us and hoped that it continued into the next generation. Maybe moving back home would create that connection for the cousins living together under one roof, however flawed that roof turned out to be.

Jake grunted and I patted his shoulder. He grunted again, adding a foot kick for emphasis. Mitchell tugged on Roni's leg and lifted his arms. She picked him up.

I rubbed Jake's shoulder, responding to his unspoken demands, but not really paying attention. Raised voices halted our conversation.

"We didn't have anything to do with sabotaging the Halloween party." Allyson Wright's voice easily reached my ears. Curiosity prompted me to move Jake's chair closer. Roni, carrying Mitchell, moved with us.

"Oh, please," Dana Franklin drawled a reply. "Why else did your daughter volunteer to help out if not to be your spy? Taking off before the first group of children went through the haunted house practically guaranteed failure."

"I hate being short," I muttered and slid a sideway's glance at my tall sister who stands a half-inch shy of six feet.

She grinned down at me. "You're not missing much. No blows exchanged yet."

"Sorry," I apologized to Jake, "but I need some help here." With quick ease, I reached down and secured the brakes on his chair. I stepped onto the back wheel and raised myself up to Roni's level. "Not the best position, but I can see now."

Jake whipped his head as far around as he could so he could glare up at me. His body went into full reflex. A loud grunt of protest burst from him.

"I'll get down as fast as I can," I assured him. "I just want to see what's going on."

Brown eyes, usually soft and full of humor, turned dark. He grunted again and his foot kicked out with anger. Accomplishing eye contact, he turned his with deliberate slowness to the side.

I followed his gaze and saw an opening. Jake wanted to see too. I sighed, hopped to the floor, released the brakes, and pushed him forward.

With a minimum of bumping and pushing, people parted, and I moved Jake to a position where he could see. Roni, still carrying Mitchell, moved in our wake.

"My daughter is missing. I don't need to listen to this..." Allyson's angry voice stopped in mid-screech when an even louder shriek reached our ears.

"Put me down. I'll get you for this. See if I don't."

"Darn it," I grumbled to Jake. "If we'd stayed where we were, I'd be able to see who's shrieking like a banshee."

"That's a no-brainer," Roni drawled. She shifted Mitchell from one hip to the other. "The missing body has been returned."

Without thought, and without bothering with the brakes, I hopped back onto the wheel of Jake's chair. One hand on the handle, I balanced precariously. "Oh, my, I hope those boys don't get in trouble."

Jake gave a loud grunt, and I glanced down at him to see his head and neck cranked as far as he could manage. Most of the time, I don't think about what Jake can't do. But at odd times, in strange ways, it hits me. I slid one hand from the chair handle and squeezed his shoulder in wordless sympathy and started a running commentary.

"The screech you hear is Karen. The kids found her and she's not coming willingly. It looks like they rounded up a couple of Keira's classmates, football players by the size of them. They have Karen trussed up, hands and feet, and are carrying her between them like a log of wood. I hope they realize the police are here, and they don't get arrested."

"No danger of that," Roni added. "They're standing her on her feet and melting into the crowd as we speak. Ghosts couldn't vanish faster."

I nodded. "I doubt anybody will squeal on them. Karen can make any accusation she wants, but with the others denying, I don't think the police will waste much time trying to find them."

I tuned out the noise, looked around the room, and didn't envy Uncle Claude trying to bring order to this madhouse. Jake grunted, louder when the first sound didn't get my attention.

Mitchell reached out and tugged on my hair. I ignored him, my attention firmly fixed on Karen. I could finally distinguish the questions being asked and the answers being given.

"Where were you? What happened in the basement?" Allyson sounded angry, but underneath the loud words, I heard the remnants of her fear. No matter what I thought of the woman personally, I understood love for a child.

"I'm sorry," Karen mumbled. "I knew how much you disapproved of the party. I thought if I left, it would shut down the haunted house. I didn't mean to scare you. And I know what I did was mean."

"Where did you get the bones? Were you responsible for digging them up?" The sternness in Uncle Claude's voice reminded me of Dad, and a wave of homesickness washed over me.

Karen gaped at him. "Bones? The bones from the cemetery? Are you crazy? I wouldn't touch real bones." I could hear the horror in Karen's voice and knew she spoke the truth.

Again I tuned out the roar as everyone started talking at once. Jake whipped his head around and grunted at me. A low, guttural sound, agonizing to hear.

Mitchell reached out and pulled my hair again with enough force that it hurt.

"Ouch, what did you do that for?" I glared at Mitchell only to see him glaring back, his big blue eyes fierce as only a young boy's can be.

"Jake is telling you something. Why aren't you listening?"

Roni and I locked eyes and then looked back at Jake. Why wasn't I listening? I'd been too busy gawking at everybody else.

Roni put Mitchell down, but held onto his hand. We moved around to face Jake and watched his eyes closely.

"You're trying to tell me something?" His eyes flew up.

"Do you know what's going on?" Again, his eyes flew up, again and again. Yes, yes, yes. The poor kid was frantic to talk.

"About the bones?" A rapid eye flutter up and up again.

"You know how they got in the basement?" Roni beat me to the question.

Eyes up, yes. A relieved sigh exploded from his body.

"Can you tell us?" He glared at me and my insides shriveled. A quick eye-flick to the side, clearly a yes, but leaving me in no doubt how stupid he thought my question.

Roni, always logical, spoke again. "I bet whoever is responsible doesn't know that Jake is as bright as he is. Non-verbal, how could he say anything?"

Jake's eyes flew up and I felt a dread chill. Goosebumps popped up on my skin. "You mean,

302

whoever did this saw Jake and Mitchell? Actually spoke to them?"

Jake's eyes flew up again. Mitchell wrapped his arms around Roni's leg. I crouched, bringing my eyes down to their level.

"Is whoever responsible in this room?"

Jake's eye's flew up; Mitchell squeezed his eyes shut and buried his face against Roni's leg

"Uncle Claude." Faster than thought, I shrieked, a sound that stopped everyone in mid-word. The silence hurt my ears.

I explained about Jake and Mitchell knowing who put the bones in the basement.

"He can identify the person?" Uncle Claude eyed Jake with doubt. Jake's eyes flew up, over and over.

"Jake says he can."

"Okay." Uncle Claude stepped back. "Let him show us."

I have faith in Jake, but once in awhile, I also have doubt. Would Jake come through? Slowly, I pulled Jake's chair in a circle. "Which way do you want to go?"

With Jake turning his head to indicate direction, I started pushing him through the crowd. It parted before us like the Red Sea did for Moses. Step by slow step, we moved through the room, Jake's head swiveling right and left as he scanned the faces, looking for one particular face. I watched him, not the crowd we moved through.

I felt Jake's body stiffen; saw the way his gaze locked onto his target. As I pushed him forward, his gaze honed in on someone. People moved, and as they moved, so did Jake's gaze. The focus in Jake's eyes reminded me of a sheep herding dog. The kind they call a gazer; a dog that can lock onto a sheep with such intensity they control the sheep with power of their eyes. Jake possesses an eye gaze with that degree of intensity.

Before us, a man moved, Jake's head whipped side to side. No escape. The man froze and I looked up into the eyes of Gary Prescott.

"You? The bones? Why?"

Now that the perpetrator was identified, the crowd surged back, surrounding us. Nobody wanted to miss hearing a word.

I murmured in Jake's ear, "People are getting more than they bargained for from this Halloween party." His eyes flew up in agreement.

Uncle Claude didn't have to ask questions. Gary, after glancing at Jake with a thoughtful expression, talked. "My name is Gary Prescott, but what I didn't tell you is my maternal grandfather's name is Gerald Whitaker."

Mr. Whitaker, reclining in my pretty teal-blue recliner, let out a guttural sound very similar to Jake's non-verbal grunts. "What did you say? Gerry's been dead for more than fifty years."

"No." Gary shook his head. "He's failing but still here. The last few years, his mental awareness of things slipped. He became obsessed with an accident that happened when he was younger. He talked about a girl dying. He'd get this wild look in his eyes and say, over and over, "I didn't do it. I didn't do it."

"Then he'd start apologizing to my mother about being disinherited. Not getting his rightful share of things."

Mr. Whitaker scowled and trembled, his face contorting into something resembling a Halloween mask any child would pay good money to wear. He struggled to get to his feet and succeeded in bumping the handle to the foot rest with sufficient force to propel the chair into a full recline.

"Gerald did it. Of course, he did it."

Roni leaned closer and spoke into my ear. "Did what? I'm getting tired of people yelling and nobody clearing anything up."

A sentiment shared by our uncle. He produced a piercing whistle that brought all voices to a standstill. The loud noise impressed me and gave me a warm feeling of connection with my Dad's brother.

"Mr. Prescott, I want the whole story, right now." For a split second I heard my Dad's voice coming out of Uncle Claude's mouth.

"I'd be glad to." Gary stepped forward. The people in the room automatically adjusted their positions, placing Gary and Mr. Whitaker at the center. We all had a clear view now.

Gary Prescott looked down at the old man, a stern, harsh look on his normally pleasant demeanor. Mr. Whitaker unsuccessfully struggled to get the foot rest down, gave up, and glared up at the younger man.

"My grandfather hasn't been in good health for several years, but as he draws closer to dying, his mind has started to wander. It soon became apparent to my mother and me that an incident from his past was causing him a great deal of anguish. I sat by his bed, listening and taking notes and what I heard....disturbed me."

"He talked about his twin brother, Evan. 'Evan,' he'd shout out, 'the window, be careful of the window.'

"Then he would let out this awful bellow and try to get out of bed. Someone had to be with him night and day." Gary ran an impatient hand through his hair. He moved restlessly, clearly wanting to pace but unable to in the crowded room. His eyes jumped from his cousin, Steve, to Ansel, then back to Mr. Whitaker.

"I pieced together enough information that I pinpointed the town and the house. It was details I had trouble figuring out. But I learned enough to know that my grandfather was disinherited without cause, that whatever happened here wasn't his fault, but I needed proof. I need to know what happened on Halloween night, and who killed Elizabeth Jordan."

"Did you dig up the grave?" Uncle Claude spoke.

"No." Gary shook his head. "What I did do was rattle the tree. I went for the weak link." He looked over at Ansel. "I'm sorry, old man. I needed answers. I figured I could shake you first. I left those notes you found. I put enough pressure on you to make you nervous."

Ansel ducked his head and looked like he'd bolt, but the crowd hemmed him in. "I thought it was him." Ansel jerked his chin toward my brother. "I started follering him around, watching him. I fixed him good."

"Fixed?" my brother asked. "As in turning on faucets and taking keys?"

Ansel moved to bolt and again the crowded room stopped him. "I got the keys. I was real careful not to lose 'em. I'm sorry about the water. I didn't think it would make such a mess. I do that a lot. Not think, I mean,"

Ansel sounded so pitiful I forgave him on the spot. I don't know if my brother did, but I do know he's a big softie and probably wouldn't hold a grudge, considering Ansel's limitations.

"You didn't handle the bones at all?" Uncle Claude resumed questioning.

"I didn't say that." Gary shook his head. "I watched Steve open the grave. He rolled the bones up in a blanket and placed them on the ground outside the grave. He seemed to be hunting for something. I thought he was recovering information that would explain why my grandfather was disinherited, why he left the family, and now, when he should be most at peace, he isn't."

"When Steve came out of the hole, he was empty handed. He left the bones lying there, so I took them. Rattling Ansel hadn't given me what I needed. I thought I'd see what messing with Steve did. I'd been asked to check the fruit cellar out, so I stashed them there for safe keeping. It didn't occur to me the children would play there."

"I heard the screams and saw the stampede toward the house."

I saw his lips twitch in a hastily controlled grin.

"The shrubbery surrounding the backyard hid the fruit cellar from view. I grabbed the bones and stashed them in the basement. I needed to get them found again. When I saw Karen sneaking away, I put them in the box where she'd been lying. I figured it was the quickest way to get them found."

Another quick, sly grin lifted his lips. "I didn't think about the uproar it would cause. I do that sometimes. Not think, I mean." His grin widened and he winked at Ansel.

Ansel ducked his head, smiling.

Uncle Claude sighed, took his hat off, and rubbed a hand over his head. He settled the cap back on his head and said, "Is there anything else you want to tell me?"

Gary turned his head, looking through the crowd surrounding him. He stopped when he saw Phoebe. "Yes. Mrs. Landon, I owe you for a cow. The cow was in the middle of the road, a pickup truck in front of me hit it. I figure the driver must have been drunk. He took off. Didn't even stop to check what happened. Knocked that cow for a loop, but somehow it got up and staggered into the ditch where the creek flows under the fence. The bottom wire was down and the cow was able to slip back under. It fell to its knees, got back up, and kept walking. My wife and I were newly arrived, out of money, and pretty hungry.

"I pulled over, grabbed the only tools I had that I thought I could use, and trailed after the cow. For about fifteen minutes I didn't dare get near it, but it walked slower and slower, fell a couple of times, and finally just dropped. I could tell it didn't have long to live, so I helped it along. I slit its throat, and using a butcher knife from the camper and a small hatchet, I hacked off as much meat as I thought I could handle.

Animals must have messed up the rest of it. I'll sure pay you for it as soon as I can get things straightened out."

"Who put Mr. Whitaker in the grave?" Buddy shouted out, his voice booming above the drone of the crowd.

I saw Jake's head move with remarkable speed, his eyes sharpened in intensity. Roni and I exchanged glances then moved forward and crouched. I followed the line of Jake's eyes straight as a beeline to Steven Whitaker.

"You?" I slowly stood up, not because I wanted to, but because slow is the only speed I've got when coming up from a full crouch. "You put your own father in the grave?"

"Hmmph," he grumped, "who would believe a dummy? The boy can't even talk."

Dozens of hands waved in the air. Not all of them were family. Gary rolled his eyes. "I would. He nailed me."

"He's wrong this time." Steve curled his lip and shot a threatening look toward Jake. Jake returned one equally threatening. A flare of pride moved through me. He might be non-verbal and non-ambulatory, but cowardly? Never.

"Going to the cemetery was Dad's idea. He insisted on going into Elizabeth's grave. I didn't argue with him."

"No, you didn't." Mr. Whitaker swung his hand down and succeeded in grabbing the lever. Face red, blue eyes blazing, he burst out. "You waited until I had my back to you, pulled the ladder up, and left me there. What kind of son leaves his father in a grave?"

Steve's face turned as red as his father's. He leaned forward. "What kind of father pushes a girl out the window, blames his twin brother for her death, and keeps quiet when said brother is booted out of the house and told to never darken the family doorway again?"

The room erupted, the noise growing in volume until I wanted to slap my hands over my ears and howl. This was my room, darn it. My part of the house. I didn't remember inviting anybody to be here. So why, when I opened my eyes, did I see nothing but people? Half of them I couldn't even put a name to. The other half was family. I sighed and waited for Uncle Claude to regain control.

"What were you doing in the grave?" Uncle Claude asked the question I most wanted an answer too.

Mr. Whitaker threw his hand in the air and leaned back. "Bah, I don't have to talk to you. My business is my business."

Jessi stepped forward out of the circle surrounding Mr. Whitaker. "I think he buried this in the dirt." She held out a gallon-size bag. Inside I could see a faded brown book.

"Where did you get that?" he whispered. "I hid it good."

"What is it?" Voices and questions rippled through the crowd.

"Have any of you handled it?" Uncle Claude took the bag from Jessi.

"Not me." Jessi shook her head. "I pulled it out of the dirt, and carried it the whole time. I haven't even laid it down."

Uncle Claude held it by the corners and turned it carefully. "It looks like a journal."

"Yes." Gary moved closer and leaned forward to look at it. "From words my grandfather mumbled, I understood the girl; I know her name now to be Elizabeth, kept a journal. The journal would prove that she had a thing for Evan, not my grandfather. I've been trying to find the journal. I knew it was hidden. I just didn't know where. I thought if I could shake up enough people, somebody would let something slip. I put my money on Ansel."

Now that the footrest was down, the teal recliner rocked. Mr. Whitaker, in his agitation, set it going, back and forth. No fierce gaze now. He looked sad and weary. His blue eyes turned watery, and I averted my eyes. I hate it when old people cry. My family tends to join in when tears flow. I blinked hard and wished again that all these people would leave.

No tears from Steve. He growled, "Whatever happened to that girl was an accident. She's been gone since 1936. There's no way my father can be blamed for anything."

"My grandfather deserves to be cleared of blame." Gary's voice sent chills down my spine. Cold, angry, implacable. "I wouldn't have had to resort to this if you'd answered my letters and my phone calls. You slammed the door in my face."

Steve glanced at Uncle Claude and snapped his mouth closed on whatever he was going to say. He gave a disgusted wave at Gary and turned his face away.

"I liked Lizzie," Ansel interrupted. "Lizzie treated me nice. She never called me names and helped me when I'd get confused."

"You knew her?" Uncle Claude eyed Ansel; a measuring look in his eyes warned me he wasn't in uncle mode. ""What do you remember, Ansel? Were you there the night she died?"

"Yes," Ansel nodded. "Yes, I was. Halloween night it was. A big party upstairs in the big room at the top of the house."

I heard a ripple of eeuws move through the room and wished my nieces weren't listening to this. All we needed was for them to refuse to sleep up there.

"The party was fun, lots of food." A smile lit his face. "I remember Lizzie's laugh. She laughed a lot but not that night. Later, after everybody left, she cried. I saw her try to talk to Evan, but he kept moving away from her. She got so upset."

I watched Ansel's hands turning and turning his hat around. "She went to Gerald. He pulled her into a corner where they couldn't be seen. She cried on his shoulder. I saw Mr. Gerald get madder and madder. He pushed her away. Told her to wait there and he'd send Evan to her."

The hat did a wild spin in his hand. The mantel clock struck the hour of midnight, the simple melody of notes and the loud bongs sounding unnaturally loud in the quiet.

The last note faded away and Ansel resumed speaking. "Gerald grabbed Evan by the shoulder. Right there, in front of the big window. I heard him say Lizzie was pregnant. Evan said, 'What do you expect me to do about it?'

"Gerald said he had to do right by her. Then Lizzie came rushing up, madder than I'd ever seen her. She hit Mr. Whitaker, smacked him right in the face. The he shoved her. That's when it happened. None of us could stop it.

"Mr. Whitaker, he must have shoved her awful hard because she fell right through the window. Broke her neck, the fall did. That's a long way down. A new window got put in. Mr. Evan's father made sure there were safety bars on the inside. Wanted to make sure nobody else would ever fall through it. But it was too late for Lizzie."

"See?" Steve broke in. "It was just an accident, nobody's fault."

"If it was an accident, why did Gerald get blamed for it?" Gary spoke.

Mr. Whitaker stopped rocking. He looked shattered. "I never meant anybody to be hurt. I loved Lizzie, but not enough to ruin my life. I didn't want a wife or a baby. We were all too young. Gerald, well, he was always in trouble anyway. I told Father it was Gerald's fault. He threw him out without listening to both sides. I knew Gerald would land on his feet. He always did." A tinge of bitterness clouded his voice.

"Gerald always got the best of everything. He was the oldest by fifteen minutes. Seeing Elizabeth go through that window scared the life out of me. I didn't know what else to do but blame Gerald. If he'd kept out of it, let me handle it... If only he'd stayed out of my face. If only Elizabeth had given me time to think." His voice faded away.

Gary sighed. "I'm sorry I caused so much trouble, but I needed to find out the truth. I didn't anticipate the fallout of learning the truth. It never occurred to me that a girl's grave would be desecrated or an old man would end up in an open grave."

I raised my hand and waved it. Mr. Whitaker wasn't the only person who ended up in that grave. Roni pulled it back down and hissed at me. "Behave. Stay off the radar."

She had a point. I leaned on the handle of Jake's chair, put my foot on a back wheel, and listened to the voices, back and forth, sometimes loud, sometimes soft. I'd already heard what I needed to hear. The rest of it was just buzz. I wished, once again, everybody would go home and give me my rooms back.

Chapter 37
Party's Over

Roni picked Mitchell up. He put his head on her shoulder. Watching his sleepy eyes droop, I figured five minutes of quiet would have him out for the night.

Jake grunted and kicked his foot. "I know, sweetie, I'm tired too."

In the quiet, the front doorbell sounded as loud as a death knell. What else could happen tonight? Who would show up this late at night? I saw one of the uniformed officers slip away to answer the door. He returned a few minutes later herding two strangers into the room.

I heard gasps and mutterings from the Weary residents. Allyson's voice, always strident, hurt my ears. "Reverend Johnson, what are you doing here?"

An even louder voice bellowed, "Jennifer, where have you been?" John Ramsey elbowed his way to the front of the crowd.

The pretty blond woman turned, as if to bolt. The middle-aged man standing next to her grabbed her elbow and pulled her back to his side. His voice, when he spoke, held the nuances of a trained speaker.

"Jenny, we have to tell everybody. I can't live in hiding anymore."

The woman dropped her head, refusing to meet her husband's eyes. Body language showed me a man embarrassed and a woman radiating guilt.

"I'm sorry," her voice faltered. She cleared her throat, glanced up at Reverend Johnson, and seemed to gain courage. She straightened her shoulders, raised her head. "John, I'm sorry I ran off. I went about this all wrong."

A frown pulled at Mr. Ramsey's face. I fought the urge to roll my eyes and would have bet money all my siblings did the same.

Reverend Johnson sighed. "This isn't really the time or the place for this, but I was afraid Jenny would run away again if we didn't just get this over with."

"What Jenny is trying to tell you is, we ran away together."

It felt like the whole room inhaled. I could hear the in-drawn breaths as everybody standing around took in the Reverend's words.

John Ramsey looked dumbfounded. "Well, I never thought that. Never once did I think you'd do such a thing. Either of you. Couldn't you just have told me? Talked about it? I've been out of my mind with worry."

Jenny whispered, "You're not mad?"

John Ramsey gave a disgusted snort. "Of course, I'm mad. You're an idiot to run off like that. I've had the police hunting for you. I was afraid you were lying dead somewhere."

Reverend Johnson looked around the room and said, "Could we go somewhere else to talk about this?

316

I don't think it's appropriate to air our problems in public."

Mr. Ramsey shook his head, slapped his cap back on his head, and jerked his chin toward the door. "Let's go."

Uncle Claude signaled the officer who had let them in. I wasn't sure how, but the officer nodded at my uncle, then followed the Reverend and Jennifer and John Ramsey out the door. One more mystery solved.

Uncle Claude started herding people toward the door. A deputy stood there, taking names and addresses. One by one, the crowd thinned out.

Jake grunted again, kicked his foot, and went into full reflex. When I started to pat his shoulder, he turned to glare at me, clearer than words, telling me now was not the time to blow him off.

"You're not tired?" He shook his head then glanced down at his fist.

"You need?" Another no.

"You're hungry?" A quick yes, then a definite head shake no. Telling me, yes, he was hungry but no, that wasn't what he was trying to tell me.

"What is it?" Frustrated, I looked around the room now holding mostly family and a few of the party committee members.

Jake stared intently at my blue recliner where Mr. Whitaker reposed.

"Mr. Whitaker?" Jake's eyes flew up.

"You're telling me something about Mr. Whitaker?" Yes, yes, yes, Jake's eyes flew up so rapidly my own eyes watered in sympathy.

I stared at Mr. Whitaker. Roni shifted her sleeping son to a more comfortable position and joined me in trying to figure out what Jake wanted to tell us.

Buddy, Jessi, Josie, Mary Lee, Samantha, Phoebe, and Katie all moved to stand with us.

"What's going on?" Katie whispered. "Why are we standing here staring at that old man?"

"Jake wants to tell me something about him. I can't figure out what."

We turned to stare at the old man.

"He sure is old," I muttered.

Jake's eyes flew up.

"If I didn't know better." Thoughtful, respectful, my brother's voice dropped to a low voice he usually reserved when he planned on spinning his sisters a ghost story. "He's so old and shriveled; I'd think he was dead."

Jake let out a loud grunt that scared me out of a year's growth. His eyes flew so high in his head, I thought they'd stick. Yes, the biggest yes he could give.

Dead? Oh, no. I opened my mouth but Josie beat me to it. Her shriek raised the roof and brought Uncle Claude running.

He moved us away from the body. We lined up against the wall, watching as the ambulance arrived. We stood, silent and respectful, as they took the body away. Of course, it was natural causes. The man was ninety-one years old. The excitement of the day, the exposure of lying in the cold grave, plus the shock of his secret revealed, had finally taken its toll.

"I'm surprised he lasted this long," Buddy said. "You'd think if he was going to die tonight, it would have happened in the grave. Being in the open grave almost did me in, and I'm in a lot better shape than Mr. Whitaker was."

"I agree." Josie nodded. "But personally, I'm glad he wasn't dead because being trapped in a hole with a dead man might have started a parade of dead bodies. I don't think I'd have survived an episode like that."

"I'm not surprised." Gloom settled on me. "He would wait until he was sitting in my room, in my new chair."

I raised my eyes and looked around. It was a pretty room, a nice, big room. My husband and older son were a world away. For just a moment, I felt sad and tired, weighed down by grief and worry. And I felt incredibly lonely.

Then I looked down where my son sat. Disabled, yes; but wise and loving and strong in character. Beside me my family stood, my sisters, brother, nieces and nephews, aunts, uncles, and cousins. It didn't matter where I lived, or traveled, or ran to. My family grounds me, defines me, and strengthens me.

Again, the mantel clock struck the hour, one in the morning. I'd survived Halloween. The party was finally over. I could go to bed, wake up in the morning, and life would be normal.

My eyes landed again on the teal blue chair. Normal? Well, as normal as my life ever gets.

"I've got to put Mitchell to bed," Roni said softly. "I'll talk to you in the morning."

Phoebe whispered, "I'm going home. I can't wait to tell Jed what happened to his cow."

Samantha went next. "I'll make sure the clean-up committee gets started as soon as Uncle Claude releases the site."

I thanked her and watched the exodus move out the door. Family that had showed up to help slipped away as quickly as they had arrived.

Steven, Gary, and his family followed the gurney carrying Mr. Whitaker out the door. A state trooper followed behind them.

Josie gathered her girls together and herded them toward the hallway. I could hear her arguing with them about where they were going to sleep. I put money on them going back to Katie's rather than face the upstairs. We'd deal with the problem of bedrooms after everybody had a good night's sleep.

Katie, Elliott, and Lili left next. "I'll be over tomorrow to help out wherever you need it," Katie assured me. From the look on Elliott's face, I didn't think wild horses would keep him from the basement.

I nodded and watched them leave. Suddenly the room seemed too big and too empty.

Buddy stayed to the last. His thoughtfulness touched me. He leaned in, put his head close to my ear, and said, "No."

I turned to stare at him. "No, what?"

He grinned, his face lighting in a way that took me back to grade school. "My furniture is ruined. My mattress can't be saved. But don't even think about giving me the death chair."

With that, he left, heading down the hallway to the living room where he'd bed down on the faithful old couch, worn, and comfortable from countless hours of use. His cheerful whistle followed him.

I headed for the bathroom where I washed my hands thoroughly. Then I helped Jake get ready for bed. I turned on his TV to an all night music station and left him to settle down and sleep.

No sleep for me yet. First, I wanted the longest, hottest shower possible. Then, I had to get rid of the teal blue chair.

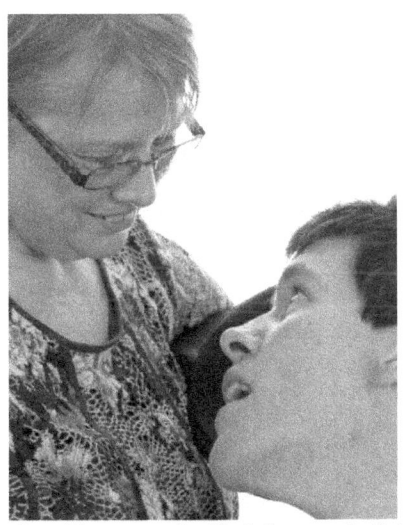

Author Photograph: Red Jasper Artistry
www.redjasperartistry.com/

C.L. Roth is an artist, caregiver, and author. She's spent twenty-five years learning her crafts. She spent a year writing articles for her local newspaper. A job that taught her to write tight and meet her deadlines.

She is a full-time caregiver for her son. Joshua was born with cerebral palsy but much to C.L.'s surprise indicated a love of art and has become a very talented watercolor and acrylic artist. C.L. manages OurHome Studio which showcases her son's artwork as well as rare pieces of her own work.

Visit her at
www.clroth.com
www.ourhomestudio.com

www.ingramcontent.com/pod-product-compliance
Lightning Source LLC
Chambersburg PA
CBHW070805180626
46818CB00001B/114